## Praise for *New York Times* and #1 international bestselling author Anna Todd and her After series

"Todd [is] the biggest literary phenom of her generation."

—*Cosmopolitan*

"I was almost at the point like with *Twilight* that I just stop everything and my sole focus was reading the book. . . . Todd, girl, you are a genius!!!"

—*Once Upon a Twilight*

"The Mr. Darcy and Lizzy Bennet of our time. . . . If you looked up 'Bad Boy' in the fiction dictionary, next to it would be a picture of Hardin alongside Beautiful Bastard and Mr. Darcy."

—*That's Normal*

"The one thing you can count on is to *expect the unexpected*."

—*Vilma's Book Blog*

"Anna Todd manages to make you scream, cry, laugh, fall in love, and sit in the fetal position. . . . *After* is a can't-miss book—but get ready to feel emotions that you weren't sure a book could bring out of you."

—*Fangirlish*

"A very entertaining read chock-full of drama drama drama. . . . This book will have you from the first page."

—*A Bookish Escape*

"I couldn't put this book down! It went with me everywhere so I could get my Hessa fix every spare moment I had. Talk about getting hooked from page one!"

—*Grownup Fangirl* on *After*

"Be prepared to have an emotional explosion!"

—*Biblio Belles*

"*Before* is brilliantly written. . . . I found myself putting it down and then pondering what would happen next between Hardin and Tessa before coming back to the story."

—*Into the Night Book Reviews*

"I'm so grateful to Anna Todd for giving me all the Hessa feels. Thank you for the 2,587 pages of insane angst and emotional turmoil. But above all, thank you for giving us, the reader, the chance to take the journey of love with Hardin and Tessa."

—*YA Book Addict*

## BOOKS BY ANNA **TODD**

*After*

*After We Collided*

*After We Fell*

*After Ever Happy*

*Before*

*Nothing More*

*Nothing Less*

### SHORT STORIES IN *IMAGINES*

"Medium"

"An Unlikely Friend"

# nothing more

## ANNA TODD

G

GALLERY BOOKS

New York   London   Toronto   Sydney   New Delhi

# G

Gallery Books
An Imprint of Simon & Schuster, Inc.
1230 Avenue of the Americas
New York, NY 10020

The author is represented by Wattpad.

First Gallery Books trade paperback edition September 2016

GALLERY BOOKS and colophon are registered trademarks
of Simon & Schuster, Inc.

For information about special discounts for bulk purchases,
please contact Simon & Schuster Special Sales at 1-866-506-1949
or business@simonandschuster.com.

The Simon & Schuster Speakers Bureau can bring authors
to your live event. For more information or to book an event,
contact the Simon & Schuster Speakers Bureau at 1-866-248-3049
or visit our website at www.simonspeakers.com.

Interior design by Davina Mock-Maniscalco

Manufactured in the United States of America

20 19 18 17 16 15 14 13 12

Library of Congress Cataloging-in-Publication Data is available.

ISBN 978-1-5011-3076-2
ISBN 978-1-5011-3077-9 (ebook)

*To those of us who put everyone else before ourselves,*
*even when we have nothing more to give.*

# Landon's

## *Playlist:*

"Come Up Short" *by Kevin Garrett*
"Let It Go" *by James Bay*
"Closer" *by Kings of Leon*
"Pushing Away" *by Kevin Garrett*
"As You Are" *by The Weeknd*
"Edge of Desire" *by John Mayer*
"In the Light" *by The Lumineers*
"Colors" *by Halsey*
"Love Me or Leave Me" *by Little Mix*
"Gasoline" *by Halsey*
"All You Never Say" *by Birdy*
"Addicted" *by Kelly Clarkson*
"Acquainted" *by The Weeknd*
"Fool for You" *by Zayn*
"Assassin" *by John Mayer*
"Without" *by Years & Years*
"Fool's Gold" *by One Direction*
"Love in the Dark" *by Adele*
"Hurricane" *by Halsey*
"Control" *by Kevin Garrett*
"It's You" *by Zayn*
"A Change of Heart" *by The 1975*
"I Know Places" *by Taylor Swift*

# chapter

## One

**M**Y LIFE IS PRETTY SIMPLE. I don't have too many complications. I'm a happy person. These things are known.

The first three thoughts that go through my mind each day are:

*It's less crowded here than I thought.*
*I hope Tessa is off work today so we can hang out.*
*I miss my mom.*

Yes, I'm a sophomore at New York University, but my mom is one of my best friends.

I miss home a lot. It helps to have Tessa around; she's the closest thing to family I have out here.

I know college students do this all the time; they leave home and can't wait to be away from their hometowns, but not me. I happened to like mine, even if it's not where I grew up. I didn't mind living in Washington for my senior year and then my first year of college—it was becoming my home. I had a family there and found a new best friend. The only, and biggest, thing missing was Dakota, my longtime girlfriend. So when she got accepted into one of the best ballet academies in the country, I agreed to move to New York City with her. I had a plan at the time I applied to NYU; it just didn't work out the way it was supposed to. I was supposed to move here and start my future with her. I had no idea that she would decide she wanted to spend her first year at college single.

I was devastated. I still am, but I want her to be happy, even if it's not with me.

The city's chilly in September, but there's barely any rain compared to Washington State. So that's something, at least.

As I walk to work, I check my phone, like I do about fifty times a day. My mom's pregnant with my little sister, and I want to be sure that if anything happens, I can get on a plane and be there for her quickly. My mom and Ken chose the name Abigail and I can't wait to meet the little one. I've never really been around babies, but little Abby is already my favorite baby in the world. However, so far the only messages from my mom have been pictures of the amazing things she whips up in the kitchen.

Not emergencies, but, man, I miss her cooking.

The streets are mobbed as I make my way to work. I'm waiting at a crosswalk with a crowd of people, mostly tourists with heavy cameras around their necks. I laugh to myself when a teenage boy holds up a giant iPad to take a selfie.

I will never understand this impulse.

When the crosswalk starts flashing its red countdown, I turn up the volume on my headphones.

Out here I pretty much wear headphones all day. The city is so much louder than I had anticipated, and I find it helpful to have something that blocks out some of the noise and at least colors those sounds that get in with something I like.

Today it's Hozier.

I even wear the headphones while working—in one ear at least, so I can still hear the coffee orders shouted to me. I'm a little distracted today by two men, both dressed in pirate outfits and screaming at each other, and as I walk into the shop, I bump into Aiden, my least favorite coworker.

He's tall, much taller than me, and he has this white-blond

hair that makes him look like Draco Malfoy, so he kind of creeps me out. On top of his Draco resemblance, he happens to be a little rude sometimes. He's nice to me, but I see the way he looks at the girls who come into Grind. He acts like the coffee shop is named after a club rather than coffee grounds.

The way he smiles down at them, flirting and making them squirm under his "handsome" gaze . . . I find it all pretty off-putting. He's not that handsome, actually; maybe if he was nicer, I could see it.

"Watch it, man," Aiden mumbles, slapping my shoulder like we're crossing a football field together in matching jerseys.

He's making record time in annoying me today . . .

But brushing it off, I head into the back and tie my yellow apron around my waist and check my phone. After I clock in, I find Posey, a girl who I'm supposed to be training for a couple of weeks. She's nice. Quiet, but she's a hard worker, and I think it's kind of cute that she always takes the free cookie we offer her each training day as an incentive to be a little happier during the shift. Most newbies decline it, but she's eaten one every single day this week, sampling the whole range: chocolate, chocolate macadamia, sugar, and some mystery greenish flavor that I think is some gluten-free-all-natural-localvore thing.

"Hey," I say, smiling at her where she leans against the ice machine. Her reddish hair is tucked behind her ears, and she's reading the back of one of the bags of ground coffee. When she looks up at me, she smiles a quick greeting, then returns her eyes to the bag.

"It still makes no sense that they charge fifteen dollars for a thing of coffee this small," she says, tossing the bag to me.

I barely catch it and then it nearly slips from my hands, but I grab it tightly.

"*We.*" I correct her with a laugh, and set the bag down on the break table where it came from. "*We* charge that."

"I haven't worked here long enough to be included in the 'we,'" she teases, and grabs a hair band off of her wrist and lifts her curly reddish-brown hair into the air behind her. It's a lot of hair, and she ties it up neatly, then nods her signal that she's ready to work.

Posey follows me out to the floor and waits by the cash register. She's mastering taking customers' orders this week and will likely be making the drinks next. I like taking orders the most because I would rather talk to people than burn my fingers on that espresso machine, like I do every shift.

I'm putting everything in order at my station, when the bell attached to the door sounds. I look over to Posey to see if she's ready, and sure enough, she's already perked up, all set to greet the morning's caffeine addicts. Two girls approach the counter chatting loudly. One of the voices strikes me, and I look over at them to see Dakota. She's dressed in a sports bra, loose shorts, and bright sneakers. She must have just finished a run; if she were leaving for a dance class, she'd be in a one-piece and tighter shorts. And she would look just as good. She always does.

Dakota hasn't come in here for a few weeks, and I'm surprised to see her now. It makes me nervous, my hands shaking, and I find myself poking at the computer screen for absolutely no reason. Her friend Maggy sees me first. She taps Dakota on her shoulder, and my ex turns to me, a big smile on her face. Her body is coated in a light layer of sweat, and her black curls are wild in a bun on her head.

"I was hoping you'd be working." She waves to me and then to Posey.

*She was?* I don't know what to make of this. I know that we agreed to be friends, but I can't tell if this is just friendly chatting, or something more.

Maggy waves, too. "Hey, Landon."

I smile at both of them and ask them what they'd like to drink.

"Iced coffee, extra cream," the duo says at once. They're dressed nearly identically, but Maggy is easily overshadowed by Dakota's glowing caramel skin and bright brown eyes.

I go into automatic mode, grabbing two plastic cups and shoving them into the ice bin with a smooth scooping motion, then pulling up the pitcher of premade coffee and pouring it into the cups. Dakota is watching me. I can sense her eyes on me, making me feel quite awkward. So when I notice that Posey is watching me, too, I realize I could—should, probably—explain to her what the heck I'm doing.

"You just pour this over ice; the evening shift makes it the night before so it can get cold and not melt the ice," I say.

It's really basic, what I'm telling her, and I almost feel foolish saying it in front of Dakota. We aren't on bad terms at all, just not hanging out and talking like we used to. I completely understood when she ended our three-year relationship. She was in New York City with new friends and new surroundings. I didn't want to hold her back, so I kept my promise and stayed friends with her. I've known her for years and will always care about her. She was my second girlfriend but the first real relationship I've had up to now.

"Dakota?" Aiden's voice overpowers mine as I start to ask them if they want me to add whipped cream, something I do to my own drinks.

Confused, I watch as Aiden reaches over the counter and grabs Dakota's hand. He lifts their hands in the air, and with a big smile she twirls in front of him.

Then, taking a glance at me, she inches away, just a bit, and says more neutrally to him, "I didn't know you worked here."

I look at Posey to distract myself from eavesdropping on their conversation, then pretend like I'm looking at the schedule on the wall behind her. It's really none of my business who she has friendships with.

"I thought I mentioned it last night?" Aiden says, and I cough to distract everyone from the little squeak that comes out of me.

Fortunately, no one seems to notice except Posey, who tries her best to hide her smile.

I don't look at Dakota even though I can sense she's uncomfortable; in reply to Aiden, she laughs the laugh she gave my grandma upon opening her Christmas gift one year. That cute noise . . . Dakota made my grandma so happy when she laughed at the cheesy singing fish plastered to a fake wooden plank. When she laughs again, I know she's *really* uncomfortable. Wanting to make this whole situation less awkward, I hand her the two coffees with a smile and tell her I hope to see her again soon.

Before she can answer, I smile again and go into the back room, turning the sound up on my headphones.

For a couple of minutes, I wait for the bell to ring again, signaling Dakota and Maggy's exit, before I realize that I probably won't hear it over the sound of yesterday's hockey game playing in my ear. Even with only one bud in, the cheering crowd and slaps of sticks would overpower an old brass bell. I go back out to the floor and find Posey rolling her eyes at Aiden as he shows off his milk-steaming skills to her. The way a cloud of steam floats in front of his white-blond hair makes him look even weirder to me.

"He said they're in school together, at that dance academy he goes to," Posey whispers when I approach.

I freeze and look toward Aiden, who is oblivious, lost in his own apparently glorious world. "You asked him?" I say, impressed and a little worried about what his answers would be to other questions involving Dakota.

Posey nods, grabbing a metal cup to rinse. I follow her to the sink, and she turns on the hose. "I saw the way you acted when he held her hand, so I thought I'd just ask what was going on with them."

She shrugs, causing her big mass of curly hair to bounce slightly. Her freckles are lighter than most redheads' I've seen and are scattered across the top of her cheeks and the bridge of her nose. Her lips are big; they pout a tad and she's nearly my height. These were things I noticed on her third day of training, when I suppose my interest flared up for a moment.

"I dated her for a while," I admit to my new friend, and hand her a towel to dry the cup with.

"Oh, I don't think they're dating. She would be insane to date a Slytherin." When Posey smiles, my cheeks flare and I laugh along with her.

"You noticed it, too?" I ask.

Reaching between us, I grab a pistachio mint cookie and offer it to her.

She smiles, taking it from my hand and eating half of it before I even manage to get the lid back on the canister.

# chapter

## Two

HEN MY SHIFT IS OVER, I clock out and grab two to-go cups from the counter to make my usual departure drink: two macchiatos; one for me and one for Tess. Not just your ordinary macchiato, though; I add three pumps of hazelnut and one shot of banana-flavored syrup. It sounds gross, but you wouldn't believe how good it is. I made it by accident one day, mixing up the vanilla and banana bottles, but my random concoction has become my favorite drink. Tessa's, too. And now Posey's.

To keep our young, college bodies properly nourished, I'm responsible for the refreshments and Tessa provides dinner most nights with leftovers from Lookout, the restaurant she's at. Sometimes the meal is still warm, but even if it's not, the food there is so good that it's edible hours later. We both manage to drink good coffee and eat gourmet food on a college budget, so it's a pretty sweet setup we have going on.

Tessa's working a late shift tonight, so I take my time in closing down the shop. It's not that I can't be home without her, but I just don't have any reason to rush, and this will keep me from thinking too hard about Dakota and Snakedude. Sometimes I like the silence of an empty home, but I've never lived alone before, and often the buzzing of the refrigerator and the clanging of steam pipes throughout the quiet apartment drives me to the point of insanity. I find myself waiting for the noise of a football game playing from my stepdad's study, or the smell of maple coming from my mom baking in the kitchen. I've nearly finished my course work for the week. The first few weeks of my sophomore year are completely different from my freshman year. I'm happy to be finished with the tedious, required freshman courses and be able to start my early-childhood-education track; it makes me finally feel like I'm getting closer to my career as an elementary-school teacher.

I've read two books this month, I've seen all the good movies that are out, and Tessa keeps the place too clean for me to have any chores to do around the apartment. Basically, I have nothing useful to do with my time and I haven't made many friends outside of Tessa and a couple of coworkers at Grind. With the exception of Posey maybe, I don't think I could actually spend time with any of them outside of the coffee shop. Timothy, a guy in my Social Studies class, is cool. He was wearing a Thunderbirds jersey on the second day of the semester and we struck up a conversation over my hometown hockey team. Sports and fantasy novels are my go-tos when socializing with strangers, something that I'm not the best at to begin with.

My life is pretty uneventful. I take the subway across the bridge to campus, back home to Brooklyn, walk to work, walk home from work. It's become a pattern, a repeated series of events that are completely uneventful. Tessa claims that I'm in a funk, that I need to make some new friends and have some fun. I would tell her to follow her own advice, but I know that it's easier to focus on the overgrown grass in your neighbor's yard than to mow your own. Despite my mom's and Tessa's strong opinion on my lack of a social life, I enjoy myself. I like my job and my classes this semester. I like living in a somewhat cool part of Brooklyn and I like my new college. Sure, it could be better, I know, but everything in my life is okay: simple and easy. No complications, no obligations aside from being a good son and friend.

I check the clock on the wall and cringe when I notice it's not even ten yet. I had kept the doors open longer than usual for a group of women talking about divorce and babies. There were a lot of "Ohs" and "Oh nos!" so I figured I would leave them in peace until they solved one another's life problems and were ready to go. At a quarter after nine, they left, their table covered in napkins, cold half-drunk coffee, and half-eaten pastries. I didn't mind the mess because it kept me busy for a few extra minutes. I spent so much time closing . . . meticulously placing stacks of napkins into metal canisters . . . sweeping the floor one straw wrapper at a time . . . and walking as slowly as I possibly could to fill up the ice bins and canisters of ground coffee.

Time isn't on my side tonight; I'm beginning to question my relationship with Dakota. Yeah, time rarely works in my favor, but tonight it's teasing me more than usual. Each minute that passes is sixty seconds of mockery; the little hand on the clock keeps ticking, slowly, but those ticks don't seem to add up—it doesn't feel like time is moving at all. I begin playing that elementary-school game of holding my breath in thirty-second increments to pass the time. After a few minutes of this, I'm bored and move to the back room with the cashier drawer and count the money from the day. The shop is silent, except for the buzzing of the ice machine in the back room. Finally, it's ten and I can't stall any longer.

Before leaving, I glance around the shop one last time. I'm positive I didn't miss anything, not one coffee bean is out of place. I usually don't close alone. My schedule alternates between closing with Aiden and closing with Posey. Posey offered to stay with me, but I overheard her talking about having trouble finding a sitter for her sister. Posey is quiet and she doesn't share much of her life with me, but from what I can gather, the little girl seems to be at the center of it.

I lock the safe and turn on the security system before I close and lock the door behind me. It's cold out tonight, a slight chill comes from the water and settles over Brooklyn. I like being close to the water, and for some reason, the river makes me feel some sort of detachment from the hustle of the city. Despite its proximity, Brooklyn is nothing like Manhattan.

A group of four—two women and two men—walks past as I lock up and step out onto the sidewalk. I watch as the two couples split into handholding pairs. The taller of the guys is wearing a Browns jersey and I wonder if he's checked their stats for the season. If he had, he probably wouldn't be prancing around in that thing with such pride. I watch them as I follow in their wake. The Browns fan is louder than the rest of the bunch and has an obnoxiously deep voice to boot. He's drunk, I think. I cross the street to get away from them and call my mom to check on her. By "check on her," I mean let her know that I'm fine and that her only child survived another day in the big city. I ask how she's feeling, but in typical fashion she pushes that aside to ask about me.

My mom wasn't as worried about the idea of me moving as I thought she would be. She wants me to be happy, and going to New York to be with Dakota made me happy. Well, it was supposed to. My move was supposed to be the glue that would keep our fraying relationship together. I thought that the distance was the thing that was chipping away at us, but I hadn't realized it was freedom she craved. Her freedom-seeking came so unexpected to me because I'd never acted possessive with her. I never tried to control her or tell her what to do. I'm just not like that. Since the day the spunky girl with the noodles for hair moved in next door, I knew there was something special about her. Something so special and real, and I never, ever wanted to hide that. How could I? Why would I? I reinforced her independence and pushed for her to keep her sharp tongue and strong opinions. For the entire five years we were together, I treasured her strength and tried to give her everything she needed.

When she was afraid to move from Saginaw, Michigan, to the Big Apple, I found a way to calm her fear. I've had the experience of a few moves myself; I moved from Saginaw to Washington just before my senior year of high school. I constantly reminded her of her very good reasons for wanting to go to NYC: how much she loved dance and how talented she was at it. Not a day passed when I didn't remind her how great she was and how proud of herself she should be. With blistered toes and bleeding feet, she rehearsed day and night. Dakota has always been one of the most motivated people I've ever met. Excellent grades came easier to her than they did to me, and she always had a job when we were teens. When my mom was working and couldn't drop her off, she rode her bike a mile to her cashier's job at a truck stop. Once I turned sixteen and got my license, she let her dad pawn her bicycle for extra cash and I gladly drove her.

And yet, in her family life I suppose freedom was something Dakota never felt like she had. Her dad tried to keep her and her brother, Carter, prisoner in their redbrick house. The sheets that he tacked over the windows couldn't keep either of his children inside. When she got to New York, she saw a new type of living. Watching her dad wither away into nothing with anger and booze wasn't living. Trying to wash away the guilt of her brother's death wasn't living. She realized that she had never truly lived. I had begun living the day I met her, but for her it wasn't the same.

As much as the destruction of our relationship hurt, I didn't hold it against her. I still don't. But I can't say that it didn't cause me real pain in addition to erasing the future we had mapped out together. I thought I would come to New York and share an apartment with her. I had assumed that every morning I would wake up to her legs wrapped around mine, the sweet smell of her hair in my face. I thought we would make memories while learning the ways of the city together. We were supposed to take strolls through parks and pretend to understand the art hanging in fancy museums. I expected so much when I started planning my move here. I expected it to be the beginning of my future, not the end of my past.

To her credit, she saw things coming, saw her feelings for what they were, and broke up with me before I moved out here. Rather than try to fake it for some time before it blew up in both of our faces, she was honest with me. Still, by the time she finally ended things, I was too invested in the move to change my mind. I had already transferred schools and put a deposit on an apartment. I don't regret it, and looking back, I think it was what I needed. I'm not completely enthralled by the city yet—its charm hasn't really hypnotized me like it does some, and I don't think I'll stay here after I graduate—but I like it enough for now. I would like to settle somewhere quiet, with a big yard and sunlight that makes everything gorgeous and browns my skin.

It helps that Tessa moved here with me. I'm not happy about the circumstances that brought her, but I'm glad I could provide an escape for her. Tessa Young was the first friend I made at Washington Central University, and she sort of ended up being the only one I had up until I left. She was the first and only friend I made in Washington, and vice versa. Her freshman year was rough. She fell in love and got her heart broken almost simultaneously. I was in a weird place, between my stepbrother, who I was trying to build a relationship with, and my best friend, Tessa, whose wounds came from the same man.

I opened my door to Tessa the moment she asked and I would do it again. I didn't mind the idea of sharing my apartment with her, and I knew it would help her. I like my place as the friend, the nice guy. I've been the nice guy my entire life and I'm more comfortable in that role than any other. I don't need to be the center of attention. In fact, I recently realized that I go out of my way to avoid any situation that would put me there.

I'm known for being the supporting act, the supportive friend and boyfriend—and I'm perfectly okay with that. When everything went down in Michigan, I wanted to suffer alone. I didn't want anyone to bleed with me, especially not Dakota.

Her pain was inevitable, and no matter what I did, I couldn't fix it. I had to let her bleed and I was forced to sit back and watch as her world was ripped apart by a tragedy that I tried my damnedest to prevent. She was my bandage and I was her net. I caught her when she was falling, and we will be bonded, whether it's by friendship or more, until the end of time because of the pain we've shared.

My mind doesn't often wander here, to the memories that I've forced myself to forget. That can of worms is closed. Sealed with super glue, and buried under nine feet of cement.

# chapter

## Three

WHEN I GET TO THE APARTMENT, I'm greeted by a medium-sized package on the doorstep. Tessa's name is scribbled in black marker, telling me immediately who it's from. I shove my key into the door and gently kick the box inside. The lights are off, so I know Tessa's not home from work yet.

I'm tired and I get to sleep in tomorrow. On Tuesdays and Thursdays, my classes begin later than the rest of the week. I'm very much looking forward to it; Tuesdays and Thursdays are my favorite days of the week because I can lie in my bed in boxers and watch television. It's a simple, somewhat sad luxury, but I enjoy every second of it. I kick my shoes off and line them up while yelling Tessa's name through the apartment, just to make sure she isn't here. When she doesn't respond, I start to undress in the living room, just because I can. Another simple luxury. I unbutton my jeans and push them down my legs. I even kick them off, letting them flop to the floor. I even leave them there. I'm feeling slightly rebellious, but mostly really exhausted.

After a second thought, I pick up my pants, shirt, socks, and boxers from the floor and carry them into my room, where I toss them on the floor to clean up later.

I need a shower.

The handle to the shower in my only bathroom sticks almost every time I turn it on. It takes at least one minute for the water to wend its way through the pipes. Our super "fixed" it twice, but it never stays. Tessa even tried to fix it herself a few times. Turns out repairwoman isn't her thing. At all. I laugh at the memory of her soaked body and how mad she was when the water burst from the pipe. The metal handle went flying across the bathroom, putting a small hole in the drywall. A few weeks later, it broke again when she turned the shower on and ended up yanking the flimsy handle off the wall. The result was her getting sprayed in the face with ice-cold water. She screamed like a banshee and ran out of the bathroom like she was on fire.

As I listen to the water moving through the lines and take a quick piss, my mind drifts through the day, how fast my classes seemed to go by, how surprised I was when Dakota and Maggy came into Grind. I still feel weird about seeing Dakota, especially with Aiden, and I wish that I would've had some time to prepare. I haven't talked to her in a few weeks and it was hard to concentrate when she was wearing such revealing clothing. I think it went pretty well, though; I didn't say anything completely embarrassing. I didn't spill coffee or stumble over my words. I wonder if Dakota felt awkward and like she was forcing conversation with me, or if she barely notices the tension anymore?

She doesn't reach out to me much—ever, really—so I have no idea how she feels or where we stand. She's never been very vocal about her emotions, but I know she's the type of girl who holds a grudge for life. She doesn't have any reason to have negative feelings toward me, but my mind immediately goes there. It's a little weird to me that we went from talking every day, to barely at all, to radio silence. After she called me to end our relationship, I tried to keep our friendship afloat, but she's given me little help.

I miss her sometimes.

Hell, I really fucking miss her.

I got used to not seeing her when I moved from Michigan to Washington, but we still talked daily, and I'd fly out and visit her every chance I had, even once I got busy with college. When she moved to New York, she started becoming distant. I could tell something was off, but I kept hoping it would get better. Still, with every phone conversation we had, I felt her slipping away from me more and more. Sometimes I would just sit and stare at my phone, hoping that she would call back and want to hear about my day. Just ask one question or give me more than a quick, two-minute rundown of her day. I hoped that maybe she was just adjusting to her new life. Maybe she was going through a phase, I thought.

I wanted her to get the full experience of her new life and make new friends. I didn't mean to take anything from her. I just wanted to be a part of her life like I always had been. I wanted her to throw herself into her dance academy; I knew how important this was for her. I didn't want to be a distraction. I tried to be as supportive as I possibly could, even as she began to carve me out of her life. I played the role of supportive boyfriend as her schedule became fuller and fuller.

I had always played that role well, ever since we were kids. I'm comfortable in this role, just like the nice guy. I stayed patient and ever so understanding. The night that she called to give me reason after reason why our relationship wasn't working, I still nodded along on the other end of the line and told her it was okay, that I understood. I didn't understand, and her "reasons" felt flimsy, but I knew there was no changing her mind, and as much as I wanted to fight for her, I didn't want to become a burden to her. I didn't want our relationship to become another thing she had to fight. Dakota spent her life fighting and I had managed to be one of the few positive forces in her life, and I want to keep it that way.

I was frustrated, and in a way, I still am. I don't really understand why she couldn't spare a little time for me when all of her Facebook updates were pictures of her at different restaurants and nightclubs with her friends.

I missed hearing about her day. I wanted to listen to her brag about how well she did in class. I missed her raving about how she couldn't wait for an upcoming audition. She was always the first person I went to with anything. That began to change after I met Tessa and started getting closer to my stepbrother, Hardin, but still, I missed her. I don't know a lot about dating, but I did know that this wasn't it.

Suddenly I realize the bathroom is filling with steam from the shower while I'm just standing here staring at myself in the mirror and reliving the failure of my only relationship. I finally step into the shower—and the water is scalding, like it's lashing out against my skin. I jump back out and adjust the water. I connect my phone to the iDock and turn on my sports podcast before I get back into the shower. The announcers' voices are deep and loud as they bicker over the unnecessary politics surrounding hockey. I try to pay attention to who they are complaining about, but the sound keeps cutting in and out, so I reach out and shut it off. My phone falls from the dock and lands in the sink. I reach over and get it out before my usual luck kicks in and an invisible house elf turns on the water. Having a house elf, preferably Dobby or his clone, would be ideal. Harry Potter was one lucky kid.

This bathroom is way too small for another body, elf or not. It's tiny—microscopic, really—with one low sink with a wonky faucet planted next to a small toilet that I can barely fit on. Whoever designed this apartment didn't do it with a six-foot-tall guy in mind. Unless said six-foot-tall guy liked to bend his knees to get his head under the shower stream. The warm water works at my back as I continue to torture myself and think about Dakota. She takes up prime real estate in my head, and I can't seem to get her to move out. She looked so good today, so damn sexy in those shorts and sports bra.

Did she notice that my body has changed since she's seen it last? Did she see that my arms have grown thicker and my stomach finally has the lines of muscle that I've been working toward?

Growing up, I was the chubby kid. My hefty build was often the topic of conversation in the crowded hallways of my high school. "Lardy Landon," they called me. "Don't let Landon *land on* you," they would joke. Maybe it sounds so damn stupid and childish now, but it bothered the crap out of me when the meatheads would walk behind me chanting it. That was only one of the many flames of the hell that was high school. It was nothing compared to what happened with Carter, but I'm not going there tonight.

The more I try to remember about our encounter at Grind, the more my brain screws with the memories and jumbles them. I couldn't tell what Dakota was thinking. I never could. Even when we were young, she always had secrets. It was appealing then, mysterious and exciting. Now that we're older and she broke up with me with little real explanation, it's not so fun.

I stare at the seaweed-green shower tiles and think about all of the things that I should have said and done during those five minutes. It's a vicious cycle, going over what I could have said and then reminding myself that it's not a big deal, then back to freaking out. I stare at the wall, remembering her standing in front of me earlier today. I wish I could have read the pages behind her almond eyes, or found some words hidden beneath her full lips.

Those lips . . .

Dakota's lips are something else. They are plump, and the perfect shade of soft petal pink. Their rosy color has always driven me crazy, and she's mastered the art of using them perfectly. We were only sixteen when we messed around for the first time. It was our two-month anniversary, and she had just adopted a puppy for me. I knew my mom wouldn't let me keep it, and she had to know it, too, but we tried to hide it in my closet. Dakota often did things that she knew she shouldn't, but her intentions were always good. We would feed the little gray fur ball the best food from the little pet shop down the street. He didn't bark much, and when he did, I would cough to try to hide the sound. It worked for a while, until he grew too big for my small bedroom.

After two months of captivity, I had to tell my mom about the dog. She wasn't nearly as upset as I thought she would be. However, she did explain the cost of upkeep of a puppy, and when I compared that to my measly check from the car wash I worked at sporadically, it didn't add up. Even with the tips added in, I couldn't cover a vet bill. After some tears and protestations, Dakota finally agreed. To ease the pain, we geeked out and watched all of the Lord of the Rings movies. We binge-drank Starbucks Frappuccinos and complained about paying five dollars a cup. We ate Twizzlers and peanut butter cups until our stomachs hurt, and I drew circles on her cheeks with my fingertips, the way she always liked, until she fell asleep on my lap.

I woke up to her warm mouth and her lips tight around my cock.

I was surprised, half-awake, and aroused as hell watching her take me between her lips, down her warm throat. She said she had wanted to try it for a while but was nervous. She worked her mouth around me perfectly, making me come with an embarrassing quickness.

She learned that she really liked to please me this way, and she started doing it almost every time we hung out. I liked it, of course.

Hell, who am I kidding? I loved it. I couldn't remember how I ever thought jerking off was an enjoyable way to orgasm. It was nothing compared to her mouth, then, later, her soft, wet pussy. We went from oral sex to fucking pretty quickly; neither of us could ever get enough. I didn't have to please myself until I moved to Washington. I missed everything about her, including the intimacy we shared. It's not so bad, jerking off, I suppose. I look down at my cock hanging, the hot water running over it. I wrap one hand around the base, teasing my own tip with my thumb the way Dakota used to with her tongue.

With my eyes closed and the warm water pouring over me, I can nearly convince myself that it's not my own hand stroking myself. In my head, Dakota is on her knees in front of my old bed in Washington. Her curly hair was lighter before and her body was just starting to really tighten up from all of her dancing. She looked so good, she always has, but as we grew up, she just kept getting hotter and hotter. Her mouth is moving faster now . . . between that and the sounds of her moaning in my head, I'm nearly there.

My body begins to tingle, from my toes to my spine. I lean my back against the cool tile of the shower wall and one of my feet slips and I step sideways, losing my footing. A string of words that I don't use often spits from my lips and I grab on to the checker-print shower curtain and pull.

*Click, click, click.* The damn thing gives way, tearing at each plastic ring. It falls, taking me with it. I yell again and my knee hits the edge of the tiny tub as I fall backward, slamming hard against the porcelain and getting hot water shooting into my face.

"Shit!" I exclaim.

My knee feels like it's already beginning to swell up and my arms feel like Jell-O as I grip the edge of the tub and try to lift myself out. The door bursts open, startling me, so I let go and smack my head against the bottom of the tub. Before I can cover myself, I see Tessa, whose hands are flying around like a hippogriff.

"Are you all right?" she shrieks. Her eyes dart over my naked body and she covers her eyes. "Oh God! I'm sorry!"

"What the hell?" Sophia screeches as she enters.

Great . . . now she's in here, too. I reach for the ripped curtain and pull it over my naked body. Could this get any worse? I look at both girls and nod, trying to catch my breath. My cheeks are on fire and I would rather disappear into a pile of dog shit than be curled up in the bathtub, naked, with one leg hanging over the edge. I push my free arm down onto the wet floor of the tub and try to pull myself up.

Sophia pushes past Tessa and grabs hold of my arm to help me. *Someone kill me.* She quickly tucks her brown hair behind her ears and uses both hands to pull me up. *Please kill me.* I try to keep the curtain covering my inappropriate bits, but it falls just as I stand up. I reach down and grab it again, just as nonchalantly as I can manage.

*Anyone listening out there? If you won't kill me, at least make me disappear. I'm begging you.*

Sophia's brown eyes have a green tint to them that I hadn't noticed before. Or maybe they don't and I'm just dazed from the fall. I look away from her, but I can still feel her eyes on me. I try to focus on the toe of her shoes: they're brown and pointy and remind me of the shoes Hardin always wears.

"You steady now?" Sophia raises one dark brow.

Could I be any more embarrassed? I don't think so. It wouldn't be humanly possible. Thirty seconds ago, I was masturbating in my shower and now I'm naked and embarrassed. This entire ordeal would be hysterical if it were happening to someone else.

Sophia's still looking at me, and it dawns on me that I haven't answered her question.

"Yeah. Yeah. I'm fine." I sound even smaller than I feel.

"Don't be embarrassed," she says quietly.

I shake my head. "I'm not," I lie, and turn my chin down and force a laugh. The worst way to make someone feel less embarrassed is to tell them not to be embarrassed.

Tessa looks at me with concern and is about to say something when a loud beeping noise pierces the air, making me flinch.

Could this get any worse?

"The chocolate is burning!" Tessa shrieks, and disappears from the bathroom, and the room feels even more compact than usual. The mirror is foggy and everything's dewy and Sophia's still in here. She smiles and her finger touches the center of my stomach, just above my belly button, with long, black nails.

I like the way they look, touching me. Dakota never has long nails because of dance. She complained about it often, but she loves dance more than nail art, so natural nails it is.

"You shouldn't be." The compliment comes out as a purr and my body responds. Sophia's finger is still making a slow line down my stomach, and I'm confused, but I don't want her to stop. Her fingers draw along the bottom of my stomach, just above where the curtain is covering enough for my cock not to show. My mind is trying to figure out why she's touching me like this while I'm simultaneously trying to keep my cock soft.

I don't know her that well, but I do know that she's much bolder than the girls my age that I've met. She doesn't have a problem cussing out the television during *Master Chef,* and she clearly doesn't have a problem touching my soaking, naked body. The trail of hair from my belly button down to my groin seems to be entertaining her as she brushes the tip of her index finger over it.

*Did she say something?* Ah, yes, she did. She said, "You shouldn't be."

When did the smoke alarm stop beeping?

*What does she mean by that? I shouldn't be embarrassed?* I

nearly busted my ass in the bathroom while jerking off and was found naked on the shower floor.

*Of course* I'm embarrassed. And just like that, the spell of whatever she's doing is weakened and self-consciousness creeps back in.

I look at her, at the reflection of her dark hair in the foggy mirror.

"Thanks," I weakly reply. I clear my throat and continue: "I took quite a tumble." I laugh, getting closer to finding the humor in the whole thing.

Her eyes are warm and her finger is still touching me, slowly tracing and teasing. It's not awkward, but I don't know what to say or do. Before I have to decide, she pulls away with a smile.

I turn from her with flushed cheeks and wipe my hand across the mirror. She stands still, her back against the towel rack. I stare at my reflection and wince when my finger touches a small but deep cut just above my eye. A trickle of blood is running down my forehead, I reach behind Sophia and grab a hand towel, dabbing at the torn skin while I make myself a promise to never try to get off in a tiny shower unless I'm wearing armor or something. I apply as much pressure as I can stand to get the bleeding to stop.

With Sophia still in the bathroom, should I be making conversation with her or something? I don't know what to think about her touching me. I don't know the etiquette when it comes to things like this. Is this the norm for young, single people?

I've only had one girlfriend ever up until now, so I can't pretend to know about this type of thing. I can't pretend to know what this girl is thinking, or what she wants. I hardly know anything about her.

I met her back in Washington briefly, when her family moved in near my mom and Ken. I know that she's a few years older than me, and that she likes her friends to call her by her middle name, Nora, which is something I constantly screw up only to have Tessa correct me with a scowl. I know that she always smells like sugar and candy. I know that she comes over a lot because she doesn't like her roommates. I know that she keeps Tessa company when I can't, and somehow they have become friends over the last few months. That's pretty much it. It sounds like a lot when I list it out, but all of those things are superficial, nothing more. Oh yeah, she just graduated from culinary school and works at the same restaurant as Tessa.

And now I can add that she likes to touch naked, wet stomachs.

I look away from the mirror and back at her.

"Are you staying to make sure I don't have a concussion?" I ask.

She nods, giving me a toothy smile. The corners of her eyes crinkle up and her lips look incredibly plump, especially when she licks over them with her tongue. Wet lips and those eyes . . . she's lethal.

She knows it.

I know it.

Obama knows it.

She's the kind of woman that will chew you up and spit you out, and you'll love every minute of it. Her index finger is tapping on her bottom lip and I'm still quiet. She can't be hitting on me? I'm confused. Not complaining, just confused.

"I appreciate your concern," I say with a wink. *Did I really just do that?*

I look away quickly, horrified that my stupid brain would have me do such a dumb thing. Winking? I'm not the winking type of guy, and I'm pretty sure that I just looked like the biggest creep. Ever.

Nora's eyes meet mine, and her lips part. She steps toward me, closing the admittedly small gap between us with one stride.

My body reacts and I retreat, my lower back resting against the sink.

"You're so cute," she says softly, and her eyes roam over my chest once again.

The word *cute* stings a little coming from someone who oozes sex appeal. From the curve of her lips to the curve of her hips, she's pure desire. I'm always the cute one, the nice one. No woman has ever fantasized about me or called me sexy.

Nora lifts her hand toward my face and I flinch slightly, wondering if she's going to slap me for imagining her naked more than once. But she doesn't slap me, probably because she can't actually read my mind despite how exposed I feel. She raises her finger to the tip of my nose, and taps it. I close my eyes in surprise, and when I open them, she's already turning away.

Without a word, she leaves the bathroom and walks into the hallway.

I rub my hand over my face, wanting to erase the last five minutes . . . although maybe keep the last two.

When I hear Tessa ask her if I'm okay, I roll my head back, take a breath, and close the door, clicking the lock into place. The shower curtain is destroyed and the tiny room looks like it's been hit by a tornado. The plastic rings from the curtain are scattered across the floor, the bottles of shampoo and Tessa's body soap are all over the place. As I clean them up, I can't help but start to laugh at this whole thing. Of course this would happen to me.

The clothes I brought into the bathroom with me are wet; the shirt has a huge water spot on the back, but the shorts aren't too bad. I pull them on and grab the wet clothes to take into my room. My dark hair is drying now; only the roots are still wet. I rake Tessa's purple hairbrush over my scalp and use a comb over the little bit of facial hair I've been growing lately. Her vanilla lotion is a little greasy, but it smells good and I always forget to buy my own. Luckily, there's a Band-Aid in the cabinet, and I stick it over my cut.

Of course it's not just a normal Band-Aid: Tessa bought *Frozen*-themed Band-Aids.

Yay. It just keeps getting better.

When I step into the hallway, Nora's laugh is as loud as Tessa is silent. She hasn't laughed since she moved here. It bothers me, but I've learned that she needs to deal with this breakup on her own terms, so I don't push her. She's not one to take other people's advice, especially when it comes to Hardin. And somehow, thinking of him reminds me I have a shift tomorrow morning. Crap. Which means I need to get up early tomorrow so I can run, so I toss my clothes into the laundry basket in the hall and walk to the kitchen to get some water and say good night to the girls. You know, try to reestablish some normalcy. A nothing-to-see-here moment to end the night on.

Tessa is sitting on the couch with her feet propped up on a pillow and Nora is lying on the rug with a pillow under her head and my yellow-and-maroon Gryffindor house blanket wrapping her up like a burrito. I glance at the TV: *Cupcake Wars*. The usual. These women watch nothing but the Food Network and the teen dramas on Freeform. Admittedly, I do like some of those shows. The one about the teenage demon-hunters is my favorite. That, and the foster-family one.

"You guys need anything from the kitchen?" I ask, stepping over Nora's fuzzy-sock-covered toes peeping out of the bottom of the blanket.

"Water, please." Tessa leans up and pauses the show. A woman with curly black hair is frozen on the screen, mouth wide open and hands in the air. She's stressed over burned cakes or something.

"Do you have anything besides water?" Nora asks.

"This isn't a grocery store," Tessa teases. Nora pulls the pillow from under her head and tosses it at her.

And Tess smiles, actually nearly laughing before catching herself. It's too bad. She has a great laugh.

Besides Gatorade, I don't know what we have in the fridge, but I hold up my finger and go to check it out. Inside the fridge, rows of bottles are lined up perfectly. Yes, Tessa even organizes our fridge, and it turns out that we have a lot to offer a thirsty soul other than water.

"Gatorade, sweetened iced tea, orange juice!" I call out.

I jump when Sophia's voice comes at me from up close. "Ew. I hate Gatorade, except the blue one," she says as if she's personally offended by my favorite drink.

"Ew? How can you say that, Sophia?" I give her a disbelieving look and rest one arm on the open fridge door.

"Easily." She smiles, leaning against the counter. "And stop calling me Sophia—if I have to tell you again, I'm going to call you George Strait every time I see you."

"George Strait?" I can't hide my laughter. "Out of every name you could have said, that was one . . . well, that's just random."

She's laughing, too, a soft laugh with sharp eyes. It suits her.

Nora-not-Sophia shrugs her shoulders. "George's my go-to."

I remind myself to look up George Strait to see what he looks like. I'm sure I've seen him before, but I haven't listened to country since I was a kid.

Nora's hair is in a ponytail now; long curls cover one shoulder and she's wearing a cutoff shirt, exposing her stomach and skin-tight capri leggings. To be honest, before, I was too busy concentrating on *my* exposed skin to really notice hers.

Is she flirting with me? I can't tell. Dakota always teased me about being clueless when it came to the advances of women. I like to think of it as uncontaminated, not inexperienced. If I were hip to all the possible advances, I would probably turn into one of those guys who are obsessed with how women perceive them. I would question everything I said or did. I might even become one of the dudes who soak their hair with gel, spiking the ends like that guy from the *Diners, Drive-ins, and Dives* show Tessa and Nora watched last night. I don't want to hide my sci-fi books or pretend that I can't recite every Harry Potter movie line for line. I don't want to try to be cool. I'm pretty sure I'll never be cool. I've never been cool, and I'm okay with that. Besides, I would rather not compete with the millions of perfect men out there and would instead keep my books on my shelves and maybe get lucky enough to find a woman who likes them, too.

Not having any blue Gatorade, I try to tempt her with my favorite, the red one. "You're so quiet," Nora says when I hand her the bottle. She examines it, raises a brow, and shakes her head.

I stay quiet.

"Better this than water, I suppose." Her voice is soft, not demanding at all, despite the fact that she has a serious Gatorade-hating problem. My mind curiously wonders what other opinions she has. Are there any other sugar-saturated drinks that she holds unnecessary grudges against? I find myself wanting to know. While I'm preparing in advance my defense of all my favorite drinks that she might hate, she twists the top from the red bottle and takes a drink.

After a moment, she says, "Eh." She shrugs her shoulders and takes another swig as she turns to walk away.

She's weird. Not in a she-lives-in-her-mom's-basement-and-collects-Beanie-Babies weird. She's weird as in I can't figure out her personality, and I definitely can't figure out what those awkward pauses or random touches are supposed to mean. I usually read people so well.

But instead of cracking the code of romance, I grab my water from the fridge, go into my room, and finish my essay, then go to bed.

# chapter

## *Four*

THE MORNING CAME QUICKLY. I went to bed around one and woke up at six. How many hours do doctors recommend again? Seven? So, I'm only like 30 percent off target. Which, yeah, is a lot. But I've gotten used to staying up late and waking up early. I'm slowly becoming a New Yorker. I drink coffee daily, I'm starting to get the hang of the subway system, and I learned how to share the sidewalks with the stroller moms in Brooklyn.

Tessa has learned all this, too, right along with me, although we differ in one maybe-significant way: I give less of my money to the homeless I see on my way to school and back. Tessa, for her part, gives away half of her tip earnings on the walk home. Not that I don't care or help, I just prefer to give coffee or muffins when I can, not money to feed possible addictions. I understand the hope Tessa feels when she hands a homeless man a five-dollar bill. She truly believes he will buy food with it or something else he needs. I don't, but I can't really argue with her about it. Maybe she has the better idea here, but I know a lot of her attitude comes from her personal connection with the homeless. Tessa found out her dad, who wasn't around in her life, was living on the streets. They got to know each other a little bit before he succumbed to his addictions and died a little less than a year ago. It was really hard for her, and I think helping these strangers heals a small part of that open wound.

For every dollar she gives, she's rewarded with a smile, a "thank you" or "God bless you." Tessa's the kind of person who tries to pull the best out of everyone. She gives more of herself than she should and she expects people to be kind, even when it's not the most accessible part of their nature. I think she sees her small mission as some kind of redemption for her failed relationship with her father, and even with Hardin, who is one of the most difficult people I know. Maybe she couldn't help those two, but she can help these people. I know it's naïve, but she's my best friend and this is one of the only positive things that actually energizes her lately. She doesn't sleep. Her gray eyes are swollen 99 percent of the time. She's struggling with getting over a catastrophic breakup, the death of her father, moving to a new place, and not getting accepted into NYU.

That's a lot for one person to carry on their back. When I met Tessa a year ago, she was so different. Her shell was the same, a beautiful blonde with pretty eyes, a soft voice, and a high GPA. The first time I talked to her, I felt like I had met the female version of myself. We immediately bonded over being the first two to arrive in the lecture hall our first day of college. Tessa and I got closer as her relationship with Hardin developed. I watched as she fell in love with him, and he fell harder, and they both fell apart.

I watched them rip each other apart and then stitch each wound back together. I watched them become one another's everything, then their nothing, then everything again. I had trouble picking sides during the war. It wasn't without causalities. It was just too complicated and messy, so now I'm taking my cue from Bella Swan and staying neutral, like Switzerland.

Yikes, I'm referencing *Twilight*. I need caffeine. Pronto.

When I walk into the kitchen, Tessa is sitting at the small table with her phone in her hand.

"Morning." I nod to her and switch on the Nespresso machine. I've become somewhat of a coffee snob since working at Grind. It helps to have a roommate who's equally obsessed. Not as picky, but even more addicted than I am.

"Morning, sunshine," Tessa says distractedly, at first barely glancing up from her phone, but then her eyes go straight to the gash above my eyebrow and concern takes over her expression. After rubbing some Neosporin on it this morning, I was happy to be able to omit the Disney Band-Aid.

"I'm fine, but damn, that was embarrassing." I grab a pod of Brazilian espresso and push it into the machine. The counter space in here is minimal, and the thing takes up half the room between the off-white fridge and the microwave, but it's a necessity.

Tessa smiles, biting her lip. "A little," she agrees, and covers her mouth to stifle her amusement.

I wish she would laugh . . . I want her to remember how it feels.

I glance over at her miniature coffee cup. It's empty.

"Need a refill? Do you work today?" I ask.

She sighs, picks up her phone, then puts it back down. "I do." Her eyes are stained with angry red lines again. Bloodshot from the tears soaked into her pillowcase. I didn't hear crying last night, but that doesn't mean she wasn't. She's slightly better at hiding her feelings lately. Or so she thinks.

"Yes to both. Work. And want more coffee. Please," she clarifies with a half smile. Then she clears her throat and her eyes fall to the table as she asks, "Do you know which days Hardin will be here yet?"

"Not yet. We're still a few weeks away, so he hasn't told me. You know how he is." I shrug my shoulders. If anyone knows Hardin, it's her.

"You're sure this is okay, right? Because you know if you aren't, I can have him stay at a hotel or something," I offer.

I would never want her to be uncomfortable in her own apartment. Hardin would fight me over this, but I don't care.

She forces a smile. "No, no. It's fine. This is your place."

"And yours," I remind her.

I put the first cup of espresso into the freezer for Tessa. She's doing this thing lately where she only drinks cold coffee. My suspicion is that even something as simple as a warm cup of coffee reminds her of that boy.

"I'm going to pick up extra shifts at Lookout. I'm almost done with training anyway. They're letting me do brunch and dinner today."

My chest aches for my friend, and for once, my loneliness doesn't seem so bad compared to the alternative of her shattered heart.

"If you change your mind—"

"I won't. I'm fine. It's been—what?" She shrugs. "Four months or something?"

She's lying through her teeth, but nothing good is going to come from me calling her out on it. Sometimes you have to let people feel what they need to feel. Hide what they think they need to hide and process it however they do.

The espresso burns my throat. It's thick and strong, and suddenly I have more energy than I did two seconds ago. Yes, I'm aware that it's a mental thing, and no, I don't care. I throw the little cup into the sink and grab my sweatshirt from the back of the chair. My running shoes are by the door, lined up in a straight row with the other shoes . . . Tessa's doing.

I slip them on and head out.

# chapter *Five*

THE AIR IS CRISP and I can actually smell fall in the air. Fall has always been my favorite season. I love waiting for the seasons to change, watching the leaves go from green to brown, smelling the cedar in the air. Football season leads to hockey season, and hockey season leads to my life being interesting for a little while. I've always loved waiting for the sports seasons to start, raking the yard with my mom, and jumping into big messy piles of loose leaves, then stuffing them into plastic bags with pumpkin faces printed on them.

We always had so many leaves to deal with because of the two massive birch trees in the front yard. Fall in Michigan never lasted long enough, though. By the third football game, the gloves and coats came out full force. And while I was sad to see fall go, I've always liked the bite of the cold air on my skin. Unlike most people, I thrive in winter. For me, the cold means sports, holidays, and a crap load of sweets piled on the kitchen counter. Dakota always hated the cold. The way her nose would turn red and her curly hair would dry out drove her insane. She always looked cute, wrapped up in layers of sweaters, and I swear to you, the girl wore mittens in September.

The best park to run the track in Brooklyn happens to be a bit far from my apartment. McCarren Park joins the two hippest parts of Brooklyn: Greenpoint and Williamsburg. Full beards and lumberjack flannels come out in droves in this part of the city. The locals bring their black-framed glasses and establish tiny little restaurants with dim lighting and small plates of heaven. I don't quite understand why men in their twenties want to dress like men in their seventies, but the food that surrounds the cool kids here is well worth having to stare into a crowd of men with handlebar mustaches. The walk to my favorite park is a little over twenty minutes, so I usually run there, then run for an hour, and cool down during the walk home.

I pass a woman loading a tiny baby into a running stroller. My knee hurts, but if she can run with a baby in a stroller, I'll be just fine. Two minutes into running, the ache in my knee shifts into a throbbing, sharp pain. Thirty seconds later, the pain is shooting from muscle to muscle. I feel every step from my fall in the shower. Forget this.

I'm off today, and even if my leg's acting up, I don't want to sit in the house on my first Saturday off since I started working. Tessa has to work tonight. In addition to her telling me, I saw it written on her little planner board on the fridge. Deciding to call my mom, I pull my phone out and sit down on a bench. She's due soon and I can feel her nerves from here. She'll be the best mom my little sister could be blessed with, whether she believes it or not.

My mom doesn't answer. Well, my only friend is busy and my mom didn't answer, meaning I don't know what to do next. I'm officially a loser. My sneakers hit the pavement and I start counting the steps as I walk. The pain in my knee isn't too bad as long as I'm walking instead of pushing my body to run.

"On your left!" a woman running with a stroller calls as she passes me. She's pregnant and the stroller has two chubby babies inside. This lady has her hands full. This is a trend in Brooklyn— lots of babies and the strollers to match. I've even seen people pushing their strollers, baby and all, into bars in the early evening.

I have nothing to do. I'm a twenty-year-old college student living in what is purportedly the greatest city in the world, and I have absolutely nothing to do on my day off.

I feel sorry for myself. Not really, but I would rather wallow and complain about my boring life than attempt to make new friends. I don't know where to begin making friends. NYU isn't as friendly as WCU, and if Tessa hadn't spoken to me first, I probably wouldn't have made any friends there either. Tessa is the first person I've started a friendship with since Carter died.

Hardin isn't included in this because *that* was a much more complicated situation to start. He acted like he hated me, but I had a feeling it wasn't as clear-cut as it seemed even then. Really, it was more that he felt the relationship between his dad and me was the epitome of everything that was wrong in his life. He was jealous, and I understand that now. It wasn't fair that I got the new and improved version of his previously alcoholic, emotionally abusive father. He loathed me for our shared love of sports. He hated the way his dad moved my mom and me into a big house, and he despised the car his dad bought me to drive. I knew he would be a difficult part of my new life, but I had no idea that I would be able to identify with his anger and see through his pain. I didn't grow up in a perfect home like he had assumed.

I had a father who died before I had a chance to know him, and everyone around me tried to make up for that. My mom filled my childhood with stories about the man, trying to make up for his early death. His name was Allen Michael, and by her report he was a well-liked man with long brown hair and big dreams. He wanted to be a rock star, my mom told me. Stories like that made me miss him without even knowing him. He was a humble man, she says, who passed away from natural causes at the unfairly young age of twenty-five, when I was only two. I would have been lucky to know him, but I didn't get the chance. Hardin's pain came from a different beast, but I've always believed that suffering is one thing people shouldn't compare.

The biggest difference between my upbringing and Hardin's is due to our mothers. My mom was fortunate enough to have a good job with the city, and we were able to fall back on my dad's life insurance from his factory job. Hardin's mom worked long hours and barely brought in enough money to support the two of them. They had it much, much worse.

It's hard for me to imagine my stepfather, Ken, the way Hardin knew him. To me, he'll always be the kind, lighthearted, and sober man he is today—the chancellor of WCU, no less. He's done so much for my mom and he loves her as much as anyone could. He loves her more than liquor, and Hardin hated that, but now he understands that it was never a competition. If Ken could have, he would have chosen his son over the bottle long ago. But sometimes people just aren't as strong as we want them to be. All of Hardin's pain festered and grew into a fire that he couldn't contain. When everything hit the fan, and Hardin—and the rest of us—found out that Ken isn't his birth father, the fire took one final massive breath and burned him one last time. He made the choice after that to take control of his life, his actions, and himself.

Whatever his therapist is doing is working, and I'm glad. And it's done wonders for my mom, who loves that angry boy as if she gave birth to him.

I pass a couple holding hands as they walk their dog and feel even sorrier for myself. Should I be dating? I wouldn't even know where to start. I want the convenience of having someone around all the time, but I'm not sure I could actually date anyone other than Dakota. The whole dating game just seems so grueling, and it's only been six months since she broke up with me. Is *she* dating? Does she want to? I can't imagine anyone ever knowing me better than her, or making me as happy as she did. She has known me so long and it would take years for anyone to know me as well as she does . . . As she did.

I know I don't have years to wait; I'm not getting any younger here. But thoughts like that aren't helping me move on.

The couple stops for a kiss and I look away, smiling because I'm happy for them. I'm happy for the strangers who don't have to spend their nights alone, jerking off in the shower.

Gah, I sound bitter.

I sound like Hardin.

Speaking of Hardin, I can call him and blow at least five minutes before he hangs up on me. I pull my phone from my pocket and tap on his name.

"Yeah?" he says before the second ring.

"One of your famous warm hellos." I cross the street, continuing my aimless trek in the general direction of my neighborhood. I should get to know this area better anyway; may as well start today.

"Warm as I'm gonna get. Do you need something in particular?"

An angry cabdriver shouts out of his window at an elderly woman as she slowly crosses the street in front of his car.

"I'm looking at your future self, actually," I tell him, laughing at my insult. I watch the scene in front of me to be sure the woman makes it across okay.

He doesn't laugh or ask what the hell I'm talking about.

"I'm bored and wanted to talk about your trip here," I say into the phone.

"What about it? I haven't booked the flight yet, but I'll be there around the thirtieth."

"Of September?"

"Obviously."

I can practically see his eyes roll from here. "Are you staying in a hotel, or at my apartment?"

The old woman reaches the other side of the street and I watch as she goes up some steps and into what I assume is her place.

"What does she want me to do?" His voice is low, cautious. He doesn't have to say her name, hasn't in a while.

"She says she's fine with you staying at the apartment, but if she changes her mind, you know you have to go."

I don't draw many lines between the two of them, but Tessa is my priority in this situation. She's the one I hear crying at night. She's the one who's trying to become whole again. I'm no fool—Hardin is probably even worse off. But he has found himself a support system and a good therapist.

"Yeah, I fucking know that."

I'm not in the least surprised by his annoyance. He can't stand anyone, including me, coming to Tessa's rescue. That's his job, he thinks. Even though he's the one I'm protecting her from.

"I'm not going to do anything stupid. I have a few meetings and wanted to maybe hang out with you and her a bit. Honestly, I'm just happy to be in the same fucking state as her."

I focus on the first part of his sentence. "What kind of meetings? You're trying to move here already?"

I sure hope not. I'm not ready to be in the middle of a war zone again. I thought I would have at least a few more months before the magical forces of insanity brought those two back together.

"Fuck no. It's just some shit for something I've been working on. I'll tell you when I have time to explain the whole thing, which is not now. Someone's calling on my other line." He hangs up before I can respond.

I look at the time on my screen. Five minutes and twelve seconds, a record. I cross the street and shove my phone back into my pocket. When I reach the corner, I look around to gauge where I am. Rows of brick town houses and brownstones line both sides of the street. At the end of the block, a small art gallery shows prints of brightly colored abstract shapes hanging from string through its window. I haven't been inside, but I can only guess how expensive the pieces are.

"Landon!" a familiar voice yells from across the street.

I search the sidewalk and see Dakota. Damn that woman and her lack of clothing. She's dressed the same as yesterday: tight spandex, workout shorts, and a sports bra. Her chest is on the smaller side, but she has the perkiest tits I've ever seen. Not that I've seen a lot of them, but hers are amazing.

She starts waving at me as she crosses the intersection, and if this isn't some sort of fate-driven meet-up, I don't know what is.

# chapter

*Six*

WHEN SHE REACHES ME, Dakota immediately wraps her arms around my neck and pulls me to her. Our embrace lasts a few beats longer than usual, and when she pulls away, she leans her head on my arm. She's nearly a foot shorter than me, though I always liked to tease that her hair, that wild mass of curls, adds four inches onto her driver's license stats.

Her nose is red and her hair is particularly wild. It's not cold yet, but it's windy and air off the nearby East River adds a chill. She's not dressed for the fall weather; in fact, she's not wearing much of anything. I'm not complaining.

"What are you doing over on this side of the tracks?" I ask.

She lives in Manhattan, yet this is the second time I've seen her in Brooklyn this week.

"Running. Crossed the Manhattan Bridge, then just kept trucking." Her eyes meet mine and then quickly dart to my forehead. "What the hell happened to your face?" Her fingers press against my skin and I wince.

"It's a long story." I touch over the sensitive spot with my fingers and feel the knot next to the cut.

"Did you get in a street brawl on the way here?" she teases, and a tingling blossoms in my chest, me missing her even though she's standing right here.

There's no way in hell I'm telling her what actually happened to my head. Or my knee. Gah, I feel like such a creep now that she's in front of me and I think of her every time I make myself come.

"Not quite." I shake my head and continue: "I fell in the shower. But I like your version better. Definitely makes me sound cooler." I chuckle, looking down at her.

My answer humors her and she bounces on the heels of her bright pink Nikes. The yellow check mark on her shoes matches her sports bra and the pink matches her tiny, tiny shorts.

"So what are you up to? Do you want to get a coffee or something?" she asks.

Her eyes dart across the street and she stares at the couple I saw earlier. Their hands are intertwined as they trot down the streets of Brooklyn. It's a romantic sight, him wrapping his coat around her shoulders, leaning down to kiss her hair.

Dakota looks back up at me and I wish I could hear what's going on inside her head. *Does she miss me? Does seeing that couple happy and holding hands make her want my affection?*

She wants to hang out with me now—*what does that mean?* I have absolutely nothing to do, but I probably should act like I have somewhat of a life outside of school and work.

"I have some free time now." I shrug my shoulders and she loops her arm through mine and leads the way. During the walk, I try to compile a list of normal conversation starters that would be nearly impossible to make come out awkward. I say "nearly" because if anyone has a talent for turning normal situations uncomfortable, it's me.

The walk to Starbucks is only a couple of blocks, but Dakota has been next to silent the entire time. Something is off with her, I can tell.

"Are you cold?" I ask. I should have asked her earlier. She has to be cold, she's barely dressed.

She looks up at me, and her Rudolph nose gives her away even though she's shaking her head.

"Here." I gently pull away from her and pull my sweatshirt up over my head and hand it to her.

It cuts me a little when she smells the gray fabric, just like she always used to. She was obsessed with wearing my hoodies when we were in high school. I had to buy one every other week to keep up with her thieving ways.

"You still wear Spicebomb," she says, not asking.

She bought me my first bottle of cologne for our first Christmas together and one every year after.

"Yep. Some things never change." I watch as she pulls my sweatshirt down over her. Her curls push through first and I help yank the fabric down over her mass of hair. The sweatshirt hits her just at her knees.

She looks down at the design printed on the front.

"Deathly Hallows." She touches the tip of the triangle with her unpainted nail. "Some things really do never change."

I wait for her to smile, but it doesn't come.

She smells the sweatshirt again.

"Is it because you like the smell, or because you probably still have a stash from me?" Dakota laughs finally, but, again, it's off.

"You grab a table and I'll get the coffee," I offer. This is what we always did back in Saginaw: she would pick a table, usually by the window, and I would order our matching drinks. Two mocha Frappuccinos, an extra pump of liquid sugar for her, an extra shot of coffee for me. I always ordered two pieces of lemon pound cake and she always ate the icing off of mine.

My tastes have changed over the years, and I can't bring myself to drink the sugary milk shake disguised as coffee anymore. I order her Frappuccino and grab myself an Americano. Two lemon pound cakes. While I'm waiting for my name to be called,

I look over at the table where Dakota is sitting staring off into space with her hands tucked under her chin.

"A mocha Frap and an Americano for . . . London!" The cute barista yells out the wrong name. She's perky as she sets the drinks on the counter, a huge smile on her face, the same as with all employees I see working for the mermaid chain.

Dakota sits up slightly when I reach the table. I hand the large plastic cup to her and she examines mine.

"What's that?" she asks.

I sit down across from her and she brings my cup to her lips.

"You'll hate that—" I try to warn her.

It's too late, her eyes are already closed and her face is already crumpling. She doesn't spit it out, but she wants to. Her cheeks are full of the espresso-and-water mixture and she looks like an adorable little squirrel as she struggles to swallow.

"Ew! How can you drink that?" she exclaims when she finally gets it down. I slide her cup closer to her for a chaser. "It tastes like straight tar—ew!"

She's always been a tad dramatic.

"I like it." I shrug, sipping the coffee.

"Since when do you drink fancy coffee?" Dakota scrunches her nose in disgust again.

I chuckle. "It's not 'fancy.' It's only espresso and water," I say, defending my drink.

She snorts. "Sounds fancy to me."

There's something behind her words. I can't pinpoint it yet, but it's like she's mad at me for something that I'm not aware that I did.

It's like we're still dating.

"I got you some lemon cake, too. Two pieces." I slide the brown paper bag across the table to her. She shakes her head and pushes her hands out, moving the bag back to my side of the table.

"I can't eat stuff like that anymore and I'm already having this coffee as my lunch." She scrunches her nose and I remember her complaining about the change in her eating habits she had to make for her academy. She has to keep a strict diet, and lemon pound cake doesn't fit anywhere into that.

"Sorry." I wince and fold the edges of the bags to close them. I'll take it home and eat it later, when she's not around to witness my gluttony.

"How have you been?" I ask her after a long stretch of silence. It's like neither of us knows how to act when we aren't dating. We're acting as if we're strangers. We were friends for years before we dated; our friendship grew as her brother and I became best friends. A chill runs down my spine and I wait for her to answer.

"I'm okay." She sighs. Her eyes close for a moment and I know she's lying.

I reach across the table and rest my hand next to hers. It wouldn't be appropriate to touch her, but I want to, so badly. "You can tell me, you know."

She sighs again, refusing.

"I'm your safe place, remember?" I remind her of her claim on me. The first time I found her crying on her front steps with blood in her hair, I promised that I would always keep her safe. Neither time nor a breakup would change that.

That's clearly not what she wanted to hear, and she pushes my hand away with a "don't."

"I don't need a safe place, Landon, I need . . . well, I don't even know what I need because my life is fucking failing and I don't know how to fix it." Her eyes are dark now, waiting for my response.

Her life is failing? What does that even mean?

"How so? Is it school?"

"It's everything—literally every damn thing in my life."

I'm not following. That's probably because she hasn't given me any information to allow me to help her.

When I was about fifteen, I realized that I would do anything to make sure she was okay. I'm the fixer, I'm the one who fixes everything for everyone, especially the curly-haired neighbor girl with an asshole for a father and a brother who could barely speak in his home without getting a bruise for the effort. Here we are, five years later, out of that slow, eroding town, away from that man, and some things really never change.

"Tell me something that I can go on." My hand covers hers and she pulls away, just like I knew she would. I let her. I always have.

"I didn't get the part that I've been training and *training* and *training* for the last two months. I thought this role was mine. I even let my GPA drop because I spent so much time rehearsing for my audition." She lets out a forced breath at the end and closes her eyes again.

"What happened with the audition? Why didn't you get it?" I need more pieces of the puzzle before I can form a solution.

"Because I'm not white." She says it loud, certain.

Her answer presses against the small bubble of anger that only holds things that I'm helpless over. I can fix a lot of shit, but I can't fix ignorance, as much as I would love to.

"They said that?" I keep my voice down, even though I don't want to. They couldn't have possibly actually said that to a student?

She shakes her head, huffing out a held-in breath.

"No, they didn't have to. Every single lead they choose is white. I'm so tired of it."

I lean my back against the wooden chair and take the first sip of my coffee.

"Did you speak to someone?" I ask timidly.

We've had this talk before, a few times. Being biracial in the

Midwest didn't trouble anyone in our neighborhood, or hardly anyone at our school. The population of Saginaw is pretty even when it comes to race, and I lived in a predominantly black area. But still, there were a few times when someone would ask her or me why we were together.

*"Why do you only date white guys?"* her friends would ask her.

*"Why don't you date a white girl?"* trashy girls with white eyeliner and gel pens shoved into their mock-designer Kmart bags would ask me. Nothing against Kmart, I always liked that store before it closed down. Well, except the sticky floors—they were the worst.

Dakota slurps on the end of her straw for a few seconds. When she pulls away, she has a dot of whipped cream on the corner of her lip. I fight my instinct to gently swipe it away.

"Remember when we would sit in Starbucks in Saginaw for hours?"

And just like that, she's closing off her real complaint. I don't push her to talk about it any longer. I never have.

I nod.

"And we would give them fake names every time." She laughs. "And that one time that lady got so pissed because she couldn't spell Hermione and she refused to write our names on the cups anymore?"

Her laughter is real now and suddenly I'm fifteen, running down the street after a rebellious Dakota, who has leaned over the counter and stolen the woman's marker right from her apron. It was snowing that day, and we were covered in dirty brown slush by the time we made it home. My mom was confused when Dakota shouted that we were running from the cops as we ran up the stairs of my old house.

I join her soft reverie. "We actually thought the cops would waste their time on two teenagers stealing a marker."

A few customers look in our direction, but it's pretty packed in here, so they are quick to find something else to look at, something more entertaining than an awkward coffee date between two exes.

"Carter said that the woman told him we were banned from there," she adds, her gaze growing somber.

The mention of Carter prickles at the back of my neck.

Dakota must see something in my eyes, because she reaches across and puts her hand on mine. I've always let her.

Taking a page from her book, I change the subject. "We had some good times in Michigan."

Dakota tilts her head and the light above us hits her hair, making her glow. I haven't realized just how lonely I've been lately. Aside from Nora's quick touch, I haven't been touched in months. I haven't been kissed in months. I haven't even hugged anyone except Tessa and my mom since the last time Dakota came to visit me in Washington.

"Yeah, we did," she says. "Until you left me."

# chapter

## Seven

**I**'M WONDERING IF MY EXPRESSION looks anything close to how I feel. I wouldn't be surprised if it did. My neck definitely jerked when she said that. *She had to have seen that*, is all I can think as I stare at her incredulously and wait for her to take back the harsh words.

"What?" she asks, deadpan.

*There's no way she actually . . .*

"I didn't want to leave . . . it's not like I had a choice." I keep my voice quiet, but I hope she can hear the sincerity in my words.

The guy at the next table looks up at us for a second, then turns his attention back to his laptop.

I grab both of her hands on the table and gently squeeze them between mine. I catch on to what she's doing. She's upset about school, so she's projecting her anger and stress onto me. She always has, and I've always let her.

"That doesn't change the fact that you did. You left, Carter was gone, my dad—"

"I wouldn't have gone anywhere if I had a say in it. My mom was moving, and staying for my senior year of high school wasn't a convincing enough reason for her to let me stay in Michigan. You know that."

I'm gentle with her, the way I would be with a wounded animal lashing out at anyone who approaches.

Her anger is deflated instantly and she sighs. "I know. I'm sorry." Her shoulders slump and she looks up at me.

"You can always talk to me about anything," I remind her. I know how it feels to be a small person in such a big city. I haven't really heard her talk about any friends except Maggy, and now I know she's friends with Aiden for some awful reason that I don't understand but I don't think I want to inquire too deeply about. The way she spun for him . . .

Dakota looks toward the door and sighs again. I've never heard a person sigh so much in my life. "I'm fine. I'll be fine. I just needed to vent, I guess."

That's not enough for me.

"You aren't fine, Baby Beans," I say, instinctively using her old nickname. Her wince quickly shifts to a shy smile and I sit back and let the familiarity of us take over. She's softening now, finally, and it makes me feel less awkward around her.

"Really?" Dakota's chair drags against the floor as she moves it closer to mine. "That was a cheap shot."

I smile, staying silent and shaking my head. I didn't use the name in order to gain some advantage. I had called her that by accident one day—I honestly have no idea why—and it just stuck. She melted then, and she's melting now. It just slipped out without me thinking, but I can't say that I'm not happy when she leans her head against my arm, wrapping her hand around it. The silly, accidental nickname has always had the same effect on her. I've always loved it.

"You're so solid now," she says, squeezing my biceps. "When did that happen?"

I've been working out more, and I'd be lying if I said I didn't want her to notice, but now that she has noticed, together with her nearness, it makes me slightly shy.

Dakota's hands run up and down my arm and I gently brush her curly hair away from my face.

"I don't know," I finally respond, my voice sounding much softer than I intended. Her fingers are still playing at my skin, tracing phantom shapes onto it, making goose bumps rise. "I've been running a lot and my building has a gym. I don't use it often, honestly, but I run almost every day."

It feels so good to be touched. I had forgotten just how good it feels to have simple companionship, let alone actually feeling the warmth of another person. The image of Nora's nails raking down my stomach flashes through my mind and I shiver. Dakota's touch is different, softer. She knows just how to touch me, what I'm used to. Nora's touch sent waves through me; this touch is calming.

Why am I thinking about Nora?

Dakota continues to caress me while I try to push Nora from my head.

I feel slightly embarrassed by her attention, but at the same time, it feels really good to have my hard work noticed. I've changed my entire body over the last two years, and I'm glad she seems to appreciate it. She was always the prettier one in our relationship, and maybe my new physique will make her want to touch me more, maybe even spend more time with me.

It's a shallow, desperate thought, but it's all I've got right now when it comes to holding on to Dakota.

She's even more beautiful now than she used to be, and I imagine she will continue to grow more and more beautiful as she transforms into a woman. We used to plan becoming adults together. We would have two kids, she said, even though I kind of wanted four. The world felt so different then, and this idea that we could grow up to be anything we wanted seemed so tangible. When you're submerged in a small town in the Midwest, bright lights and big cities seem so farfetched to most—but they didn't to Dakota.

She always wanted more. Her mom was an aspiring actress

who moved to Chicago to get into a theater production and thereby become a massive star. It never happened; the city stole her soul and she became addicted to the late nights and the things that keep you awake to enjoy them. She never managed to get out, and Dakota has always been determined to do what her mom couldn't: make it.

She leans closer. Her hair tickles my nose and I sink farther back into the chair.

"Tomorrow my meltdown will seem funny," she says, sitting back up in her chair, turning the conversation away from me.

And truth be told, I'm glad for it. I tell her I agree that tomorrow everything will look different, better, and that if she needs anything, I'm only a call away.

We sit in comfortable silence for a few minutes before Dakota's phone starts to ring. As she talks, I push a napkin around the table and then start tearing the paper into little pieces.

Finally, she chirps into the phone, "I'll be there, save me a spot" and shoves it into her bag. She abruptly stands and throws her bag on her shoulder. "That was Aiden." She takes a long slurp of her Frappuccino. My chest tightens and I stand up, too. "There's an audition and he's going to save me a spot. It's for an online ad for the academy. I gotta go, but thanks for the coffee— we need to catch up again soon!" She rests her hand on my shoulder when she kisses my cheek.

And after that flurry, she's gone. Her half-full Frappuccino remains across from me, mocking my loneliness.

# chapter
## Eight

THE ENTIRE WALK HOME I keep thinking:

A. *That was weird.*
B. *I can't stand Aiden and his creepy white hair and long legs—what the hell does he want with her, anyway?*
C. *He's probably trying to convert her to the dark side—but I'm onto him!*

When I open the apartment door, I'm met by the thick scent of vanilla. Either Tessa has gone overboard on the body spray again or someone is baking. I'm praying for baking. The smell of it comforts me—my childhood home was always full of the sweetest smells of chocolate chip cookies and maple squares—and I don't really want to be feeling this way about some body spray; the bait-and-switch would be too similar to what I just had with Dakota . . .

I toss my keys onto the wooden entry table and cringe when my Red Wings key chain chips off a flake of the wood. My mom gave me this table when I moved to New York and made me promise that I would take care of it. It was a gift from my grandma, and my mom holds anything associated with her late mother above nearly everything else, particularly since there isn't much left—especially after Hardin shattered an entire cabinet of cherished dishes.

My grandma was a lovely woman, my mom tells me. I only have one really strong memory of her, and in it she is anything but lovely. I was about six at the time and she caught me stealing a handful of peanuts from a massive barrel at the grocery store in town. I had a mouth- and pocketful of them in the backseat of her station wagon. I don't remember why I did it, or if I even understood what I was doing, but when she turned around to check on me, she found me cracking open shells and chomping away. When she slammed on her brakes, I choked on part of a shell. She thought I was faking it, which only made her more upset.

I coughed the lodged chunks out of my throat and tried to catch my breath as she busted a U-turn right in the center of the highway, ignored the honks from understandably angry drivers, and drove my butt back to the store. She made me admit what I had done and apologize not only to the clerk, but also to the manager. I was humiliated, but I never stole again.

She passed away when I was in middle school, leaving behind two daughters, who couldn't be more opposite from each other. The rest of my information about her comes from my aunt Reese, who makes it sound like she was a tornado compared to the rest of my calm family. No one messed with anyone with the last name Tucker, my mom's maiden name, lest they had to deal with Grandma Nicolette.

Aunt Reese is a cop's widow with big blond hair, teased and sprayed high enough to hold her abundance of opinions. I always liked being around her and her husband, Keith, before he passed away. She was always happy, always so funny, and she snorted when she laughed. Uncle Keith, who I automatically thought was awesome because he was a cop, always gave me hockey trading cards when I saw him. I remember wishing he had been my dad a few times. Pitiful, yes, but sometimes I just wanted another guy around. To this day, I remember when he died, and the gut-wrenching screams of my aunt resounding through the hallways, and then the way my mom's face was so pale and her hands so shaky when she told me, "Everything is fine, go back to bed, sweetheart."

Keith's death turned everyone upside down, especially Reese. She nearly got her home foreclosed on because she was just *that sad*. She no longer had any interest in life, let alone pulling out a checkbook to write a check from an account full of blood money her husband's life insurance had deposited there. She wasn't cleaning, cooking, or dressing herself; she always took care of her children, though. The toddlers were bathed and groomed, their little round bellies proof that she put her children above anyone else. Rumor has it that my aunt gave all the money from Keith's death to his oldest daughter from a previous marriage. I never met her, so I couldn't tell you if it's true or not.

Reese and my mom were close their entire lives, being only two years apart in age. While Aunt Reese has only visited Washington once, they talk on the phone a lot. My grandma's death didn't seem to affect Reese the same way it did my mom. My mom dealt with it with a gentle approach and a lot of baking. Still, it was hard on her, and this table that I just scratched is about the only thing she has left.

Bad son, I am—

"Hello?" Tessa calls from the kitchen, interrupting the picture of little Yodas swimming around in my head.

I bend down to remove my shoes and spare the spotless, old wood floors. Tessa spent all of last week polishing them, and I learned quickly not to wear my shoes inside for a while. For every footprint, I swear she spent twenty minutes on the floor with the little polisher tool in her hand.

Given all the crap on New York's streets, probably best to just always do that anyway, I guess—

"Hello?" Tessa repeats, her voice closer now.

When I look up, she's standing a few feet from me.

"You scared me," she says, her eyes meeting mine. She's been so nervous since someone broke into an apartment on the first floor a couple months back. She doesn't say it much, but I can tell by her anxious glance to the door every time there's a creak in the hallway.

Tessa's wearing a WCU T-shirt and her black leggings are covered in what appears to be flour.

"Sorry. You okay?" I ask. The dark hollows under her eyes are evidence that she's not.

"Yeah, of course." She smiles, shifting her feet. "I'm baking, and how can anything be wrong when you're doing that?" Her words turns into a wry laugh. "Nora's here, too, in the kitchen," she adds.

My brain skips past the latter part for now. "My mom would be proud." I smile at her and toss my jacket on the arm of the chair.

Tessa eyes it, but decides to let this slide. Aside from the cleaning, she's a great roommate. She gives me my time and space in the apartment, and when she *is* here, I like her company. She's my best friend and she's not in the best place right now.

"Yes!" I hear Nora yell.

Tessa rolls her eyes and I shoot her a questioning look, to which she just she nods her head toward the kitchen.

"Thank God," she says sarcastically as I follow her into the kitchen.

The sweet scent grows stronger with each step. Tessa walks straight to the small cart we call an island. At least ten baking pans are stacked on top of one another on the small space.

Tessa lets me in on their reason for celebration. "She must have gotten this batch right."

"We took over your kitchen," Nora tells me. Her greenish-brown eyes catch mine for a moment before she looks over at the mess.

"Hey, Sophia Nora de Laurentiis," I say, opening the fridge and grabbing a water.

Hearing "Sophia," Tessa opens her mouth to correct me, but then I think she gets my little joke and doesn't say anything.

For her part, Nora says, "Hey, Landon," and barely looks up from her task.

I try not to stare at the streaks of purple icing smeared on the chest of her black shirt, which is pretty tight, stretched out over her breasts, and the purple icing so bright . . .

*Look away, Landon.*

I look down at the purple mess in front of her, except it's not a mess. It's a three-layer cake, painted purple and covered in big lilac-and-white flowers. The center of the icing flower is yellow, dusted with glitter. The cake almost looks fake because the icing is so detailed. The candy flowers look as if they could actually have a lovely scent, and before I realize what I'm doing, I lean down and take a whiff.

A small giggle sounds from Nora and I look up at her. She's watching me like I'm animated.

She's really very beautiful. The high angles of her cheekbones make her look like a goddess. She's exotic-looking, with her tan skin and light-brown eyes. Her hair is so dark, it's shining under the buzzing light in the ceiling.

I need to fix that light.

A knock at the front door interrupts my stare-fest.

"I got it," Tessa says, then adds with a smile, "It's so pretty, right?" She nudges Nora's hip with her spatula and heads to the door. I'm happy to see her smiling.

Nora blushes and turns her chin down. She hides her hands behind her back.

"Indeed it is," I agree.

Reaching over, I cup my fingers under her chin and lift her face up to me. She gasps, full lips opening under my touch. My spine tingles when she jerks away.

*Whyyyy, oh why, did I just touch her like that? I'm an idiot.*

And embarrassed.

An embarrassed idiot.

This seems to be a recurring theme when she's around. In my defense, she started the random touching the other day with the dark-fingernails-on-the-naked-stomach bit.

Nora's eyes remain on me. A touch of boredom is there, hidden behind the sheepish pride in her edible creation. I get the feeling that it takes a lot to please this woman.

"What?" she says, like I'm halfway between being rude to and flattering her.

I shrug. "Nothing."

I lick my lips, and her eyes scan my face, resting on my mouth. Her energy is kinetic; there's something insanely electric about this woman. Before my thought can finish, she's crossing the small space between us and has wrapped her hands around me, resting them behind my neck. Her mouth is harsh at first as her lips crush against mine. My mouth opens, welcoming her after I get over the initial shock of her action. Her lips are warm and her kiss is unforgiving as she slides her tongue over mine. I fight the urge to pull her closer and let the kiss soak into me. Nora's hands are moving from my neck now. Her hands are small, but not dainty in the least. She has long, crimson nails today. She must get them done a lot. Her hands are sprawled out, rubbing against the tight muscles on my chest.

Kissing, teasing, kissing.

Kissing her is like touching hot wax. The brisk burn of surprise stings, but the burn quickly fades into the opposite, transforming into something else entirely, something softer. My hands find her hips and I push her body against the counter. Soft moans escape her, and her teeth bite at my bottom lip. My body responds before I can stop it. I try to take a step back so I won't be pressing my arousal into her, but she's not having it. She grips the top of my sweats and pulls me flush against her soft body. She's swearing a tight shirt, and even tighter leggings. I know she can feel every inch of me pressing against her.

"My God," she breathes into my mouth.

I sigh into her.

She twists and pulls away, and instantly, I feel a pang of emptiness.

Her red fingernail taps me on the tip of my nose and she smiles at me, cheeks red and lips swollen from our kiss. "Well, that was unexpected."

Her hand covers her mouth and she pinches her bottom lip between her thumb and forefinger.

*Unexpected? You think so?*

I play it cool, leaning against the counter. I rest my elbows on the cold stone and try to think of something intelligent to say. My body is still humming, silent electricity shooting through my veins, while she looks like she's completely unaffected.

What was that about?

I decide to be bold, like her. At least for a moment.

"Why did you kiss me?" I question.

She watches me, eyes narrowing, and takes a deep breath. The bottom of her shirt is pushed up slightly, caught on the tanned curve of her hip. She's distracting me in every way without even trying.

"Why?" she asks, seeming genuinely puzzled. Her hair escapes from behind her ear and she pushes it back. Her neck is exposed; it seems to be begging for my lips to cover her skin. "Didn't you want me to?"

*Yeah, I did* would sound desperate.

*No, I didn't* would sound rude.

I struggle with the right answer. It's not that I wanted her to kiss me. On the other hand, I didn't *not* want her to kiss me. I'm confusing myself, so I know if I try to explain it to her, it will be an even bigger jumbled mess.

As I stand there in stupid silence, she suddenly looks bored again, and I watch as the heat around her fades into a warm blur.

But then she quickly changes the subject. "You should come out with me and my roommates tonight."

*Okay . . .*

Part of me wants to continue the conversation and find out why she kissed me in the first place, but I figure that she clearly doesn't want to talk about it, so I won't push it. I don't want to make her uncomfortable or give her the impression that I didn't enjoy it.

I'm trying to learn how to "adult." It's getting easier each month, but sometimes I forget that instant intimacy is something only young people desire. If we were teenagers, her kissing me would automatically make us committed to each other in some way, but adult dating is so . . . so much more complicated. It's a much slower process. It's usually like this: You meet someone through your friend, you hit it off, you go on a date. By the end of date number two, you usually kiss. By five dates, you have slept together, twelve dates before you start sleeping over on a regular basis, a year before you move in together, another two you get married. You buy a house, a baby follows.

Sometimes the last two are reversed, but most of the time this seems like how it goes. According to television and romantic movies. Sure, not for people like Hardin and Tessa, who clearly didn't google the SparkNotes of Dating 101 and moved in together within five months of meeting, but still.

"Is that a no?" she presses.

I shake my head, trying to remember what we were talking

about. Her roommates . . . Oh yeah, going out with her room-mates.

I look toward the living room when I hear Tessa talking to someone, and when I turn back to Nora, she's stretching, holding her arms up in the air, exposing more skin. She's tall and curvy; she looks to be at least five foot seven.

It's distracting, for sure.

"Where will you be going?" I ask. I don't want to decline, I'm just curious.

"I don't know yet, honestly." She grabs her cell phone from the counter and swipes her finger over the screen. "Let me ask. We have this group chat that I usually ignore because it's mostly just three horny chicks spamming pictures of hot, naked men, but I'll ask."

I laugh. "Sounds like my kind of chat."

I immediately recoil at my own joke, but humor fills her eyes. Why won't my mouth just stay closed around her? I need a lameness filter. Though if I couldn't say anything embarrassing around her, I probably wouldn't have much to say at all.

"Well then . . ." She laughs. My awkwardness is drowned out by the sound. Her laughter is light, like she doesn't have a care in the world. I want to hear the sound again.

"Sometimes I try too hard," I admit, laughing with her.

She tilts her chin up at me. "You don't say." Her lips are pouty now, as if she's testing me. It's like they are begging me to kiss them again.

Her phone starts to play the theme song from a show I immediately recognize.

I raise one eyebrow. "*Parks and Rec?* I didn't think you were the type," I tease.

I loved that show until the internet stole it from the actual fans and turned it into a cool, memeworthy thing that I can't wrap my mind around.

She quickly ignores the call, but the phone starts ringing again, and Nora immediately swipes to ignore it and puts the phone on the counter. I consider asking her why she did that, just to make sure she's okay. I can't help it. It's become some sort of habit of mine, making sure everyone is okay. Before I butt into Nora's business, Tessa walks back into the kitchen followed by a young man wearing a red work vest and utility belt.

"He's here to fix the garbage disposal," she explains. The man smiles at her, looking at her for a beat too long.

"We have a garbage disposal?" I ask. This is news to me.

Both women look at each other and do that thing where women use their eyes to say, *Oh, men!* like back in the fifties.

Not fair. I help with dishes. I load them. I scrub them. I dry the silverware if Tessa doesn't beat me to it. So I'm not just a dumb dude who doesn't know there's a garbage disposal because I'm lazy—I just hadn't noticed it. Or used it. Come to think of it, I don't think I've ever used a garbage disposal in my life.

Nora grabs her phone from the counter. It's lighting up like it's ringing again, but she must have switched it to silent. Her eyes close and she sighs. "I better go," she announces. Her eyes move back down to her phone. She shoves it into the pocket of her jacket, which is hanging on the back of the chair, and which she then grabs.

I move to help her and hold the jacket behind her as she maneuvers into it. The repairman takes notice of her, watching her as she hugs Tessa and then kisses me on the cheek. Something hot, with a shot of bitter, boils inside of me as he stares at her ass. He's not even trying to hide it. Not that I blame him for wanting to look, but come on, be a little respectful.

Before I smack some manners into the guy, Nora gives me a wave and says, "I'll text you when I know where we're going!"

I'd be lying if I said I wasn't interested, and just a tad worried that she won't actually text me. I don't know how many options she has lying around. I don't know my competitors' stats—oh Lord, I'm comparing dating to sports. Again. I've repeatedly come to the conclusion that they're not that much different, but I'm better off looking at things from a different angle.

But why am I already jumping to the conclusion that Nora wants to date me? Because she kissed me, then invited me to go out with her?

Yes, that's exactly why. I can't tell if this a regression in my "adulting" progress or not.

When Nora is gone, Tessa looks like a little chipmunk that has just found a stash of nuts hidden under some leaves. "What was that about?" she asks nosily.

I'm so used to her intrusiveness it doesn't bother me. I run my hand over my chin, tugging slightly at the hair growing there. I lift my hands up in defense.

"I have no freaking clue, she just kissed me. I didn't even know she knew my name—"

"She *what!*" Tessa shrieks.

This little sip of gossip is enough to keep Tessa Young going for days. I'll definitely hear about it later. My mom may hear about it, too.

The repairman cocks his head to the side like he's listening to a daytime drama. He could at least be subtle about it. Then again, if I fixed appliances all day, I would want some comic relief or some kind of entertainment. Like adding a little splash of color to a black-and-white painting.

"I didn't know either! Well, I know she knew your name," Tessa says, being as literal as ever.

"I don't know. I'm just as confused as you."

Something is off in the way Tessa is looking at me, like she's trying to hide her disappointment. I'm not sure what to make of this. My guess is because she misses Hardin, but I'm probably wrong. I haven't got a clue what to think about any of this.

Instead of indulging in gossip that may or may not be worth it, I tighten the drawstring on my sweats and head toward the door.

"We aren't done here, Landon Gibson!" Tessa shouts after me.

And somehow it all makes me feel a little like a criminal on the run.

# chapter

## Nine

*I* CLOSE THE APARTMENT DOOR BEHIND ME and nearly slam into someone in the hallway.

When his hood falls down, I don't recognize him. He's wearing a black coat and gray Windbreaker pants. He nods at me,
being friendly enough, and lifts his hood back over his head. Our
apartment building has about twenty units and I've seen nearly
every person or couple who lives here, but not this guy. Maybe he
just moved in.

"Excuse me, sorry!" I say as I move out of his way, but he just
grunts in reply.

At the corner of the block, I break out into a run. I wait for
the ache to resurface in my knee, and it does, but it's bearable
now. The low, simmering pain is no longer a sharp throb.

I pick up my pace. My Nikes hit the sidewalk with hardly
any noise at all. I remember when I first started running and my
legs would burn and my chest would feel like it was going to ex-
plode. I pushed and pushed—I needed to be healthy, and now
I am. Not healthy like the stroller moms in Brooklyn who take
shots of wheatgrass for breakfast and feed their babies kale and
quinoa for lunch. But healthy insofar as being active.

I often empty my mind when I run, though sometimes
I think about my mom and the baby, about Tessa and Hardin, or I

stew with frustration if the Chicago Blackhawks beat the Detroit Red Wings. Today I feel like I have a lot on my mind.

First: Dakota's behavior. She's barely spoken to me since she broke up with me, and now she's acting like we will see each other every day. She was so worked up over her audition and I wish there was something I could do. I can't go to one of the most prestigious ballet academies in the country and knock on their door claiming racial discrimination without any proof. Especially with all the madness going on in the country already. The last thing that I want to do is to cause Dakota to get too much negative attention while she's trying to start a career there.

The shit that I'm used to helping her with is so different from this. Her career is something that I absolutely can't do anything about. The obstacles that we used to battle together seem so distant now, a part of our past. Our problems felt much heavier back then, much more immediate. I don't know what to do with practical, day-to-day problems like school or career choices.

This is one of the few times that I would like to be Hardin for about an hour. I would rush down to that academy, pound on the door, and demand justice for her. I would convince them that Dakota is the best ballerina they have there, that despite her reminders that she's not a ballerina yet, she is indispensable to them. The best.

Ballet to Dakota is what hockey is for me, only ten times more so because she actually does it. My school didn't offer hockey as a sport, and when my mom signed me up to play at the local rec center, it was the worst two hours of my life. I learned very quickly that hockey is a sport I can love to watch—and never play. Dakota has been dancing since she was a kid. She started with hip-hop, moved to jazz, and settled on ballet in her teens. Believe it or not, beginning ballet as a teen is a huge disadvantage and in some circles is considered to be too late. But Dakota smashed those assumptions during her first audition at the

School of American Ballet. My mom sent her the money to go to the audition for her birthday present. She cried grateful tears and promised my mom that she would do her best to pay her generosity back someday.

My mom didn't want to be paid back, she wanted to see the sweet neighbor girl rise above her circumstances and make something of herself. The day she learned of her acceptance, Dakota came running through the house with her letter waving above her head. She was screaming and jumping and I had to pick her up and flip her small body upside down to get her to stay still. She was so happy. I was so proud. Her school may not be Joffrey, but it's a highly rated academy and I'm damned proud of her.

All I want is for her to be happy and for her talent to be recognized. I want to fix this for her, but it's out of my control. As frustrating as it is, I can't think of one realistic solution to this problem. I should have asked her what else was going on; there has to be more to work with . . .

I file that away for later and shift my focus to Nora. She does look more like a Nora than a Sophia, and luckily I'm not as bad as Hardin with names. He refuses to call Dakota anything other than Delilah, even to her face. Enough about brooding Hardin.

Hardy.

That makes me laugh. I'm calling him that next time he calls Dakota "Delilah."

As I pass a grocery mart, a woman with her hands full of paper bags is staring at me, so I stop laughing at myself and my corny plans to stick it to Hardin. Or Hardy.

I laugh again.

I need more coffee.

I'm only about a twenty-minute run from Grind, but it's the opposite direction from my apartment than the park . . .

Coffee is worth it. You can get coffee on nearly every corner here, but not good coffee—*ugh,* deli coffee is the worst—and I need to check if next week's schedule is up, anyway. I reverse course to run back toward the coffee shop. I pass the woman carrying the shopping bags again and I watch as one of the sacks slips from her hand. I rush over to help, but I'm not fast enough and the brown bag tears and cans of food roll onto the sidewalk. She looks so frustrated that it wouldn't be a surprise if she screamed at me just for helping her.

I grab a can of chicken soup before it rolls into the street. Another bag tears and she curses as her vegetables tumble to the ground. Her dark hair is covering her face, but I would guess she's about thirty. She's wearing a loose dress and has a slight bump underneath. She may be pregnant—or she may *not* be: I know better than to ask.

Two teenage boys cross the street and come our way. For just a moment, I believe they may actually help us.

Nope. While we're scrambling to clean up her grocery disaster, they don't bat an eye in our direction. No neighborly assistance; they just pick up their boots and are nice enough to step over a box of rice directly in their path. Sometimes not crushing things in your way is as much kindness as you can get in this city.

"Do you live far from here?" I ask the woman.

She looks up from the sidewalk and shakes her head. "No, just one more block." She pushes her deep brown hands against her hair and groans in frustration.

I point to the pile of groceries from the two bags. "Hmm, okay. Let's get these under control." Seeing as I don't have any extra bags hanging around in my pockets, I pull my sweatshirt over my head and start scooping the groceries into it. They may not all fit, but it's worth a try.

"Thanks," she offers, slightly out of breath. She moves to bend to help me, but I stop her.

A car honks, then another. I barely have one foot in the street, but they honk anyway. The best thing about living in

Brooklyn is the lack of honking (usually). Manhattan is a chaotic, angry little island, but I could possibly see myself settling down in Brooklyn, teaching at a public school, and raising a family. My daydream plans usually include other cities, quieter ones. Still, I've got to get a girl to go on a date with me first, so this may take a while. Let's just say it's my five-year plan . . .

Okay, ten-year plan.

I push a bottle of cooking oil into the crook of my arm. "I've got it. It's fine," I tell the woman.

I look into her hooded eyes. She's watching me now, skeptical and unsure whether I'm sketchy or okay. *You can trust me*, I want to promise her. However, chances are that if I say that, it will only raise her suspicion levels. The wind picks up, instantly bringing the temperature down a bit. I move faster, and once I get most of the groceries inside my sweatshirt, I tie the sleeves together, creating my best version of a bag. I toss in a box of crackers and a pack of lunch meat.

I stand to my feet and place the sweatshirt bag in her hands. Her eyes soften.

"You can keep the hoodie, I have a ton of them," I say.

"I bet you'll make a lady very happy one day, young man," she says to me with a smile. She gathers up the remainder of her grocery bags that didn't break, readjusts the sweatshirt in her arms, and starts to walk away. I'm flattered by her compliment but I quickly wonder why she assumed that I'm single. Do I ooze desperation and loneliness?

Probably.

"Do you need help? I can help you get them home?" I offer, sure to pose my tone as an offer, not a demand. It's going to take her a while to get home, carrying those bags like that.

She shakes her head and looks past me, in the direction she was headed. "It's just right here. I've got it."

I hear a tinge of an accent in her voice, but I can't make it out. As she walks away, it dawns on me that she actually doesn't need my help—she's carrying the bags and the sweatshirt full of groceries just fine. I'm guessing this is supposed to be some metaphor sent by the cosmic forces to show me that I don't have to help everyone, like Augustus and his cigarettes in *The Fault in Our Stars*. Well, not exactly the same, but still. He obviously had it worse than me, poor guy.

I let the woman go on her own and continue my journey south, deeper into Bushwick. I love the neighborhood I live in. It's close to the cool things in Williamsburg, but with much lower rent. Definitely our rent is already high—it shocked the heck out of me when I moved here—and is basically more than my mom's mortgage. But if the cool factor of our neighborhood keeps rising, it will double in no time. Still, things aren't as expensive here as I thought they would be. They're not cheap, by any means, but those rumors of a gallon of milk costing ten dollars in New York City aren't true . . . for the most part. The Russian guy who owns the corner store below my apartment does like to hike his prices, but I suppose I'm paying extra for the convenience of being able to get down there in under a minute. I could always walk two more minutes and find another. One of the best things about the city is the endless options. From corner stores, to restaurants, to people, there's always another option.

# chapter

## Ten

*W*HEN I GET TO GRIND, Posey is behind the counter pouring a bucket of ice into the bin. Jane, the shop's oldest employee, who sometimes likes to call herself the "elder statesman" in a corny little voice, is cleaning the stained wood floors. She dips the mop into the bucket and soapy water overflows. A little girl gets up from a table near the back and walks over to watch Jane as she swipes the mop over the mess, soaking up the water. I look around the various tables for her parents, but the shop is pretty empty. Out of the ten tables, only two are occupied. Two girls with their laptops and textbooks filling the table and a guy with four empty espresso cups are the only people I see.

Noticing me, Posey greets me with a silent smile.

The little girl, who looks to be about four, sits down on the floor and pulls something out of her pocket. A small red car wheels across the puddle and I watch her eyes light up. Jane says something to her that I can't make out.

"Lila, please don't do that." Posey lifts the partition and steps out from behind the counter. Approaching the girl, she bends down to her level.

The little girl grabs the red car before Posey can reach it. She hugs it to her chest and shakes her head furiously. "Want car," her little voice chimes.

Posey reaches her hand out and cups the little girl's cheek.

Her thumb caresses the child's skin and turns her panic into comfort. She must be familiar with Posey.

Her sister, of course. This little brown-haired girl must be the sister she's mentioned a few times.

"You can keep the car, but please don't put it in the water." Posey's voice is different when she talks to the girl. Softer. "Okay?"

Posey taps the little girl on the nose and she giggles. She's cute.

"'Kay." Her little voice is even cuter.

I walk toward them and sit down at a nearby table. Jane finishes with one more swipe of her mop and says hi before she excuses herself to go to the stock room to finish inventory. Posey looks around to assess how busy the store is, politely checks in on the two tables, then walks back over to the girl and me.

"Please don't tell Jacob that I brought her to work with me." Posey slides into the chair in front of me.

"I would never," I tell her with a smile.

Jacob can be an ass. He's just a little too young to be a manager and is the type of guy that when given just a taste of power, he runs with it. He's a little too bossy and a little bit of a douchebag.

"My grandma had an appointment and I couldn't call in." Posey nervously justifies herself.

"Well, lucky for you, then; you get to hang out with your sister all day."

Posey smiles and nods in agreement, relief clear on her face.

Little Lila doesn't turn to look toward my voice. The bell on the door chimes, alerting Posey of a customer. She looks at Lila and I nod, telling her I can sit with the girl. Going back behind the counter, Posey greets two men in suits and I turn to watch the little girl play with her toy. She's not paying any attention to me. That car is fascinating her and she's awfully cute while she rolls the little Camaro along the uneven floor. She crawls behind it, despite being clearly old enough to walk. Her little sneakers light up when her toes hit the floor, and her little fingers wrap around the body of the car, which she flips over and spins upside down, smiling all the while.

"That's an awfully cool car you've got yourself," I tell her.

She doesn't look up at me, but she speaks. "Car," she says.

Posey looks over as she pours soy milk from a carton into the blender. I smile at her and her shoulders relax. She purses her lips into a modest smile and gets back to work. Her fingernails are dark with little yellow dots painted on them. I watch her hands as she pours premade green tea from a pitcher into the cup full of soymilk and ice. She blends the concoction and sways her head back and forth to the Coldplay song playing on our speakers. I look back over to the little girl staring adoringly at her little plastic Camaro.

"Zoom," Lila says softly. She lifts the car into the air and gazes off into the distance after it.

I sit quietly until the customers disappear. Posey is wiping down the bottles of flavored syrup with a wet rag. The tables are dirty, eight out of ten of them. I walk over to the trash area and grab the busser tub from inside the cabinet next to the trash can. Lila is still saying "car" and "zoom" as I start to clear off the first table. A three-dollar tip.

Not too bad. You'd be surprised at the number of customers that leave their tables a mess but don't think to leave a tip for the person cleaning it up. I'm not sure if it's rudeness or if it's just ignorance. Like Uber drivers: we assume that they get their entire tip, which is charged automatically, but I've heard people say it's not. Even if you mark the 15 percent tab, they don't actually see that money, so this one guy in my class told me you're supposed to tip them in cash. Then again, he said he was from France, but his accent was clearly German, so the possibility of him lying is probably fairly high . . .

Either way, baristas should be tipped way more than they are. Public-service announcement complete. Moving on.

The next table has at least four sugar packets emptied out into a pile. I'm impressed when I see the sugar packets folded into little stick figures. There's a toothpick with a piece of napkin for a flag stuck right into the center of the sugar hill. I try to remember what the guy looked like who was sitting here. Actually, I think it was a girl. Or woman. I didn't get a clear look at her face, but whoever she is, she's clearly an awesome force in the miniature sugar sculpture scene.

"Lila." I call to get the little girl's attention. She looks up but doesn't move her body from its now full-on lying-down position on the floor.

"Do you want to come see this little scene over here? It's pretty cool." I point to the sugar hill and stare at the fake sword in one of the sugar-packet people's arm.

A hearty "no" comes out of her mouth and I nod, not entirely surprised, flattening the hill with my washcloth. I go back and forth between clearing the remaining tables and keeping an eye on Lila. As I'm taking a last swipe over the second-to-last table, Posey walks from behind the counter and stands in front of me.

"You didn't have to do that," she says; the brown of her eyes is barely noticeable because of how bloodshot they are. "It's your day off."

"Are you okay?" I ask.

She glances around the shop and nods, sighing as she sits down at the table closest to her sister.

She shrugs. "Just tired. Work, school, the usual." Her smile is perky still, despite her words. She doesn't like to complain, I can tell, even though she totally has reason to, or to at least vent.

"If you need to have some shifts picked up or anything, let me know. I don't mind helping and I have some free time this semester." I actually don't have that much free time, but I would like to help her if I can. She clearly has more going on than I do.

Posey shakes her head, and her cheeks flush. Light red strands are escaping from the tiny black elastic band that's too small to hold her hair. In the light, her hair looks lighter, as if she dyed it red. Her complexion doesn't give any of her secrets away.

"I need the shifts. But if you know anyone who makes bubbles to put little four-year-old daredevils inside of while I work, let me know."

I smile with her and look at Lila, who is still lying on the floor.

"She's autistic," she says. Somewhere inside my head, the pieces were put together within a few minutes of meeting her. "We aren't sure how severe yet. She's learning to talk now"—she pauses briefly—"at four."

"Well, sometimes that's not such a bad thing." I gently bump her shoulder with mine, trying to find a dash of humor in something so scary. She uncrosses her arms and her face relaxes into a wide smile.

"True." She presses her fingers against her lips.

Posey bends down closer to her little sister and rests her hands on her knees. I can't hear what she says, but I can see that it makes Lila happy.

I check the time; it's close to six. If I'm going to go out with Nora and her friends, I need to get back to my apartment and shower. I'm not nervous really, I just don't know what she's thinking about me. Does she randomly kiss people often? If so, that's okay, but I wish I had some inkling of what she's feeling, or how she acts on a date. She'd been flirty before today—well, I take it as her flirting, but so far she hadn't given me any indication or warning that she was open to kissing me like she did this morning. She was so confident when she leaned into me, pressing into me, running her hands over my chest. Remembering the way her tongue tasted makes my cock ache. I need to do something about it, and this time, I won't rip the shower curtain and fall on my ass and cut my face and bruise my knee. Safe sex: I'll stay safely in my bed. With my door locked. I'll even push my dresser against the door.

I look over at Posey, who's sitting back at the table again. She has her phone next to her ear and is frowning. I watch her shake her head and mutter something into the phone before hanging up. I want to be nosy, to ask her if she's okay, but at the same time, I don't want to pry into her life without her wanting me to.

"Do you need anything before I go?" I ask while I walk behind the bar to check my schedule and make my espresso. Double espresso. I consider doing a triple, but that might not be the best idea.

Posey's shift should be close to over by now. She shakes her head, thanking me, but says she's fine. I wave goodbye to Lila and Posey, shouting goodbye to Jane loud enough for her to hear me from the stock room.

# chapter

# *Eleven*

*A*S I PUSH ON THE HEAVY SHOP DOOR and walk out into the coming night, my phone pings in my front pocket. Heavy bags of trash line the street, nearly bursting open to spill their litter onto the sidewalks. It's the same every day, but I don't see myself getting used to it. Manhattan must be even worse, with all the shops and a million and a half people sharing the smaller space. It's an impossible city to live in if you don't want to be bumped into, honked at, or hassled.

It astounds me that so many people can be shoved into so many little apartments with tiny windows and tiny kitchens. The rooms in my place are bigger than I had expected (the bathroom is snug), but I knew I couldn't afford to live in an expensive place in Brooklyn that was any bigger than five hundred square feet. My stepdad, Ken, helps pay our rent, but I've been putting money aside since I got a job and I plan on repaying him someday, at least some of it. I'm not very comfortable with the idea of him helping me with my bills. I'm responsible enough, partly thanks to him and his lectures about money management and student expenses. I don't blow my money on booze or going out. I pay my bills and occasionally buy books or tickets to a hockey game.

Having a parent who occupies such a high position at a university has unquestionably made my college life one hundred percent easier. I got help with each and every form, I had a help-ing hand in choosing all my classes, and I managed to get into some that were supposedly full. Ken had a lot more pull at Wash-ington Central than at NYU for sure, but it still helps to know the ins and outs of admissions departments.

I often think about how life would be if my mom had stayed in Michigan. Would I have left her alone there and moved to New York with Dakota? I feel like I would have been less likely to move if she didn't have Ken and her group of friends in Washing-ton. My life would be so different if she hadn't met him.

Sometimes I think that outside of the few obvious things, New York City isn't *that* different from Saginaw. The sun is often hidden in Manhattan, keeping the light from the city's residents in a small box on a beach somewhere on the West Coast. I've be-come so used to the overcast sky shadowing every town I've ever lived in that when the sun shines here in Brooklyn, my eyes burn for half of my walk to work. I bought a pair of sunglasses, which I quickly lost. But the sun shows its face in Brooklyn often enough that I would actually use them, marking one of the many rea-sons I chose to live here instead of Manhattan. In September, the overcast has blotted out everything close to the skyline. The far-ther you get away from the towering buildings, the more lumi-nous the sun becomes.

A short, stocky bundle of layered coats with a hat on top moves past me on the sidewalk, the man beneath them push-ing a shopping cart full of aluminum cans and plastic bottles. His hands are encased in thick, faded brown gloves covered in black dirt. Patches of gray hair poke out from under the red-and-green plaid hat he's wearing and his eyes are half-closed, like time and hardship have wilted him to the point of near collapse. He stares straight ahead, paying me no mind, but my heart aches for him.

To me, the poverty in some parts of the city is the hardest thing to deal with. I miss my mom, but seeing the sad, shameful look on the weathered face of a middle-aged man sitting against a bank window using the words printed on a piece of cardboard to beg for food money—that kind of thing is especially hard for me. Even so, it must cut even deeper for men like that to be leaning against a building that is home to millions of dollars. To watch, with an empty stomach, as groups of suits walk past on their lunch break and spend twenty dollars on a grain salad while they are starving.

Saginaw doesn't have a large population of homeless. Most of the city's poor have homes. The siding on their old homes is almost collapsing, the walls are rotting with mold, and the beds are infested with little bugs that feed on them in their sleep. But they have roofs over their heads. Most of the people I know in Saginaw try and try to get ahead, but it's hard there. All of my friends' parents were farmers or lifelong factory workers, but since all the factories closed over the past decade, there just aren't any jobs. Outside of heroin, the city can't boast of any growth industries. Families that were doing well ten years ago can barely put food on the table now. Unemployment rates are at an all-time high, along with the crime rate and drug problems. The happiness ran away with the jobs, and sometimes I think neither will ever return.

That's the biggest difference between my hometown and this city. The hope that buzzes through New York City makes all the difference in the world. Millions of people move to the biggest city in the entire country based solely on this emotion. They hope for more. They hope for more happiness, more opportunity, more experience, and—most of all—more money. The streets are crowded with people who leave their native countries and build a home and a life for their families here. It's pretty amazing when you think about it.

People pack up and move here, some crazy statistic like over a hundred people a day. Twenty-four-hour subways—heck twenty-four-hour services of every category—and no large pick-ups or tractors taking up half of the road, like in Michigan. The small brown municipal buildings that we called "downtown" Saginaw aren't even close in comparison to the soaring skyscrapers in New York City.

So the more and more I think about it, New York and Saginaw have absolutely nothing in common, and I think I'm okay with that. Maybe I keep trying to make them similar to try to reassure myself that living here won't change me . . . that whatever growing up means, I will still be myself when I get there, only different.

My phone pings again. Pulling it out, I see my mom's name twice, making my heart race. When I read the messages, I relax. One of them is a link to an article about a Harry Potter–themed bar that just opened in Toronto, and the other is an update on my little sister's weight. She's a little one so far, but my mom still has four weeks to go. The last month should give little Abby enough time to bulk up in there.

The thought of my wrinkly little baby sister wearing a pink headband while lifting little pudgy arms into the air makes me laugh. I don't know how it will be to be a big brother, especially at my age. I'm too old to possibly have anything in common with the little one, but I want to be the best brother I can be. I want to be the older brother that I needed when I was young. It will be an adjustment for my mom and for Ken, to have such a young baby at home again when both of their other children are grown and finally out of the nest. My mom kept telling me that she couldn't wait to have her house to herself, but I could tell she would be lonely without me around. It's always been her and me, through the best and the worst.

As I wait for the crosswalk sign to change and show that glowing white silhouette, I remind myself how damn lucky I am to have the mom I do. She never once questioned my move and has supported every one of my whims since I was a child. My mom was that mom who would dress up in costumes with me months away from Halloween. She even told me I could live on the moon if I wanted to. When I was a child, I often wondered if I ran fast enough, if I would land on the moon. Sometimes I wished I would.

When the light changes, a woman in high heels struggles to cross the street before me. I don't understand why women put themselves through so much torture to look taller. The intersections here change quickly, usually giving pedestrians less than thirty seconds to cross. I type a quick response to my mom and promise to call her tonight. I shove my phone back in my pocket, deciding to read about the bar later.

I really want to go to Toronto, I always have, and a flight from here is only an hour, so maybe I can plan a trip over winter break. I'll most likely go alone, even though a wild part of me suddenly suggests that I take Nora—she would be fun to travel with, I bet. I have a feeling she's traveled more than I have. Even without knowing her, I see her as someone who's been a few places, or just knows more about the world in general than me. There's only so much a textbook can teach you. I'm proof of this. I would love to travel, and soon.

But why am I imagining Nora and me on some tropical beach somewhere, imagining her in a tiny bikini top, her full ass peeking out from the bottom? I barely know her, and yet I can't get her out of my head.

The deli just below my building is never crowded, and sometimes I feel bad for Ellen, the young Russian girl who works behind the counter. It worries me that she sits in there alone at night. The bell above the door rings as I enter, and Ellen pops her head up from a thick textbook and gives me a polite smile. Her short, wavy hair is tucked behind a thin headband that matches her red sweater with small white dots.

"Hi there," she says to me as I scan the refrigerated section in the back for milk.

"Hey, Ellen," I say, grabbing a container of milk; I check the dates because I've left here with expired products more than once. Then I search for a blue Gatorade, to grab for Nora the next time she comes over, but they don't have any. I have time, so I'll just walk down to the next-closest store after I leave here.

And for the second time today, I find I could have used one of the tote bags Tessa keeps a supply of near the door. She likes to discourage the use of plastic, and now every time I open the door, I hear her voice, reminding me of the damage plastic bags wreak on the environment. That woman watches way too many documentaries. Soon she's going to boycott wearing shoes or something.

Ellen closes her textbook as I approach. I grab a pack of gum from the shelf in front of the counter. She looks a little stressed, so now I really wish I had brought a tote, the one with a watermelon and a cantaloupe on it. Next to the watermelon is a text bubble that says, *We should run away and get married* and the cantaloupe replies, *I'm sorry*, and underneath that, the cantaloupe's face is larger and it's saying, *I CANTaloupe*.

Ellen finds the fruit humor just as funny as I do, which makes her quality people. And maybe a joke would make her smile.

"How's it going?" I ask.

"Good, just studying."

The old register beeps when Ellen types in the cost of the milk and gum. I pull my card out and swipe it.

"You're always studying," I say. It's true: every time I come here she's alone behind the counter and is either reading from a textbook or filling out work sheets.

"I need to get into college." She shrugs, and her brown eyes flash away from mine.

*College?* She's in high school and works here this late, and this often? Even on the days when I don't stop in, I see her working through the window.

"How old are you?" I can't help but ask. It's none of my business, and I'm not much older than her, but if I were her parents, I would be a little worried about my teenage daughter working alone, at night, in a store in Brooklyn.

"I turn eighteen next week," she says with a frown, which kind of runs counter to the typical teenage girl, who beams at the idea of getting another year closer to the golden age of eighteen.

"Nice," I tell her as she hands me the receipt to sign.

She's still frowning when she hands me a red pen tied to a small clipboard with a dirty brown string. I sign it and give it back to her. She apologizes profusely when the printer machine jams before my copy of the receipt comes out. She pops the top off and I tell her that it's fine.

"I'm not in a rush," I tell her. I don't have anywhere to be except home to study for Geology. Oh, and my date with Nora that I'm pretty damn nervous about. No big deal.

She rips the jammed paper roll out and tosses it into a trash can behind the counter.

Thinking about her, I realize that Ellen has never really seemed as carefree as a seventeen-year-old should be. Often I forget that most people in the world don't have a mom like mine—heck, most kids I knew growing up didn't. I didn't have a father figure growing up, but it never bothered me much, honestly. I had my mom. Everyone reacts to things differently based on their own personal experience and how they're built. Hardin, for example . . . his experiences had different effects on him than mine had on me, and he had to take a different path to understand them. It doesn't matter why; what matters is that he's taken responsibility for them and is busting his ass to understand his past and shape his future.

When I was twelve, I began to count down the years and months leading to my eighteenth birthday—even though I wouldn't be going anywhere right away, my eighteenth birthday being right at the beginning of my senior year. Because of the enrollment cutoff, I was always older than everyone else in my grade. I hadn't planned on leaving my mom's house until after college, but that was before Dakota started mentioning me moving to New York with her during *her* senior year. After I spent months applying for a transfer, applying for FAFSA at NYU, finding an apartment for the two of us that was easily accessible to the campus using the subway, coming to peace with leaving behind my best friends, my pregnant mom, and my stepdad, Dakota's life took a change and she forgot to tell me.

I'm still happy that I moved, happy that I'm becoming an actual man who's socially aware, with responsibilities and plans for the future. I'm not perfect—I can barely do my own laundry, and I'm still getting the hang of paying my own bills—but I'm learning at a pace that I can keep up with and having a good time doing it. Tessa helps a lot. Tessa likes to keep things much tidier than a normal person, but we both clean and do an equal share of the chores. I've never left a dirty pair of socks in the living room, or forgotten to pick my damp, dirty clothes off of the bathroom floor after a shower. I'm conscious that I share an apartment with a woman who I'm not intimate with, so I never leave the toilet seat up or freak out if I see a tampon wrapper in the trash can. I make sure she's not home when I masturbate, and I always make sure to leave no evidence behind when I do.

Though perhaps yesterday disproves that last claim. My mind keeps going back there, to the encounter with Nora.

After turning the machine off and back on and changing the roll of paper twice, Ellen prints my copy of the receipt. I decide to linger just a little longer; I have a feeling that she doesn't get much interaction outside of the characters in her history books.

"Are you doing anything special for your birthday?" I ask her, genuinely curious.

She scoffs and her cheeks flare. Her pale skin turns red and she shakes her head. "Me? No, I have to work."

Somehow I knew she didn't have plans outside of sitting in a stool behind the high counter.

"Well, birthdays are overrated anyway," I say with the biggest smile I can manage. She half smiles, her eyes lighting up with just a touch of happiness.

Her back straightens slightly and her shoulders sag a little less. "Yeah, they are."

I tell her to have a good night and she says she will. As I close the door behind me I tell her not to study too hard. Man, what it would be like to be seventeen and growing up in the city; I can't really imagine it.

During my walk to the store at the end of the block, I read about the bar my mom texted me about and call her. She tells me that Ken just got home from a conference in Portland, and he hops on the line so we can talk about the score of the last Giants game. With their loss, I won a little wager we had going, and I can't keep myself from bragging just a touch. We play quick catch-up and get off the phone so he and my mom can eat dinner.

I used to eat dinner with them nearly every night and talk about current events, school, sports, among other things. While I'm glad for the time I spent with my family before I moved, thinking about them only reminds me all the more that I've got to make some friends.

# chapter

## Twelve

*a*FTER FINDING NOT ONE, but three red Gatorades, I head back to my apartment.

At my building, a loud delivery truck is idling in the middle of the street. The deli below the building has deliveries at all times of the night; the trash collectors come at around 3 a.m. nearly every night and the loud pounding of the bins being emptied into the metal truck used to wake me up all the time. I recently made the best purchase of my life and got one of those machines that play sounds of the sea, the rain forest, the night desert, and the only setting that I actually use: white noise.

I wait patiently for the elevator to reach the first floor and step inside. It's small, only suitable for two medium-sized people and one shopping bag. I usually don't mind taking the stairs, but my knee's started throbbing a little again.

As it lifts me up to the third floor, the elevator creaks and groans and those sounds, along with my anxiety about tonight, make me wonder when one of the old elevators in this city is finally going to trap me for hours. If it happened tonight, I wouldn't be able to go out with Nora—

No, tonight will be fun.

*It will be so fun,* I tell myself as I put the milk away and the Gatorade in the fridge.

*It's a normal thing to go out with a woman and her roommates, even if I don't know them,* I think as I feel the soothing hot water of the shower. An uneventful shower, during which no curtains or egos are hurt, and one that I very much enjoy.

Totally normal, and nothing to be nervous about.

But the moment I convince myself of this, a tiny, curly-haired wrench is tossed into my plans. Lying back on my bed, my hair still wet from the shower, I check my text messages. I scroll through two texts, one from Tessa about taking an extra shift. She says she will meet us out if she can and that Nora is going to text me soon with the information about tonight.

The other is from Dakota.

**Hey what are you up to?** I read, then repeat it aloud, a little confused.

Staring at the screen, I wait a few moments before responding. I don't want to tell her that I have plans with someone else, especially not another woman. It's not that I want to lie; I would rather do anything than that. I just don't see anything good coming from telling her what I'm *actually* doing. I don't know if there's even a reason to tell her. We aren't dating. Nora and I are only friends, no matter how much time I spend thinking about her.

But I lie anyway.

**Studying. You?**

I close my eyes before I hit send and my memory guides my thumb to pull the trigger. I immediately feel guilty for lying, but know that it's too late to backtrack now.

I plug my phone into the charger and walk to my closet to begin getting ready for tonight. I grab a pair of dark blue jeans with rips in both knees from my closet. The jeans are tighter than I usually wear, but I like the way they look on me. Until two years ago, I would have never fit into these without looking like an overflowing cupcake. Not even a cupcake . . . a muffin. An ugly muffin.

I stare and stare at my closet, trying to locate any bit of fashion knowledge I may have stored somewhere inside my brain. There's nothing. I've got elves, wizards, hockey pucks, and plenty of warlocks inside my head, but no fashion tips. There's nothing in my closet except button-down shirts, plaid everything, and too many WCU hoodies. I walk over to my small dresser and open the top drawer. I'll wear gray briefs, one of the few pairs I have that don't have holes in them. My room is a little muggy, so I lean over and pull my window open.

The second drawer is filled with T-shirts, most of them with words printed on the front. Should I have gone shopping?

Where is Tessa when I need her?

Getting ready to go out for a night of partying is something I'm not even close to being familiar with. I usually wear plain T-shirts with jeans or slacks, and since I've moved to Brooklyn, I've added a few jackets to my wardrobe. I would say I'm right in the middle stages of being able to dress myself.

I don't know what type of place we're going to, or what Nora will be wearing. I don't know much about dates in general.

I reach for a gray shirt and toss it over my head. The sleeves are weirdly long, so I roll them up and pull my briefs over my legs.

My hair is getting long in the front; it curls down slightly on my forehead, but I can't decide if I want to cut it. I put some of Tessa's spray stuff in my hair and try to comb the unruly whiskers on my face. I like the scruffy look but really wish I didn't have the patches of skin at the bottom of my cheeks that refuse to grow hair.

By the time I'm dressed and my hair is somewhat tamed, I have a text from Nora.

The only thing written is the address with a heart emoji.

Which makes me excited . . . and a little more nervous.

And which is also when I realize what time it is and that I

need to hurry the hell up or I'll be late. I push my feet into my brown boots while I put the address into Maps on my phone, relieved that I can walk there in around thirty minutes.

I use the walk to quiet my mind and try to think of interesting talking points to keep Nora and her friends somewhat entertained. God, I hope they're not into politics: discussions about that never end well.

I'm so preoccupied that I don't even notice that Dakota hasn't texted me back.

# chapter

## Thirteen

WHEN I GET TO THE CLUB, it's smaller than I expected a night-club to be. I've been to a club once in downtown Detroit that was twice the size of the brick building we are waiting in front of now. The setup of this club isn't like in the movies, where there's always an overmuscled, bossy man controlling the door, a guy whose little clipboard and earpiece hold the power to make or break the self-esteem of women who would never otherwise give him the time of day. A simple nod from him while he unhooks the velvet rope validates the two hours they have spent getting ready. If you're made to wait very long, you are nothing. That's what he wants you to feel like anyway, and it's pretty messed up.

It's all a charade, though; he still probably sleeps alone at night and he doesn't feel any better about himself the next morning. His power trip has a twelve-hour expiration date. After that, he still hates himself and he's still mad that he didn't get that one big shot he deserved with the lady he pined for or the phone number of that one hot woman who he didn't make an effort to treat with any sort of respect. It makes me a little sad to know that in 2016, people still care about getting into nightclubs based on their looks. I try my hardest not to buy into that stuff, but I know it's what happens.

That said, I'm extremely relieved that this place isn't like all that. The small redbrick building is on the corner of the street, right next to a row of food trucks parked on a vacant lot. The street isn't as busy as the sidewalk; only a few green cabs and a Tesla drive by.

While I'm watching the Tesla's black paint shine under the lights, a hand touches my arm. I look around to see Nora; her eyes are made up, smoky gray makeup shadows them. She's wearing black pants that look as if someone painted them on her thick thighs. Her hips are hidden behind a black shirt with an Adidas symbol printed on it. It looks like she took scissors to the top of it, cutting a V neckline into the soft cotton. She's wearing a black blazer over it and white tennis shoes. She looks casual and so put together and so out of my league.

She's way too pretty.

Too hot.

Too everything.

After Nora lets go of my arm, she just stands silently in front of me, seeming to be waiting on me. I don't know what to do, so I stare back at her. More than a few people join us on the sidewalk as we wait to go inside.

Finally, she glances toward the door of the bar.

"Shall we?" I nervously ask.

Her shiny lips turn into a smile and she nods. I watch her eyes take in my outfit and I can't help but feel a little self-conscious about my choice of clothing.

Should I have worn looser pants? Are the rolled-up sleeves too much?

Nora's eyes finally leave my body and she looks over toward the plate-glass window of the bar. "Yep. We shall." Then, pointing inside, she adds, "They already have a table."

I feel like I look out of place. I text Tessa while I follow Nora to tell her I'm here. I feel a little bad that I pestered her into coming out with us via text. I know she would rather be in her bed, reading the highlighted pages of her favorite book. She would much rather be buried under her blanket, crying over the mistakes and regrets of these characters, wishing her relationship had ended like one of her novels.

But lying in bed being miserable isn't good for her. Besides, I could use another familiar face in this unfamiliar territory.

When the door of the club opens, smooth electric music tumbles out onto the sidewalk. The beat is nice, slow yet fast, soft but complicated. I speed up and take an extra step to get closer to Nora to try to make conversation.

"So do you dance here much?" I ask as we enter.

She turns and runs her index finger down the center of my lips.

"No one dances here." She smiles at me the way a mother smiles at her child when she has to explain the simplest logic to them.

When I look around, I realize it's not a club at all. Why the hell did I not just google the name of the joint? The place is a typical hip hangout, and it's crowded. Small wooden tables, dark lighting, industrial theme. Groups of people congregating at the bar, laughing and downing handcrafted cocktails. A man with white hair shakes a tumbler of neon-colored liquid and everyone watches, cheering him on as he pours it over a bed of ice. It sizzles and a cloud of smoke rises from the cup. I'm impressed.

As we walk up to the bar, I look at Nora and watch her expression change from curiosity to complete skepticism.

"*Barkeep—that's the lamest trick in the book!*" she yells, loud enough for the bartender to hear her over the music.

I look from side to side, taking in all the faces turned to us now. Nora doesn't turn away; she stares straight into the man's eyes when he turns toward her.

"Ugh. I should have known that was you." His expression is pure annoyance, but it's all pretend. The way he doesn't stop looking at her, I know that he knows her quite well, enough to tease her.

Briefly and irrationally, I wonder if they have dated . . . or are maybe dating now.

She smiles and leans against the bar. "Hey, Mitch."

She's using the bar top as a shelf for her chest. And he notices. He clearly likes it. I watch him stare, unashamed, at her open cleavage.

Her shirt is just so low, the neck cut into a V shape is very distracting, and in combination with those damn jeans, I've never seen someone look so good in such a simple outfit.

"Don't scowl, it doesn't suit you," Tessa chimes in my ear.

Am I that transparent? I straighten out my face and try to rationalize this. I've never been a jealous person. Dakota would have driven a jealous person totally insane with her flirty personality and the pull she seemed to have on every guy at our high school. She did a good job at never making me feel like I had to fight for her—she was always mine and I didn't feel the need to be immaturely jealous or dramatic over it.

"When did you get here?" I ask, distracting myself from staring at Nora.

"Just now; work was weirdly dead." She sighs, shrugging her shoulders like she would rather be anywhere but here. She's in her work uniform, black pants and a button-down white shirt; her apron strings are hanging out of her purse. What a trouper and a friend.

Horny bartender prances over, his smile wide and his hair perfectly coiffed. I'm sure he's nice. He has the shoulders of a linebacker and the build of Adam Levine. He's a tiny thing, yet muscular. It's an odd combination, but I can see the appeal.

Nora stretches over to hug him and he leans over into her arms. The bar is the only thing keeping the two of them from full body contact. I look away and pretend to scan the scene, but out of the corner of my eye, I can see that they are still hugging.

I look around the place. All of the names of the drinks are written in chalk on a big blackboard behind the bar, and when I hear Nora order two of them, I look them up. "Letters to Your Lover" contains gin, raspberry, and something that I can't read. The "Knot-So-Manhattan" is a blend of whiskey, vermouth, and bitters. A little hand-drawn knot is doodled next to the handwritten ingredient list.

I continue to read through the quirky list of crafted cocktails, assuming that since Nora is about twenty-five and definitely knows the bartender, we won't have any problem getting served alcohol. I don't drink often—a six-pack would last me a month probably—but I would like a drink tonight. Tessa and I have gone out a few times, and when we were offered a cocktail menu, we often managed to get drinks without being carded. Yeah, we walk on the wild side every once in a while.

Tessa looks out of place as she tugs on the bottom of her baggy white shirt. "I'm going to the bathroom," she says, and I nod and stand awkwardly in place, waiting for Nora to remember that I'm here.

I stare at Mitch and he keeps getting more and more attractive . . . and more and more obnoxious. Shouldn't he be making drinks or something? Now it's just me, Nora, and one of the most attractive men ever created.

These types of men are brought into this world to make guys like me feel inadequate. His teeth are so straight, and whiter than a new pair of sneakers. I look at them again, tilting on the heels of my boots and trying not to stare. Maybe I should have taken a bathroom break with Tessa—you know, like girls do?

Before I can walk away, Nora breaks off from Mr. Hot—who's too hot to work at a small bar—and links her arm through mine. Her hands are cold when she touches my skin. I reach for them, take them in mine, and rub them together. They warm up almost immediately, along with my cheeks, which are burning at my forwardness. Thank God it's dark in here.

She looks up at me, her eyes curious. She looks down at our hands, at my gesture, and smiles. The lights suspended from the ceiling are moving, casting shadows and casting light on her body. The exposed skin of her neck and chest is glowing under their slow dance. She's staring at me, and I'm staring at her, and I can't stop.

I look over at Mr. Hot and he's not paying any attention to us. I sort of wish he would. I wish he could see this . . .

*What's wrong with me?* I've got to stop talking to Hardin so much. He's turning me into an asshole.

A neurotic asshole.

Nora keeps eye contact with me. "Let's go sit down?"

It's slightly unsettling, keeping eye contact with anyone, especially a beautiful girl who I've already sort of admitted that I'm attracted to. When she kissed me, my body responded in a way that had me convinced my body had always been waiting on her, on such a kiss.

She turns back to the bar, thanks Mitch, and then hands me a drink with a strand of red licorice tied into a knot in it. There's a little stick in the drink with an upside-down skyscraper on the end of it. It appears to be made from wood. I'm impressed. Nora's drink has a little note clipped on its side. I'm going to assume that it's a little letter. I'm doubly impressed.

Nora continues to stare at me and I remember that she said we should sit down. I nod, wanting to move away from the crowded bar area. The row of tables looks pretty crowded, too, but at least we can sit down there. The music is nice, low and steady with a good beat. There's no dance floor; it's a cocktail bar that has a small snacks menu, not a nightclub. I still can't believe I didn't just look up the place instead of overthinking it.

Nora wraps her fingers around my wrist and leads me toward the back of the bar. The space gets darker and darker the farther we move away from the bar and finally we stop at a table full of women who look up and smile and nod at us. It still amazes me how close to one another people are willing to sit in this city. The small tables are all lined up next to each other and you can hear everything the people around you are saying, though the music is so loud that it may not be a problem. A few of the seats at the table are empty and Nora gestures for me to sit down at one. She sits across from me and raises her drink to mine. Clinking our glasses, I poke at the licorice and at the little wooden building and move them out of the way before I take a drink.

*Holy hell, this tastes like gasoline!* I somehow knew that it would.

I smile at her, but shake my head and wave my hands over the drink. "I'm going to sit this one out."

She laughs, covering her mouth and nodding. "I don't blame you! He made them *strong*." She pushes a tumbler full of water toward me with a smile. She grabs my drink and sniffs it, scrunching her nose at the harsh smell before pushing it away, toward the edge of the table, farther away from me.

I like that Nora doesn't mind if I choose not to drink. She takes another sip of her cocktail and licks at the pink sugary rim of her glass. She unclips the note and rips open the flap on the little envelope. I give her a moment to read the words, then I reach for the card. She huffs, rolling her eyes at the corny message. Her fingers play at the thin chain of her necklace as I read:

> *Dear Lover, don't open a new door*
> *if something is hiding behind the other.*

I laugh and hand the letter back to her. It's clever marketing. While I wonder if they actually change the notes out and if so, how often, Nora looks slightly uncomfortable as she begins to introduce me to her friends.

"Melody." Nora points to a pretty Asian girl. Her eyeliner is thick, drawn in a perfectly straight line and out to a point.

"Hi," Melody says, looking from Nora to me.

The next girl's name is Raine, then Scarlett, then Maggy, and quickly the faces are blurring together because, really, I just want to talk to Nora alone. I want to ask her things like what she's been doing since she came out here from Washington, how she likes her coffee, what season she prefers—basically get to know her a bit more since, even though we met a while ago, we never really hung out.

I notice that the friend of Nora's named Maggy says something and taps the shoulder of the girl next to her—and realization strikes me like a damn match.

Maggy is *Maggy*.

*Maggy* . . .

Which means . . .

The girl whose shoulder she taps turns around, and her face twists in confusion when she sees me. Surely my mind is playing games with me.

Dakota is staring back at me; her eyes immediately widen and her lips tighten into a bewildered frown.

"Landon?" she says, wide-eyed. Still, something about her tone of voice seems off, and I get the feeling that she noticed my presence much earlier than I noticed hers.

Her eyes are tight on me, draining out every ounce of excitement I was feeling when I walked through the door. This is when I would desperately love to have a portal to jump through, to take me anywhere but here. I would even take being zapped into the middle of the Battle of Helm's Deep. Unfortunately for me, I haven't found a way to portal into my favorite movie series.

When I was sixteen, my aunt got me a Lord of the Rings

LEGO set and I attempted to put together that exact battle scene. It was too complicated, and I gave up. Dakota lasted longer than me, putting little bows and arrows on at least fifty elves. She was better at LEGOS as a kid than I was, and now, as an adult, she's much better at coming up with words to say when words are needed. So, here I am, and here she is, staring at me and then at Nora, then back to me. I watch as she pieces it together, the fact that Nora brought me here.

Her almond eyes narrow into slits and she turns to Nora with a huff. "*This* is the hot guy you were talking about?"

*Hot guy? What?* I look toward the bar, wanting to crawl behind it. This gathering isn't going to go well.

Nora rolls her eyes at Dakota with a quick laugh and sticks out her tongue. "Way to bust my balls, Dakota."

Oh no. She doesn't even understand what's happening here. And there's something odd about Nora's tone with Dakota; something unpleasant is threaded through her words.

Tessa approaches us, and when she notices Dakota sitting at the end of the table from Nora and me, she freezes, and looks just as confused as Dakota. My problem-solving skills have suddenly evaporated and I'm sitting here like an idiot with nothing to say.

Dakota turns her attention back to Nora and I try to think of something to say to get all of this to make sense. I don't want a scene. I want one thousand other horrible things to happen before I'd want to cause a scene here.

"So, how long have you been seeing each other?" she asks.

"We haven't been," I say just as Nora, her voice louder than mine, says, "Just a little while, it's a new thing."

Nora looks at me and my chest caves in. She's confused by my answer.

*A little while?* What does she mean, *a little while?* Are we seeing each other? Is that what this is?

She's only kissed me once, and outside of a few minutes while Tessa was in the shower or on her way home from work here and there, we haven't spent any time alone together. We've really barely talked, I'd say.

Dakota's eyes begin to water and I can see her loading her guns. She's building up accusations, brewing some theory to make sense of the situation. I've rarely been on this side of her anger, and for some reason, a part of me feels satisfied. We hardly fought when we were together. She yelled often, but not at me. Never at me.

"We aren't dating," I feel the need to tell her again.

The other three ladies at the table begin to whisper, probably creating their own version of the live soap opera that's unfolding in front of them.

I look at Nora and she's beginning to catch on. "You two know each other?" she asks.

*"Know each other?"* Dakota's voice is deep now, guarded, as she waves her hand back and forth between Nora and me.

*Come on, portal. Pull me in and get me the hell out of here.*

Dakota is eyeing me like I'm some kind of predator, something she has to escape from. I hate it. She's several seats away, but I can still see how upset she is. Her fingers grip the edge of the table and she bulges her eyes at me, probing for my response.

"Yes, we *know each other*. We've known each other for a long time."

Dakota's putting on a show. She's detached herself from this. She's trying to remain cool and calm, trying not to let anyone know how much this bothers her. She grabs one of the glasses in front of her and doesn't look to see what it is before she downs it in one quick motion.

Nora's shoulders rise and fall with deep breaths and she doesn't say anything. Everyone is looking at me now.

One glare.

One expectant look.

Two more glares.

Tessa is looking at her phone now; she's no help.

Make that three glares . . .

. . . and an eye roll.

Dakota grabs her purse from the back of her chair and pushes past me. I try to reach for her shoulder, but she jerks away, nearly tripping over the chair next to me.

I watch her go. And when I turn around, I'm face-to-face with Nora.

"You're the fucking guy. You're the nerdy ex from Michigan." Her voice is flat, unimpressed, with a splash of embarrassment. I stand up.

*Nerdy ex?* Is that what Dakota thinks of me?

Is that how Dakota refers to me? Is that how she describes me to the new friends she's made in this city?

I look back toward the door and spot Dakota's hair just as she pushes the door open and disappears.

I can't imagine how she must feel. She thinks I'm dating Nora and I lied to her earlier about having to study.

This is exactly why I never lie. I don't know why I thought it was a good idea to lie, I should have known it would backfire, nothing good ever comes from a lie. Aside from a few times when I pretended to know what she was talking about when really I didn't, I never needed to lie to her.

A hand grabs my shoulder, spinning me. Face-to-face with Nora again, I can see she's challenging me, making me choose. Her brow is raised above her sharp eyes, eyes that I thought I would be staring into all night. I thought I would be getting to know the woman with enough confidence to fill this bar, enough spark to light the city.

How can I choose? I barely know her.

Nora is completely silent and still; only her eyes speak to me. If I leave with Dakota, will she ever speak to me again?

Why does the idea of that bother me so much?

But I can't let Dakota leave this place alone, this late at night. She's upset and I get the feeling that I have no idea just how volatile she can be. Her self-destructiveness is her greatest enemy.

"I'm sorry," is the only thing I have time to say to Nora before I follow Dakota out into the night.

# chapter

## *Fourteen*

WHEN I STEP OUT OF THE BAR, Dakota is standing on the sidewalk, raising her hand to hail a cab. I run up to her side and push her hand down.

"Don't touch me," she spits, a cloud of smoke puffing out of her mouth from the chilly fall air. I drop my hand and step in front of her. She keeps her arms down, crossing them in front of her chest as if to protect herself.

I immediately begin to explain myself. Or try to.

"It's not what you think," I say in a rushed voice.

Dakota turns away from me. She's not going to let me explain. She never has.

I gently grab her arm, but she wrenches her whole body away as if I've burned her. I ignore the judgmental glances of the people walking by and step in front of her.

"*Bullshit!*" she shouts. "Are you kidding me, Landon?"

The liquor on her breath and the way her bloodshot eyes are focusing, I can tell she's had more than a few. Since when does she drink like that? Or at all, really?

In my mind, she's sixteen again, her curly hair pulled up into a bun. She's wearing gym shorts and high socks, the kind with the red stripes around the top, sitting cross-legged on her bed. We're flipping through college applications over pizza. Her house is quiet for once. Her dad is gone. Carter is out with Jules. She's talking to me about how she's never been drunk, but wants to be.

Her first experiment didn't work out the way she expected; alcohol doesn't taste as good as the characters in *Gossip Girl* make it seem. Ten minutes and three swigs of eighty-proof vodka later, she was hugging the toilet and I was holding her hair while she swore to never drink again. Before I put the bottle back into her dad's crowded freezer, I dumped out half and added water, figuring in a naïve way that maybe if the alcohol were diluted, his temper would be, too.

Apparently, vodka doesn't freeze—but water does. And the next morning Carter came to school with a black eye and a sore rib cage because of my mistake.

I never made that mistake again.

"She's Tessa's friend," I say. "I barely know her. I know what it looks like—"

Dakota cuts me off, not even looking at me as she speaks. "She's been talking about you for weeks now!" Her voice is loud, cracking at the end like a whip.

*"He's sooo sweet,"* she croons, mocking a sultry female voice.

Passersby on the sidewalk stare at us as I try to calm her down. One guy in a beanie gives me an I-would-save-you-if-I-could-bro look as he passes with his girlfriend. His *quiet* girlfriend, who doesn't seem to hate him. Lucky guy.

I attempt to defend myself, but it comes out as babble. "I don't know what she's been saying, but I didn't—"

Dakota raises her hand in front of my face, waving for me to shut up. Her dress is bunched at her hips, exposing the line of her tights underneath. The more she moves, pacing on the side-walk, the higher her dress rises. She doesn't even notice as she continues to stew in her rage.

After a few more seconds of pacing, she turns back to me,

her eyes alight as she seems to remember something. "Oh my God! She kissed you! She told us!"

She takes a few steps across the sidewalk and bumps shoulders with a man walking a Saint Bernard. "That's who she was talking about! It's been you this entire fucking time."

Jesus, has Nora been giving Dakota a play-by-play of our every encounter?

Dakota raises her hand to hail a cab again. "Get away from me," she warns when I touch her elbow to steady her.

I haven't said anything and I know to be careful about how I approach this. I hadn't expected the two of them to be sharing stories about me. I didn't think Nora liked me enough to even mention me to her friends, and if she did, I would have never imagined that Dakota was one of her roommates. How can the world be so small?

"I'm coming with you. How much did you have to drink?" I ask her.

She shoots fire at me; her eyes are damn near glowing red now. I get no answer. Not that I expected one.

Regular cabs being fairly rare in this part of Brooklyn, I say, "I'll order an Uber. I'll have it drop you off at your place," and reach into my pocket for my phone.

She doesn't stop me, which I take as a good sign.

While we wait for the car, I decide to keep my mouth shut. Dakota's not going to be very reasonable until we can get away from the crowd. This is all one huge misunderstanding and I need time alone with her, and some quiet, in order to be able to explain.

After three minutes of complete silence, Daniel of the blue Prius and five-star rating pulls up to the curb and I put my hands on Dakota's shoulders to guide her to the car. She twists herself away from my touch and stumbles off the sidewalk to get to the other door. A car is passing at the same time and I rush to her, pulling her out of the way and guiding her into the car. She grunts, mumbles something about not touching her, and I walk back around and climb into the other side.

This is going to be a long night. I put my address into the app, not hers, since I'm sure she won't want to see Nora, although I'm pretty positive she will be pissed about this, too.

"How are you guys tonight?" Daniel asks.

Dakota ignores him, presses her cheek into her hand, and leans against the window.

"We're good," I lie.

No need to drag him into the mess; he seems like a nice guy and his car smells like caramel.

"That's good to hear, it's getting chilly out. I have some waters back there if you're thirsty, and chargers, too," he offers.

Now I see why he has a perfect five-star rating.

I look at Dakota, thinking she might want some water, but she doesn't seem interested in much of anything at the moment.

"We're good . . . thank you, though," I respond.

Our driver looks into the rearview mirror and seems to take the hint. He turns his music up slightly and drives in silence the rest of the way. He'll be getting a five from me.

"Where do you have him taking us?" Dakota finally decides to talk to me a few minutes into the drive. I stare out the window. We're about halfway to my apartment, having just passed Grind.

"To my apartment. I don't even know where yours is," I remind her.

The reason I don't know is because she has barely kept in contact with me since she moved here, and certainly has never invited me over. Does she really have the right to be this mad over my seeing Nora—if you could call what I've been doing "seeing her"? Even though it seems to me that Dakota's being completely irrational, I wonder if I actually deserve the cold silence.

She huffs but doesn't fight me on it. I assume that's because

I was right and she doesn't want to deal with Nora or the other roommates who witnessed the entire awkward exchange at the bar. I get the feeling that their living situation is one of those weird frenemy types of relationships Tessa explained to me once while we binge-watched *Pretty Little Liars*.

Tessa. Ugh, I just left her there. I pull out my phone and send her a text, apologizing. When Dakota gives me the side-eye, no doubt wondering if I'm texting Nora, I sheepishly say, "Just wanted to let Tessa know I left . . ."

Five-star Daniel pulls up to my apartment building and gives me one last sympathetic glance before I step out. I quickly pull out my wallet and hand him a five-dollar bill. Dakota is quick to climb out of the car and slams her door as I step onto the side-walk.

"Let me help you." I hold my hand out for the big purse she's wrestling with.

The straps are wrapped around Dakota's shoulder in a tan-gled mess of brown leather. She shrugs and stands still, allowing me to help her. I quickly untangle the straps, trying not to actu-ally touch her, and when it's free, I carry it for her. I don't think she wants to, but she leans into me as we walk toward the door of my building. The moss growing on the brick walls of my building seems thicker tonight, more strangling.

Dakota lets go and stumbles to the front entrance. I pull it open for her and she sighs in relief when we step into the warm hallway. My apartment doesn't have a doorman or any fancy security, but it's always clean and the hallways usually smell like chemicals. I'm not sure if it's a good thing, but it's better than some of the alternatives.

As we walk in silence down the hall, I realize that she's never been here before. When I first moved to Brooklyn, we were sup-posed to get together for dinner at my house, just to catch up, but she canceled an hour before our meeting. I had made a full meal, four courses—with Tessa's help, of course. It felt like I had searched nearly every corner store in Brooklyn for Dakota's favorite drink, blue cream soda in a glass bottle, finally finding it after an hour. I even stopped myself from drinking any of the six-pack before she arrived. Well, I had two, but I left four for her.

Dakota's flat shoes squeak against the floor, and I can't remember it ever taking so long to walk to my apartment. The elevator seems to be taking forever.

When we finally reach my door and I unlock it, Dakota pushes past me and enters. I lay her purse on the table and kick off my shoes. She takes a few more steps until she's in the center of the room.

The living room feels much smaller with her in it. She's a beautiful storm, all waves and anger as her lungs fill with air. Her chest rises up, then down, in a ragged pattern.

I step toward her, right into the eye of it all. I shouldn't know how to approach her. I shouldn't remember the exact way to talk to her, to cool her temper.

But I do.

I remember how to slowly step to her and wrap my arms around her waist. When I do, they fall into their protective place, trying to shield her from anything and everything. In this case, from myself.

My fingers should have forgotten how to gently raise her stubborn chin and let me look into her eyes. But they haven't, they couldn't.

"We have to talk about this," I whisper through the heavy air between us.

Dakota takes a breath and tries to look away from me. I bend at the knees, leaning down to her height. She looks away again and I refuse to give in before she listens to me.

"I met Nora a while ago, back in Washington," I begin to explain.

"In *Washington*? You've been seeing her that long?" She hiccups at the end of her question and pulls away from my embrace.

I wonder if I should offer her something to drink. I don't think this is the best time, but when an inebriated person hiccups, it sometimes means they're going to get sick, doesn't it?

Where did I even hear that?

This is one of those times when I wish I knew more about drinking and the effects it has on your body. Dakota's toe catches on a pile of textbooks on the floor and she stumbles, taking a few unsteady steps toward the couch. Better safe than sorry, I'll get her that water after all.

I shake my head. "No, no, no. She came over a few times because her parents live close to my mom and Ken."

I know it sounds like a lie, but it's not.

"I barely know her. She helped my mom with baking and now she's Tessa's friend—"

"Your mom? She met *your mom*?" Dakota shrieks.

Everything I say seems to add another shovelful of dirt to the hole I'm digging myself in.

"No . . . well, yes." I sigh. "Like I said, her parents live near mine. I didn't have her over for family dinner or anything like that."

I hope something clicks within her and she sees that this isn't what she thinks it is.

Dakota turns away and her eyes scan the living room. I watch her as she walks over to the couch and sits down on the side closer to the door. I pull my jacket off and drape it over the chair. I hold a hand out for Dakota's jacket, but she isn't wearing one. How did I not notice? I remember looking at the line of her tights, the outline of her bra through the thin cotton of her dress. I'm not used to seeing her dressed like this, in such tight clothing.

That's my excuse for being a pervert who didn't even notice

that she wasn't wearing a jacket? It didn't even cross my mind to offer her mine—what's happening to me?

While I wait for her response, I walk over to the thermostat and turn up the heat. If we're lucky, it'll make her drowsy. I pop into the kitchen and pour each of us a glass of water.

When I return, she shakes her head and looks past me; I can see that she's struggling within herself. "For some reason, I believe you, but should I? I mean, this fast? Just like that?"

She rests her chin on her elbow and stares across the room. "I didn't think I would care this much if you dated someone," she admits.

Her words take me by surprise, and as I mull them over, something shifts in my reasoning. I guess I saw that from the beginning of the small almost-catfight that she was annoyed I was with Nora, but for some reason I thought she was more upset because I'd lied to her about what I was doing tonight. That she would feel weird at seeing me with someone—even though I'm really not *with* anyone—wasn't the first thing on my mind, given everything. *She* broke up with *me* over six months ago and has barely given me the time of day since.

Part of me wants to shout at her, *Where's the logic in that!?* but another part reminds me that she must feel that she's justified in some way. I do my best to try to see it from her side before I say anything or react because I know that if I do speak right now, my words will do more damage than good. Especially if I'm only thinking of my point of view. Of myself. Still, I'm mad, too. She thinks after six months that she can yell at me for dating someone who I'm not even dating? I want to tell her that, tell her that she's wrong—and I'm right—and I'm pissed, too! But that's the problem with this type of quick anger: discharging it would make me feel better for a few moments, but then I'll feel like crap after. Anger doesn't often offer a solution, it only creates more problems.

Still, part of me wants to say something. I take a big drink of water instead.

I know anger.

The type of anger that I know isn't some small thing that pops up when you see your ex of six months hanging out with someone else. My experience with anger isn't getting pissed off because your neighbor drove his car into yours. The anger that I know cuts at you when you're watching your best friend get his eye split open because his dad heard someone down at the bar whispering about him looking at another boy just a beat too long.

The anger that I know seeps inside of you and turns you into lava, burning slowly as it rolls down the hills and covers the town. It's when your friend's bruises are in the shape of knuckles and you can't do shit about it without causing more destruction.

When you've been host to that type of anger, it's very, very hard to fly off the handle over small things. I've never been one to add fuel to a fire. I've been the water, extinguishing the flames, the salve to heal the burns.

Little problems come and go, and I have always avoided confrontation at all costs, but sometimes things become too much to bear or too big to ignore. I'm terrible at fighting, I can't keep an argument going to save my life. My mom always said I was born with a gift: an enormous amount of empathy. And that it could quickly become a fault instead of a virtue.

I can't help it . . . I can't stand to see other people suffer, even if holding back causes suffering to *me*.

I'm struggling to understand Dakota's anger when she finally breaks the silence.

"I'm not saying you can't date," she says.

I sit down on the arm of the couch farther away from her.

"Just not so soon. I'm not ready for you to date," she adds, and takes a long drink of water.

*Soon?* It's been six months.

I can tell by her expression that Dakota's completely serious, and I don't know if I should call her out on it, or just let it blow over. She's pretty drunk, and I know how stressed she's been lately with her academy and all. I'm smart enough to pick and choose my battles, and I don't feel strongly enough about this one to let it snowball into a full-fledged war.

What she's asking of me isn't remotely fair, and I'm frustrated by how easily I've let myself slide into this passive role again. I'm enabling her . . . but is it really that bad? We are communicating. No one is yelling. No one is losing their cool. I want to keep this going. If she's handing out secrets, I'll take a few.

"And when will you be ready for me to date?" I ask softly.

She sits up straight, immediately defensive. I knew she would be. I stare at her, my eyes telling her that there's nothing to be upset about, we're only talking. No judging here.

Her shoulders relax.

"I don't know. I haven't really thought about it." She shrugs. "I assumed it would take you longer to get over me."

"Get over you?" I ask, worried for this woman's sanity. What would have given her the assumption that I *could* get over her? My kiss with Nora? It's not like this girl before me even gave me a choice about getting over her.

But, man, do I wish she didn't know about that kiss. Not because I want to hide it, but because some things really are better left unknown. I keep my distance still, leaving two cushions of space between us.

"I'm not over you," I calmly say, "but you didn't give me much of a choice here, Dakota. You've barely spoken to me since you moved. You broke up with me, remember?"

I look at her. She's staring at the floor.

"You wanted to focus on yourself when you moved, and I got that. I let you have your space and you didn't do anything to stop me. You didn't reach out to me at all. Not once did you call me first, not once did you answer the first time I called. Now here we are and you're acting like I'm a villain because I went out on a casual date with someone."

So much for biting my tongue and letting it blow over.

I truly don't want to fight with her. I just want to communicate openly and honestly.

She looks at me with a pointed glare. "So you *did* go out with her."

It's frustrating as hell that after everything I said, that's all she picked up on.

I'm trying to find some logic behind her accusations, but I'm coming up short without knowing what Nora has been telling her. All night I've repeated over and over that Nora and I aren't dating, but she's not listening. And then she's holding me up to this no-dating standard she'd never voiced before.

If the roles were reversed, I would believe her. I know her well enough to know that she wouldn't lie to me. She's complicating things. Why is she complicating things?

"Stop lying to me." She waves her hands through the air and the metal bracelets on her wrists clang against each other. "I get it, Landon, she's beautiful and older, and aggressive, and men like that kind of shit. You like that, and I've been replaced again."

I can either sit here and get mad that she's cooking up her own explanations for everything, or I can bite my tongue and remember that she's drunk, upset, and has been under a lot of pressure lately.

With a sigh, I move from the arm of the couch and kneel on the rug in front of where she's sitting. I look up at her stoic expression. "I would never lie to you about something like this. I'm telling the truth."

My hands grab at hers in her lap. Her skin feels cold and the chill forces a memory into my mind. I'm thrown back into a back-yard make-out session that happened when we were fifteen. Her hands were so cold and she put them up my shirt to rest on my warm stomach. We kissed and kissed and couldn't stop. We were frozen by the time we went inside, but we didn't care. Not one bit.

"Can I ask you something?" Her voice is soft and melts something inside of me.

I'm a sucker for her.

A goner.

I always have been.

"Always."

Dakota draws a long breath and pulls one of her hands away from mine to tuck her hair behind her ear. I turn her other hand over and trace the lines in her skin, the scar there. She flinches out of instinct and I feel the throbbing ache of the memory behind her reaction.

"Do you miss me, Landon?"

Her hands are soft and light in mine.

This moment feels familiar, yet foreign. How is that?

Do I miss her?

Of course I miss her.

I've missed her since I moved to Washington. I've told her how much I've missed her. I've expressed how much I miss her more times than I've heard anything remotely close to that come from her.

I lean into her farther and squeeze her hands between mine while repeating her question back to her. "Do you miss *me*?"

Without giving her time to answer, I continue: "I need to know this, Dakota. I think it's more than obvious that I miss you, that I've missed you since I left Michigan. I missed you before and after you visited me in Washington. I would say that me moving across the country to be with you shows that I missed you."

She seems to think on my words for a beat. She looks at me for a second and then stares past me. The clock on the wall is ticking, humming in the silence.

Finally, she opens her mouth to speak. "But did you miss *me*? Or was it just the idea of me, the familiarity of me? Because there were times when I literally felt like I couldn't do anything without you, and I hated it. I wanted to prove to myself that I could take care of myself. After Carter died, I clung to you, and so when you left me, I had nothing. You were my safe place, and when you moved away, you took that safety with you. But then, when you said you would move to New York with me, I felt like I was going to be stuck in that safe place with you. That I would be a child forever. There would be no chance for adventure, nothing unexpected could possibly happen with you around to save me."

Her words burn as I digest them. They pull at the most insecure part of me, the little voice in my head that's worried about what people think of me. I don't want to be the nice guy. I've been the nice guy for twenty years now, even when it's extremely difficult, and I still can't grasp why women want drama over normalcy.

Just because a man doesn't bash the face in of someone for hitting on his girlfriend doesn't mean he doesn't care about her. Just because he doesn't guard her jealously or wince every time she talks to another male of the species doesn't mean he's uninterested or weak. It only means that he has his temper under control, that he's respectful and mature enough to be a functioning member of society. That he understands that everyone needs their own space and every woman needs a chance to develop her own independence.

I will never understand why the nice guys have it so damn bad.

However, if you think about it, the nice guys usually end up being the husbands. The women go through a period of trial and error with the hot bad boys, but eventually most of them want to trade in the motorcycle for a Prius.

That's me.

The human version of a Prius.

Dakota would be a Range Rover, sturdy and luxurious, yet still beautiful.

Nora would be a Tesla, sleek and new and fast. Her curves are smooth and assured . . .

"Until I broke up with you . . . then there was adventure. I was alone to navigate this big city and all the trouble that comes along with it," Dakota continues.

*And what the hell is wrong with me?*

I'm here, inches away from Dakota, her hands in mine. Nora shouldn't be on my mind. This is the worst possible time to think about Nora and the way her eyes are impossible not to get lost in, the way her bottom lip pouts out farther than the top.

And then I realize it: thinking about Nora is much less complicated than trying to understand the logic of Dakota's emotions. I don't have a clue what to say to my ex right now. She's telling me that I did too much for her, that in some way I prevented her from doing things for herself, and I'm too afraid of pissing her off to come up with anything decent to say in response. I certainly can't point out that I *didn't* put her in a box. That I was a safe space, but never a jail. That I never curbed her freedom on purpose. That all I ever wanted was to help her in any way possible . . . her and her brother, Carter.

Dakota shifts on the couch and tucks her feet under her, still holding my hands, waiting for my response.

All I can do is speak the truth, with as little anger as possible. "You can't expect me to apologize for being good to you."

Her hands are still in mine. She pulls one away and again tucks her hair behind her ear before she looks at me.

"I don't expect that." She sighs and licks her lips, wetting them. "I'm just saying, at the time I needed a break from you, from us." She moves our joined hands back and forth between us.

*At the time?* She's speaking in the past tense, like our breakup is something that we are . . . moving past? Forgetting about?

I look up to catch her eyes. "What are you trying to say? That you don't need a break anymore?"

She pushes her upper teeth over her lower lip as she takes my question in.

The weirdest part of this is that I don't know how I feel. One week ago, if this conversation played out the exact same way as it's playing out now, I would've felt differently. I wouldn't feel so reluctant to go over past history. I would've been excited, grateful, happy. Now it just feels weird. It doesn't quite settle the way that it should.

Dakota hasn't answered me yet, and her words already feel somehow stilted as her eyes scan the room and her chest fills with a breath too deep to hold good news.

"Can I have some more water?" she asks, keeping her response to my question to herself.

I nod and get up, meeting her eyes one more time in hopes for an answer. Half of my brain tells me that I should ask again, that I should make sure she doesn't want to change the status of our relationship. Would we fall back into old routines so easily? How many days would it take before she'd be effortlessly falling back into my arms, forgetting about her need for independence and adventure?

I grab her glass and once in the kitchen open the small drawer next to the fridge where the Tylenol is. If her hiccups and stumbling steps are any indication of how much she's drunk, she won't be feeling so hot in the morning. I open the bottle and dump three into my hand, then fill her glass with more water. In the sink is a cake pan. On the counter next to it, the elaborate tiered cake with purple icing and flowers Nora and Tessa made earlier.

Nora has left traces of herself all over my apartment.

I debate whether it would be worth it to eat a piece before I go back into the living room to deal with Dakota. Or I could cut one for each of us. I doubt that she'd eat it, though, with her strict diet and all. I lift up the corner of the plastic wrap and dip my finger into the icing.

Dakota walks into the kitchen just as I shove my finger between my lips.

*Shit.*

"Really, Landon?" Her lips lift into a smile and I lean against the counter and face her. She looks at the cake, then back at me. All I can do is shrug and smile.

I grab the glass of water and hold it out to her. She inspects it for a moment, thinking of something to say, I'm sure. Dakota's lips press to the side of the glass and I move back toward the delicious cake.

"You always had a serious sweet tooth." Her voice is warm and delicious like the icing on my tongue. "It was irresistible."

"There are a lot of things I never could resist." I look at Dakota and she looks down at her bare feet.

With my fingers I tear off a small corner of the cake. Little pieces of it break off and a chunk of icing drops onto the countertop. I look at Dakota and try to lighten up the conversation.

"At least now I work out," I joke.

I was a pudgy kid, always a little thicker in the middle than the other kids. I blame my mom's baking and my own laziness about going outside to play. I remember wanting to stay home, like actually wanting to be inside my house on the weekends, with my mom. I ate a lot of sweets and I wasn't as active as I should have been for my age, and when my doctor talked to my mom about my weight, I was embarrassed, and in that instant I knew that I never wanted to overhear a conversation like that again. I still ate what I wanted to, but I became more active than before. I was a little shy about asking my aunt Reese for help, but once I did, she came over the next day with an exercise bike in her trunk and little weights in her hands. I remember laughing at her eighties-style pink-and-yellow workout outfit complete with matching arm warmers.

Despite how absurd we looked exercising together, she and I got healthy. My mom joined in, too, just for the fun of it, though she had always been in good shape. Reese was always more plump than my mom, but she became a machine and we both lost weight together. My aunt was happy that she could finally fit into some dress that she had been eyeing for a year at some expensive store, and I was just happy not to have the extra weight on my body, making me self-conscious.

I felt great for a while and Dakota began to notice that the chubby boy next door wasn't so chubby anymore. The problem was that my weight loss wasn't good enough for my peers. I lost too much weight and didn't put on any muscle, so that's when the "Lardy Landon" name-calling switched to "Lanky Landon."

First I was too fat, then too skinny. Nothing I did would please those bullying assholes. And as soon as I stopped trying to, my life became easier.

"What are you thinking about?" Dakota asks; her hand is warm now as she wraps her fingers around my wrist and lowers my arm to my side. Her body presses against mine and she leans her head on my chest. She takes another drink of water and sits the cup down on the counter.

I haven't responded yet, I'm aware of that. I just don't know what to say other than reposing my question about whether she wants to get back together.

*Do* I bring it up again, or wait and see which way she takes the conversation?

I take a sip out of my own glass and decide to wait it out. I shouldn't trust myself to keep my mouth from saying something stupid. I've never been the best at knowing what to say or when to say it. I'm not that cool guy who can lean against the counter and be all *I was just thinking about us getting back together and running off into the sunset and living happily ever after, yo.*

Ugh, even my self-mocking fantasy is lame.

I don't know how to keep eye contact when I'm nervous about her answer. I simply just suck at being *that* guy.

Surely, this is one of those things that I can blame on my father. I've been patiently waiting for one of these moments when I could cash in my "crappy dad" coupons and blame him for dying too early to be able to teach me how to be a man. But even as the thought passes through my mind, I know it's irrational and not true. My lack of assertiveness wasn't his fault, and still isn't, but I want someone to blame other than myself.

If I'd had a man to talk me through my teenage years, to explain how to talk to women, I would know what to say. It must be his fault that I overthink everything.

"Landon," Dakota says in a soft breath like she's coming to some sort of resolve. And I'm just standing here, disappointed in myself and stuck in playing the blame game.

"Dakota," I say back to her, and she turns her cheek. I gently push her hair down, caressing the thick curls with my fingers. I've spent hours, probably days, of my life touching these strands, calming this girl. Her hair has always been one of my favorite things about her. Her fingers grip at the back of my shirt, and I can practically hear the starchy fabric crunch. Never again will I iron my shirts under Tessa's watchful eye. She went a little overboard on the starch spray that day.

Dakota holds me tighter and I dip my head down to kiss the top of her head.

She sighs, melting into my chest, her voice soft as she says, "I made a huge scene."

I keep one hand on the counter to hold us up and wrap the other around her back.

"Oh God, this is so embarrassing. *Of course* you and Nora aren't dating."

My arm tenses. Something about the way she says this sits weird with me. Is she assuming that since I'm hugging her in my kitchen, I couldn't be dating Nora, because I just wouldn't do that kind of thing? Or that the idea of nerdy me dating someone like Nora is impossible and ridiculous?

Either way, I remind myself that I shouldn't care. I'm not dating Nora and I'm pretty sure that *she* has absolutely no desire to actually date *me*. She eats guys like me for breakfast. I need to stop thinking about her. I already have.

Dakota lifts her cheek from my chest just long enough to speak.

"I feel like shit," she says.

"Because you drank too much or because you made a scene?"

"Ugh," she groans against my chest. "Both?"

I pat my hand against her back. I can tell she's exhausted. Her hands are on my back, at the waist of my jeans. She reaches up, untucking my shirt. Her hands are a little cold against my back. The ache of familiarity as her fingertips move in circles over my skin mixes with the coconut smell of her hair, and suddenly I'm a man obsessed.

I've been here before, immersed in her scent, her touch. I feel her fingers press into the small of my back and I mold myself to her body. I'm ever so accustomed to this. To her. It's only natural that I fall back into this routine. Once she touches me, I see only her.

"Let's go to your room," she says just as her lips touch mine. She keeps them there, barely skimming mine. "No one is here, right?"

Tessa's gone. Check.

For a second I feel a pang of guilt about Tessa being gone

because I left her somewhere. But when Dakota kisses me again, deeper, all guilt disappears in a wave of desire.

At last, we don't have to sneak around like we did when we were kids. I've never been able to actually fuck this love of mine in the privacy of an empty house. All of our encounters have been hushed kisses and subdued moans, rushed hands and sloppy tongues. I've never been able to slowly devour her body in the way I dream of. I want to run my tongue down every inch of her caramel skin and spend extra time where she needs it the most. I want to taste all of her, hear every sound of hers.

Now that I have my own place, I could take her in my bed and do everything I've longed to do since we were teens. I remember how amazed I was the first time she wrapped her lips around my cock. I think back to the many times she wanted to try things. It all felt so experimental then, it felt exciting, other-worldly, and our list of favorite things to do quickly became sexual. That's all we did for a while, all we wanted to do.

Dakota's hands move to the front of my body, circling around my belly button, her fingertips slipping into the top of my briefs. I grow under her touch, hard now, and I can't begin to fight it. It's biology, after all. I haven't been touched, save for that one kiss and a few touches from Nora, in months. Dakota proves that she still remembers my body when she rubs her index finger over the sensitive skin above my hipbone. I jerk away from her tickling, and she laughs, pulling me closer.

She's in a much better mood now, but this feels an awful lot like throwing a blanket over a raging fire. Eventually, it will burn up just the same.

Eventually, but not right now.

# Fifteen

DAKOTA TAKES MY HANDS and pulls me out of the kitchen. I follow her like the lost puppy I am.

"Don't forget your water," I remind her, and she pouts at me, but I point to the water on the counter. She really will need it.

With a sigh, she removes her hands from mine and goes back to grab her glass. While she's doing that I grab the TV remote and turn it on for Tessa, hitting mute. I always make sure she has some light when she gets home later than me, and the lamp on our end table has a blown lightbulb that I keep meaning to replace.

But as I put the remote back down on the couch, I hear the ominous sound of voices and a key ring jingling.

The lock finally clicks and the door opens, bringing Tessa inside . . .

. . . with Nora.

As I stand there somewhat dazed, Tessa takes off her purple beanie and closes the door behind her. Nora pulls her jacket off and her cleavage nearly spills out from her shirt as she shakes her hair.

Then both of them look over at Dakota and me, suddenly realizing they're not alone.

*Please, dear God, let Nora think I was looking at her face at least.*

And more importantly, where is that damn portal?

"Landon?" Tessa starts.

"Hey, I didn't know—" Nora begins, but stops as soon as Dakota walks out of the kitchen, seemingly unaware of her.

Dakota approaches me and, walking between me and Tessa and Nora, wraps her hand around mine. As her fingers play with my own, Nora's eyes stay fixed on me. She doesn't look down to Dakota's and my joined hands, though I get the feeling she wants to.

"Let's go to bed?" Dakota says, pulling me toward the bedroom with her, without looking at either of them.

When I look again, Nora's eyes are on our connected hands and Tessa is staring with her lips sucked in against her teeth and her eyes wide.

I turn to Dakota. She's giving me a look. One that says, *You better not stop and talk to that girl instead of coming to your bedroom with me.*

I look at Nora again and then at Tessa. I'm confused, and seemingly without my permission, my mouth says, "Uh, yeah. Good night, guys."

I follow Dakota into the room and she closes the door behind us.

Dakota is fuming when she turns to face me.

"She has *some fucking nerve!*" she roars. She tosses her hands into the air and then presses them to her temples.

I step toward her and cover her mouth with my hand. "Hey, be nice," I softly advise.

Dakota talks under my hand and I bring my free hand to her neck. I spread my fingers wide and cover her shoulder. I rub at the tense muscle there and she stops talking.

"She knew who you were all along," she half whispers. "I know she did. She had to remember your name."

I try to be the voice of reason. Maybe she did, but she honestly seemed just as clueless about my connection to Dakota as the rest of them.

I shrug. "Are you sure you said my name? Do you have our pictures out anywhere?"

I wince after that last question; I kind of don't want to know the answer.

I don't know Nora very well, but I don't see her as the type of person who would purposely go after her roommate's ex, knowing it would all blow up sooner rather than later. Plus, it's not like there aren't three million other guys in the city who would happily return any interest she showed in them.

Dakota huffs. The gray dress she's wearing is falling off her shoulder and she looks so small next to me.

"I don't know . . . maybe I never said your name, exactly." She looks around my bedroom. Her eyes stop at the picture of us on my dresser. "And I didn't keep any pictures of us around."

She looks guilty when she says this. And it's not like I expected her to build a shrine for me or anything, but is it possible that she didn't even mention my name to her roommates? Not once?

"Like at all?" I ask.

She shakes her hand and pulls at my shirt. Her fingers are struggling to loosen the fabric, so she moves to the buttons of my jeans. I steady them, cupping my hands around hers and pulling them to her chest.

"Not tonight," I say against her cheek.

With a pouty grumble, she pulls her hand free and dips it into my pants. I groan as she grips me and slowly moves her hand up and down.

*Think logically*, I remind myself.

I have to think logically, and I can't do that while Dakota's teasing me like this. I reach for her hand and gently unwrap her fingers from me. She looks up at me in confusion.

"You had too much to drink," I say, and lead her by the elbow to my bed. She stands in silence while I reach for the zipper of her dress.

She gathers up her hair and holds it out of the way to allow me access to the fabric. When the dress begins to fall she holds it to her chest and I pull her tights down her smooth legs. She steps out of them and lets the dress drop to the floor. She isn't wearing a bra.

Fuck me, she isn't wearing a bra.

Clearly I'm meant to be tempted tonight. For panties, she's wearing a red thong made of lace. Her ass looks so good in them, petite and toned. She turns around to face me with a devilishly sly grin.

"I don't remember these," I tease. I hook my finger around the hip of her panties and she moans when the fabric snaps back against her tawny skin.

I back away and she glares at me.

"You're mean," she says, sticking out her tongue as she shakes her ass a little. She's in a playful mood now, and I'm very aware that I'm in for it. There's nothing she can do to make me sleep with her tonight, no matter how sexy she looks standing here in only panties. We haven't touched each other in months, and we aren't dating. Tonight isn't the night to change all that. Not while she's wasted and we're both confused.

She'll understand in the morning.

I wrap my hands around her shoulders. "Let's get you to bed."

I can hear Tessa and Nora talking in the living room, but I can't make out anything they're saying. Dakota grabs the picture frame from my dresser and holds it to her face.

"We were *soooo* dorky!" She laughs, running a finger over the hideous plaid shirt I'm wearing in the picture.

Her bare breasts are distracting me, but I steer my attention toward grabbing her a shirt from my drawer. I reach around her and blindly pull something out, only to find it's my Adrian High School track shirt.

Of course it is, because we are in some mystical land where we can't seem to outrun our past no matter what we do. Dakota snatches it from me and brings it to her chest. She lifts it up, smelling the worn-out fabric.

"This shirt, oh my God!" She seems genuinely happy, and I don't think she notices when the talking in the living room quiets again. I do.

"We had sooo many good times in this shirt," she muses, her tongue licking at her lips.

I look away from her bouncing body.

"Put me out of my misery and put it on, please," I plead with her.

She giggles, thoroughly enjoying my compliments and admiration of her dancer's body, as she should. She should always feel like this, beautiful and empowered. She's still a little drunk, but she's glowing at my words.

Which makes me want to be a little more wild.

"You are so beautiful, you know that?" I say, wanting her to bathe in my words, to wrap herself in the kind words she deserves to hear. I keep a straight face, experimenting. "You're fucking smoking, and if you hadn't gotten yourself drunk tonight, I would tear your little ass up."

I sound like a damn idiot, but according to most erotic novels, this is what girls are into.

Dakota bursts into laughter. She holds one hand up and looks at me.

"You would *tear my little ass up*?" She cracks up. Her eyes are closed and I can't help but join in.

"Hey!" I try to breathe, but my stomach aches from laughing

so hard. "I read it in a book and wanted to see what it sounded like to say it."

Dakota pauses and struggles to hold her laughter in. "Let's just stick to the plain stuff that you're good at and leave the sexy stuff to the books." She covers her mouth and dips her head, snorting laughter.

*Plain stuff I'm good at?* Hey, I know we haven't experimented very much, or ever, but that's not because I wasn't willing. She never brought it up, and once, after I tried to talk about porn to her, she broke up with me for three days. So if any of the things that I'm good at are "plain," they're not that way for my lack of trying.

"I'm not that plain," I retort, defending my skills, but making sure to keep my voice down. I do not want Tessa or Nora to hear this.

I sit down on my bed. Dakota walks over, her mouth still turned up into a smile. She pulls the corner of her lip between her teeth. "Um, maybe now you aren't, but you were with me."

Maybe I'm being overly sensitive, but I feel like she's diminishing every intimate time we've had together. Our sex was *teenage* sex, rushed and quiet, even though I was hopelessly in love with her. It's not like I could've taken her any way that I wanted to with Carter in the next room, or her dad asleep downstairs. I never felt shortchanged with her, and I don't remember feeling like anything was missing in our sex life. I thought we were active and happy and satisfied.

Apparently not.

Dakota sits down on the bed next to me and crosses her legs. She puts on a pair of my socks sometime between teasing and laughing at me.

She clears her throat. "How many girls have you been with since we broke up?"

When I look at her, she's twirling a chunk of her hair between her thumb and forefinger.

"How many? None," I scoff, trying to force a nonawkward laugh.

She raises her eyebrow at me and cocks her head. "Really? Come on, I know—"

"You have?" I interrupt.

If she's acting this surprised that I haven't slept with anyone, how many people has she slept with?

Dakota shakes her head. "No. I haven't, I just assumed you did."

"Why would you assume that?"

And sitting here in the night, bringing all of these things up, I'm starting to think this woman doesn't know me at all. Dakota doesn't say anything, she just shrugs her shoulders and lies down with her head propped up against the headboard. She stares up at the ceiling before finally proclaiming, "Today was not fun."

I should change the subject. I finally got her in bed and calm and mostly sober.

"It's fine, it's over anyway. It's gotta be like two a.m. by now," I tell her.

She smiles and I lie down and turn off the lamp.

"Thank you for everything, Landon. You're always my safe place," she whispers in the dark.

I can feel her eyes on me even though I can't see them.

"Always," I reply, and gently squeeze her hand.

Today *wasn't* fun, she's right. Today was stressful.

I started the day thinking I was going on a first-date-like thing with Nora, but then ended up with a drunk Dakota in my bed and Nora in my living room probably listening to every embarrassing word Dakota and I say in here. The hallway is short and the walls are thin.

Even worse, I feel guilty for leaving her at the lounge. I didn't know what else to do. I've known Dakota half of my life. I've already gone through those terrible early stages of love with her. Together we made it through the awkward adolescent sex stage, where you can't find where to put it and come almost instantly when you do. We worked out most of our kinks and already know each other's backstory. We have no secrets, tell no lies. We've shared tragedy. I've already confessed my love for Dakota, and to start again would be daunting. Especially if she really has missed me as much as she says.

Just as I think Dakota is asleep, she jerks her hand from mine and brings it to her face. That's when I notice the sounds of crying.

I sit up. My hands gently shake her shoulders and I ask her over and over what's wrong. She shakes her head and catches her breath. I wait to turn on the light, knowing that the truth is easiest told in the dark.

"I . . ." she cries, "I slept with two people."

Her words slice through me like her cries slice through the darkness, and as if I've been burned, I suddenly don't want to be near her.

My instinct is to run. To get far, far away.

My stomach aches and she cries again, trying to cover her mouth. She reaches for a pillow and presses it to her face to keep herself quiet. Regardless of my pain, I can't stand to see her like this. And so I do what I always do. I put my feelings on hold. I pack the anger down. I tell my desire to run off without me. I reach for the pillow and remove it from her face. I toss it to the floor and lift her into my arms and lay us both down, an intertwined pair.

"I'm so sorry," she chokes.

Her cheeks are soaked with tears and I thumb at them, catching them before they roll down her face. Her shoulders are shaking, and I can feel her pain, or guilt maybe, or our lost history, and it's throbbing inside of me, too. I gently push at her shoulders to keep her still and raise my hand to her forehead. I brush back her hair and gently caress the strands, rubbing her scalp.

"Shhh," I say.

"Today is over," I say.

"We'll deal with this tomorrow," I say. "Get some rest."

I continue to massage her head until she falls asleep.

If she wants to work this out, I'm willing to listen to her. There has to be some explanation that makes sense, and now that she's told me the truth, she's going to be okay with telling me what happened. As soon as she wakes up, she will explain everything.

Except she didn't.

When she woke up, she snuck out of my apartment without a word.

# chapter

## Sixteen

WHEN I WALK OUT OF MY ROOM, I'm quiet so as not to wake Tessa. I know she's going to want to discuss last night, but I need coffee before attempting any such thing.

As I tiptoe down the short hallway, I glance at the square picture frames that Tessa spent hours hanging up, making them all perfectly parallel with one another along the wall. Inside of each frame is a portrait of a cat dressed in different types of hats. The one closest to me is a tabby, its gray panama-style hat streaked with black and brown to match the wearer's fur. A big white feather sticks up from the front.

I've never really paid attention to the portraits, but in the strange mood of this morning, I feel a pull to examine them, and find them really pretty entertaining. I had noticed that they were cat-related, but that was the extent of it. The next cat is another tabby, but instead of gray and black, it's all orange and cream. It's fat, this one, and I chuckle at the bowler hat it's wearing. A tuxedo cat exhibits his top hat, naturally. These are pretty clever and I want to shake the hand of whoever created them for taking something so simple and making it quirky and giving me the perfect distraction this morning. I glance at the rest of the pictures and stay as quiet as possible as I reach the end of the hall.

I'm a little surprised to find Nora sleeping on the couch. I had thought maybe she'd go home now that she knew Dakota and I weren't over at their place.

But there she is, her arm hanging over the edge of the cushion and her fingertips dangling just above the wood floor. Her dark hair is pulled up high on her head, and her knees are folded up, her lips parted slightly as if in a sigh. Her eyes are closed tightly. I walk by on my toes; my soft socks barely make a sound as I pass through into the kitchen.

After I realized that Dakota left before the sun came up, I went back to sleep for a while. I wasn't actually surprised that she left. I was mostly disappointed that I let any bit of me actually believe I would wake up to her next to me. She was being silly last night, being the old version of herself that loved to be around me, the silly girl who I've loved half of my life. Now the sun has come up and she's disappeared from my bed, taking the light with her.

The wind must have picked up sometime in the night, and it howls through the open kitchen window, making the yellow curtain flap against the glass. I can hear the rain picking up as I draw closer. And when I look out of the window and down at the sidewalk, I see a garden of umbrellas amid the downpour. Green-and-White Polka Dots is walking faster than Tan-and-Army-Green, and Red is the slowest of them all. The umbrella tops sort of look like flowers from here, and I'm surprised by how crowded the sidewalks are, even in the rain.

I glance over at Nora and quietly close the window before the noise of the rain and wind wakes her. I was going to make something for breakfast, but that's too noisy, so I'll probably just walk down and grab a bagel from the shop on the corner.

Though . . . if I leave now, I might not be here when she wakes up, and I would like to talk to her about last night. I want to apologize to her for being so quick to leave with Dakota, without giving her a proper explanation. She's not really the type of woman to be jealous of another; I've heard her ramble about shows like *The Bachelor* and claim that she would be the ultimate contestant precisely because she isn't jealous. Not that I want her seething with jealousy, but I would hate to think it didn't matter to her at all that Dakota inadvertently crashed our date and I ended up being a jerk and leaving with her.

On the other hand, of course, I don't want her to feel any pain or discomfort around me, and I want to make sure she's not upset over last night. It was a big misunderstanding and I'm sure she gets it.

But do I get it?

Actually, I don't think that I *do* get anything that has happened between me and either of these two women in the last twenty-four hours . . . at this point, I would probably kill to have both of them explain our situations to me in layman's terms. I do not understand dating in this city despite the fact I always hear that men have some sort of "upper hand" here.

I try to break everything down in my head while staring at the bright yellow curtain covering the window.

One, Nora touched my stomach after she found me in the shower, then she kissed me, then she invited me out with her friends.

Two, I left with Dakota in the middle of our datelike thing, in front of her friends; even if she doesn't *like me* like me, that couldn't have been good for her ego.

Three, she watched Dakota walk into my room last night, most likely heard at least some of our conversation, and most likely assumed we had sex.

This is so damn awkward. I don't even know if Nora likes me—she's a huge flirt.

I sigh, wishing that I had a clue about women and their minds.

I open the fridge slowly and wince when two root beer bottles clink together on our wobbly door shelf. I grab the one closer to me and steady it, resting the refrigerator door on my hip. I grab a two-day-old take-out box, noodles with some sort of peanut sauce and chunks of questionable chicken, and close the fridge.

I turn and Nora is standing there, her eyes sleepy and her hair messy. I jump in surprise and nearly drop the leftovers, but she just smiles up at me. Her smile is a lazy-morning smile and her eye makeup is smeared around her eyes.

"You woke me up," she says, and rolls the sleeves of her sweatshirt up her forearms. Her black shorts are so short that when she turns around and walks toward the fridge, I can see the curve of her ass where it meets her thigh.

She tugs at them, trying to cover more of her body, but there just isn't enough fabric.

No complaints here.

I look away when she opens the fridge and bends down. Half of her ass has to be hanging out of those little shorts, and I have to force my feet to stay planted here, not to grab a handful of her. This is something new for me, this urgency, this gnawing throb from my chest to my groin. She pulls out a red Gatorade and I raise my brow to her. I point my index finger at her.

Nora smiles and pulls a straight face and covers the bottle's label with her hand.

"Two th-things," I begin, awkwardly clearing my throat when my voice breaks.

Now that she's up, I don't care so much about being quiet. Tessa's probably been lying awake in her bed since seven, anyway. I toss the box of dicey leftovers into the trash and open the fridge again. I grab a carton of eggs and a container of milk and set them on the counter.

"Make that three," I correct myself. "Do you want an omelet?"

I open the egg carton and look at her. She glances toward the living room and back to me like she's looking for someone.

"She went home," I say.

At least, I assumed it was home. She's not here and doesn't have many options that I'm aware of. But given how little I know about her new life, she probably has an entirety of things I don't know about. For example, she could be hiding a Hippogriff in her apartment and I wouldn't even know—because I've never even seen her apartment building, let alone been inside of it.

"Oh," Nora says, seeming surprised. "Last night—" she begins, but I want to finish my three things, or I won't remember them later.

"Wait." I hold my finger up between us. She smiles and dramatically closes her mouth. "First things first. Omelet?"

I reach into the cabinet in front of me and grab the frying pan with one hand while turning on the stovetop with the other. Honestly, it's the smoothest, most coordinated move I've made in the past twenty-four hours.

"Yes, please," Nora responds in a voice that sounds like it should still be in bed.

I can hardly imagine how it would be to wake up to this woman every morning. Her hair would be messy and probably tied up on her head. Her legs would be smooth and tanned and I bet she doesn't even have a tan line.

"I'm a vegetarian, though. So only cheese for me."

"I have some onions and peppers?" I offer.

She nods, giving me an impressed smile. "Don't talk dirty to me so early in the morning."

Her smile is contagious and I'm impressed that I caught on to her kitchen humor. Though my two-egg omelet won't be very brag-worthy, it will be competent, and as a pastry chef, she likes when men can stand their own in the kitchen. Or so I assume.

Using a small bowl, I crack two eggs on the side.

"Now, for my second thing." I look at her to make sure I have her attention.

Her eyes are on mine as she lets her hair down. It falls in thick waves of deep brown around her shoulders, and when she shakes her head, I'm convinced that I've been thrown into a shampoo commercial.

*Would it be weird to say that? Will I sound like a guy who's trying too hard?*

I choose not to say anything. Comparing her to a shampoo commercial can't be a normal compliment, and I really don't need to dredge up any more reasons for her to think I'm lame.

Instead of taking a chance on being a creep, I dive straight into the pile of things I would like to figure out between us.

"I didn't know you two were roommates," I begin to explain. "I didn't know that Dakota would be at the bar. I'm sorry if me leaving there embarrassed you in front of your friends. I really was looking forward"—my throat is dry and I may cough mid-sentence but keep going—"to spending time with you. I don't know how much you know about Dakota and me, but—"

Nora holds a hand up. I shut my mouth and pour a splash of milk into the bowl of beaten eggs and open the fridge again. Nora walks over to the stove and turns down the heat. That's probably a good thing.

She looks at the floor and then up at me. "I know you didn't know. And I had no fucking idea that you were the guy she was talking about. She never told us anything about you that would even make me begin to think that you knew her at all. She didn't even mention your name."

And when she says that, there's something in her tone that I'm not sure I want to figure out. She lifts herself onto the counter a few feet away from me. Her feet dangle over the wooden cabinets.

"But I'm not mad or anything." Her tone is flat, paper-lying-under-a-pile-of-books flat. "So don't worry about it. I get it and it's fine."

Nora is being incredibly understanding, but she has that look glazing over her face again, and it's disconcerting. The one where she looks bored enough to pick at her nail polish.

Oh, and what do you know, there she is, one thumb beginning to pick at the other, trying to chip away her black polish.

"We aren't back together," I tell her.

The sting of Dakota's confession still burns at me, nagging at my mind.

Nora grins, looking up from her hands. "It wouldn't be any of my business if you were." She shrugs her shoulders as if I just told her the sky is blue, and I cock my head to the side.

The eggs are cooking now, hissing at me from the steaming pan, and the cheese is nearly melted, so I grab her veggies and a slice of ham from the deli bag.

"Meat." She makes a disgusted face. "And lunch meat, at that. I was starting to get a little too impressed. Good thing you brought out the Hillshire Farms."

When she laughs, I realize I don't think I want to let her change the subject. I want to know why she thinks my relationship is none of her business.

Were we not out together last night? Everything was fine for five minutes, before you-know-what hit the fan. Also, this meat isn't your typical packaged lunch meat. It's cut from the deli. I pay an extra three dollars a pound for that difference written in red ink on a yellow sticker—this is worth mentioning.

"That's how you stay so fit, then?" I point to her body with the spatula that I just used to flip the omelet. "Not eating processed lunch meat?"

She nods, shrugging her shoulders. She scoots a little closer to me.

"No, I don't eat meat, but I still have to watch what I eat. I could easily gulp down this entire bag of cheese and I may do just that," she says, pointing to the cheese on the counter.

I finish up her omelet, then drop it onto a paper plate and start cooking up my own. All the while I watch as she mentally adds another demerit to my score sheet, that list that women make inside of their heads when they first meet a guy.

> *Cuteness: 8 points. (Realistically anywhere between*
>   *6 and 10. I would say I'm a solid 7.5.)*
> *Height: 8 points. (For some reason, at five-foot-eleven,*
>   *I get eight points.)*
> *Cooking skills: 5 points.*
> *Using lunch meat in his omelet: −2.*
> *Paper plates: −1.*

I'm electing to ignore the fact that I had to lose at least ten points for last night. More than likely, I'm close to a two-point average right now.

"But I realized as I got older that to stay in shape, I have to work a little harder than most people do." She pokes at her leg and I get distracted by a small freckle in the center of her thigh.

Her shorts are *so* short, and my eyes follow the freckle, up to another one, to another one. It's like the brown speckles have aligned perfectly to form a trail to the edge of her shorts. It's only human nature to follow the dots.

She turns slightly and looks at her own ass and thighs. "But I like to keep some things the way they are."

I'm sweating.

I may pass out from the rise in temperature induced by the pushing of her ass out slightly, subtly. And because now I'm staring at the *back* of her thighs. Her hand grabs a chunk of her own flesh of her ass and she looks at me.

I look away, I have to.

I should speak.

I should say something cool back to her.

Problem is, I can't think of anything remotely cool to say, and I don't want her to think that I'm thinking that she's thinking . . .

Dammit, I'm overthinking again.

"Especially when I bake for a living and a hobby," she continues, as if she had not just discombobulated my brain. "I would rather go without Wi-Fi than sweets." She turns back to me, and somehow I manage to not return to the freckles on the front of her thighs.

Her declaration is serious and I can tell by the way she's bugging her eyes out and pursing her lips that she means business.

I almost pretend that I'm one of those trendy techy people who immediately ask for the Wi-Fi password wherever they go, but after last night, I don't have the energy to pretend much of anything.

"You make it sound like this is life or death," I tease.

She grins at me wholeheartedly . . . and then I make a U-turn in our conversation: "Second thing, part B: if you want to talk about Dakota, we can."

Nora shoots me an annoyed glare. I ignore it. I want her to know that I'm not one of those guys who doesn't tell you what's on his mind and makes you guess, and by the time you figure it out, you've already forgotten what the problem was in the first place. That guy is not me.

I was raised by a single mom, and I credit her for my communication skills.

I don't just swallow half-truths, and I don't give them out. I wouldn't just leave with my ex and not want to explain everything to the girl I was actually on a date with. I don't want her to create this version of me that she thinks she knows. I want her to base her opinion of me on facts and good experiences.

But so far, I haven't given her a great example of what type of man I am. I wipe out the pan and spray the nonstick spray onto the nonstick surface. Neither product actually works completely, but still, only half of my meals get stuck to the bottom of the pan. That's a win, the way things go for me.

"Come on," I say, trying to guide her into the conversation.

Nora eyes me tentatively. "Since I get the feeling that you aren't going to let this go, I'll talk about how insane it is that she's my roommate and you're Tessa's roommate. Talk about a small fucking world."

She tilts her head back and shakes it.

It *is* such a small world—*too* small, if you ask me. I'm so curious as to how it could be possible that my ex-girlfriend ended up rooming with my . . . friend Nora.

"How did you meet her? If she's in the ballet academy and you're a baker—"

Nora's neck rolls and she holds up her hand. "I'm not a baker. I'm a chef."

Her tone lets me know that she gets that a lot and she doesn't care for the generalization. Oops.

"Anyway," Nora continues, "my old roommate from college, Maggy, posted an online ad for a third. Dakota showed up one day with one bag around her arm and the biggest attitude I've ever seen."

I can tell by the face she's making that she regrets saying this in front of me. "No offense," she adds hesitantly.

"None taken."

I feel as if I should be defending Dakota, but I don't want to just yet. Nora's entitled to her own opinion of her, and I'm in no place to be her defender. Who are the two guys she slept with? Do I know them? It's more than likely that I don't. I know a handful of guys in New York and she's been single the whole time she's lived here. I don't want to begin to consider that she slept with anyone we knew in Michigan.

"Well, it's just my luck that I tried to go on a date with my ex's roommate. I'm sorry," I say with a laugh, aiming to lighten up the energy in the room.

Her expression tightens and she shrugs her shoulders again. "It's fine. It wasn't much of a date. I don't really have the time to date anyone anyway. So what was your third thing? There's the omelet, the uncomfortable date not-date, and then there was something else."

When I pause for a moment to remember, she leans over and pokes at my cheek. My heart leaps. "What. Was. The. Third. Thing?"

She leans back and rests her head against the cabinets, then opens the top of her Gatorade bottle and takes a sip. Perfect timing.

"This!" I point to the red perpetrator in her hand.

Nora closes her mouth, cheeks full of Gatorade, and widens her eyes.

"You hated it just the other day and now *this*!" I tap the bottle with my fingers as she swallows a huge gulp.

A dribble spills down her chin as she tries to hold it in, and I laugh, leaning across her. Her thighs separate and she doesn't move away when I take the towel from the counter and gently dab at the corner of her chin.

I'm between her thighs now and my entire body couldn't be more aware of it. She swallows, then reaches up and holds on to my forearm with both hands. Her fingers press into my arm and I lean closer. My chest is touching hers now and her ankles are wrapping around my legs. I'm so damn attracted to her that it hurts. Physically and mentally, in every place it could hurt, it stabs at me—want and need mixing together into a cocktail of confusion.

She's no longer a silly, giggling girl sitting on a countertop batting her lashes at me. She's a seductive, sensual woman wrapping one of her arms around my neck, letting her nails drag along behind her smooth fingertips. Goose bumps rise on my skin, and there's no way she didn't just feel me shiver, and there's no way I'm letting that bother me when she's wrapped around me like this. I'm only a little taller than her when she's sitting on the high countertop, but when I look down at her, she's breathing heavily, her lashes dark, resting on her cheeks as she looks down.

I move my hand to her chin, lifting gently until her eyes meet mine. She inches closer. Her breath whispers into my mouth and I grip her thighs with my hands on instinct. Only it shouldn't be an instinct because I've only touched this woman once, yet I can't seem to convince my body otherwise. It has a mind of its own and I'm in no shape to stop it.

She breathes my name and I take it in, appreciating the way her tongue seems to wrap my name in sugar. My hands move up, and up, until they reach the side of her thighs where her ass begins. In the wake of my hands, red streaks blotch her smooth skin. Her breathing accelerates again when she looks down at her thighs and up to my eyes. I gently nudge her cheek with my jaw and she turns her head. My mouth delicately touches her neck in small pecks of admiration and need.

She moans; her legs tighten around my waist and she reaches up and grips my hand. She rocks her body against mine and I move my mouth to her ear, drenched in lust for her. It's coating me, covering me.

She puts her hands on mine and presses them into her legs. She moves both of our hands closer to the apex of her thighs and the drawstring on my sweats rubs against her. She moans again, her nails press into my hands, and I'm in a daze. This woman who I know close to nothing about has me dry-humping her on the kitchen counter with Tessa at home in her bedroom, after Dakota skipped out on me this morning, and despite these things, I am completely at her mercy. It's like I'm sucking in laughing gas, like I can't tell black from white, or innocent touches from sexual advances. This kiss is strong enough to bring me to my knees. She looks like a dark angel through my hooded eyes, and though I've never been religious, now I'm a devout Nora-ite.

I shouldn't be doing this, and she shouldn't be doing this, but I want to keep doing this. I desire this, I need to do this. On this counter, on the kitchen table, even on the kitchen floor.

I feel her pull away when my teeth brush against her ear.

"This . . . is . . ." she breathes. "This is bad for me. For both of us." She pushes her hand against my chest and I back away.

"Good God." She touches her hand to her chest and takes a few deep breaths. "You are soooo bad for me. And I'm even worse for you."

She jumps down from the counter and tugs at her shorts in frantic desperation to conceal her body from my eyes.

I try not to stare, knowing that with every second that passes she's letting doubt creep up her spine and is checking off the list of reasons why Tessa's loser roommate isn't good enough for her. She's trying to tell me something, and I'm doing that stereotypical man thing where I stare at her instead of listening to what she's saying.

Except I'm not. I'm trying to keep a good grasp on reality and what's happening between us. Good thing I'm not completely clueless, and I'm fully capable of looking back up at her eyes and listening to her list of the reasons why we can't jump each other's bones every time we are alone in the kitchen.

# Seventeen

*I*T'S THE KITCHEN," I add when she touches on the third reason we can't sleep together.

I missed the first two reasons she stated because I couldn't stop being one of those guys who stares, the category I was just claiming to be excluded from. In my defense, she was fumbling over words strung together as excuses while adjusting her bra. It was hard not to stare at her soft tits pushing one way, then the other.

"The kitchen makes us crazy," I say, then turn and crack two eggs into the bowl and stir them with a spoon.

If she doesn't want me to kiss her, I won't kiss her. The way my body aches for her can be ignored.

It can.

I'm pretty sure.

Nora watches me, looking pleased that I'm continuing with breakfast after all. I reach over and grab a third egg. When I oil the pan, she walks over and takes the milk jug from the counter. She adds at least a half cup more to the bowl and opens my silverware drawer. She grabs a fork and stirs the eggs with it. Her fork moves much quicker than my spoon and I back away, bowing slightly to her chef-ness.

She appreciates my gesture and laughs, although the rain

outside nearly drowns out the sound. I wish it would stop so I could hear her cute laugh better.

Nora opens the top of one of the plastic containers of pre-cut vegetables. She adds a handful of onions to the pan, then peppers, and waits to add the eggs. While she's effortlessly out-performing me in the kitchen, she leans against the counter and looks at me.

"Tessa's my friend, and if this gets too messy, it could ruin that."

That was reason number four? Or maybe five?

"We have too much baggage, both of us," she adds.

Seven, maybe eight if we count our scores separately?

"How many reasons do you have, *ten*?" I say lightly. "Or would you like to come on my run with me so you can finish telling me all of the reasons why we can't be friends?"

"I wasn't saying we couldn't be friends. I was talking about all of this," she says, and waves her hands around in front of herself.

I imagine her running beside me, listing off reasons word by word. I have a few, too; I'm just not as eager to say them as she is. She's still waving between our bodies. I decide to fuck with her, just a little.

"The air? You mean the nitrogen and oxygen—"

Reaching her free hand over to me, she clamps it over my mouth and gives me a shut-the-fuck-up-you-adorable-bastard look that shoots through me like Cupid's arrow.

Yikes, good thing I didn't say that out loud.

"I meant the making-out. The heavy petting." Her eyes glance over to my lips and stay there.

"I fail to see how petting animals is a problem—" I start, but the hand goes right back over my mouth.

"We can't keep doing that and keep everything from getting out of control. Your ex is my roommate, she lives with me, she knows where I sleep." She smiles, and I think she's only half teasing. "I was only thinking we could take each other's mind off of whatever baggage we had—Tessa told me about your breakup."

Her eyes fill with sympathy . . .

And I sort of hate when people feel sorry for me.

But I nod. "I understand. I wasn't sure what you were thinking, how you were feeling, and I was trying to get over Dakota," I explain.

She nods her head. "I'm glad you were. But let's just agree to be friendly. No touching, no kissing"—her voice slows and her eyes glance away from me—"definitely no thigh-grabbing . . . And no ear-nibbling, no throat-kissing . . ." She clears her throat and straightens her back.

I clear my throat, too, and look for a towel to wipe my sweaty palms on.

I'm getting caught up in her words and whirled back to two minutes ago when I was possessed by one of those guys in romance novels. She was about one more moan away from me saying things like *I shall ravish you* in my best attempt at a seducer's voice.

A list of romantic comedies pops into my head, guiding my thoughts. "The next step in this agreement is for you to propose a friends-with-benefits type of relationship, and then we bicker over it for about thirty seconds before we agree," I say. "One month later, one of us will be in love and it will be messy. Cut to another month later, we have ourselves a perfect relationship or a complete disaster. There's no middle ground. It really is an indisputable fact that the movies have proved."

I like that I can be completely unfiltered around her. I've made a fool out of myself more than once, so she should be used to it by now. There's no history, I don't have any expectations placed on me. She laughs and nods. Her omelet is browned now and my kitchen smells amazing. She slides it onto the plate and blows at the light puff of steam coming from the dish.

"Agreed." Nora tucks a lose strand of hair behind her ear. "We can easily avoid all of that mess now and agree to be friends. I don't have time for catfights in restaurants with twenty-year-old girls who shouldn't even be drinking in public in the first place."

Somehow the way she says that makes her sound much older, and I feel like a child being scolded by his mom.

"I'm building a career in a thriving city and I don't want to fuck that up for some cute college kid."

Her use of the word *kid* stabs at my already wounded ego. I'm nearly twenty-one and I have more in common with the people my parents' age than I do with college "kids." I've already been stopped twice on campus by students who thought I was a professor; I have that mature look. It's true—my mom says it, too.

Ugh. Using my mom as a standard—maybe I *am* just a kid. That hurts a little.

I wouldn't have thought Nora would see me as anything other than a peer, but apparently to her, I'm just some college kid who was going to be her distraction from whatever.

"Friends, then." I deliver her a smile and she nods. From here on out, I will be only friendly to Nora and Dakota.

I will not let things get messy.

No chance.

# chapter

## Eighteen

*I*T'S BEEN TWO WEEKS since I've heard from Dakota. She hasn't reached out to me once since she slipped out of my bed in the middle of the night, nor has she answered either of my calls or the two texts I've sent. Maybe I've overdone it, bothering her too much when she obviously doesn't want to talk, but I want to make sure she's okay. No matter how many times I try to remind myself that that's not my job anymore, my head just won't listen. Or maybe it's my heart, possibly both. I know Dakota well enough to know that when she needs her space, she will take it and no one can change that.

The unfamiliar part is that I'm not used to being the one she needs space from.

Since we decided to be friends I've seen Nora twice, but only spoken to her once. Friends without kissing. Friends don't kiss and friends definitely don't think about kissing.

I'm still working on that part. She hasn't started to come around less; she's just leaving earlier and I'm coming home later than I used to. I've been staying a little later at work to help Posey close. She's been picking up so many of Jane's shifts lately that I have a feeling she could use the help. She seems overwhelmed. I don't want to be too pushy and probe too much into her life, but I've always been pretty good at reading people. We have become something close to friends during our long shifts together, and she's been sharing more and more of her life with me while we scrub dishes and clean coffee grounds from every nook and cranny of Grind.

I'm enjoying the extra hours and her company. I'm lonely and soaking our conversations up like a sponge, like the details of her life somehow make me feel more involved in the wider world. She was born and raised here—a dyed-in-the-wool New Yorker, something millions of people in this city strive to imitate. Her family used to live in Queens, and when she was fifteen, her mom passed away and Lila and Posey moved to Brooklyn to live with their grandma.

It's nice having someone to talk to about random stuff. It's nice to hear about someone else's life and opinions and thoughts when I don't want to think about my own.

I don't want to think about Dakota, and I don't want to miss Nora. Am I a bad person for liking two people?

Really, though, I don't know if I like Nora or if I'm just attracted to her. I don't know enough about her to compare to my feelings for Nora . . .

I mean, *Dakota*.

Shit, I'm a mess.

Am I being too hard on myself by keeping my distance from both of them? I've loved Dakota for years; I know her inside and out. She's my family. In my heart of hearts, she owns half the real estate.

Nora is another story; she's wishy-washy and hot and cold, and undeniably sexy and flirtatious. I'm half-attracted, half-curious about her, and I keep having to remind myself that we killed our potential relationship before it ever had a chance to bloom into anything anyway, so I can't sit around moping over losing something that wasn't mine to begin with.

So it's been two weeks of avoidance of the women in question: picking up later shifts at work, joining more study groups, or staying home and watching cooking shows with Tessa. She's ob-sessed with them lately and they provide good background noise when I'm doing my schoolwork. I can pay just a little bit of atten-tion to the shows, but I don't care enough to have to give my full attention to them—and I'm not convinced that Tessa does either.

One night during *Cupcake Wars*, my phone buzzes on the leather couch and Hardin's name lights up on my screen. Tessa's eyes follow the noise and flash at the sight of his name. Her eyes dart back to the screen and she pulls her pouty bottom lip be-tween her teeth.

She's freaking miserable and I hate it. Hardin's miserable, and he deserves it, but I still hate it. I don't know what kind of mountain Hardin will have to move to earn her forgiveness, but I know damned well he would even *build* a mountain if he had to—a whole row of them with her face carved into them—before he would live his life without her.

That sort of desperation, that kind of burning, throbbing love—I haven't known it.

I have loved slow and deep with Dakota . . . it was—still is—a steady kind of love. We had our share of complications and fights, but nine times out of ten, it was her and me fight-ing against the world. It was me, sword drawn, cannon loaded, ready to charge at any enemy who crossed a line. Mostly the foe was her dad, the biggest, nastiest troll of all. I spent many a night rescuing my princess from the yellow-stained walls and worn *Cinderella*-printed curtains tacked over the windows of her house. I climbed the dirty, sun-damaged siding and opened the dust-covered window, and pulled her to the safety of warm choc-olate chip cookies and the soft voice of my mother.

Times were rough at her house, and when Carter was gone, even the best cookies, the softest voices, and the tightest hugs couldn't comfort Dakota. We shared pain and pleasure, but the more I think about it and the more I compare it to the relationships I see around me and the ones I read about in my books, the more I realize that while Dakota and I were family, we were also nothing but kids.

Is someone even supposed to spend his whole life with the one who helps him grow? Or is that person simply a stop along the way to who he will become, their role ending when he learns what he needs to make it to the next stop? I once felt like Dakota was my entire journey and my destination, but I'm starting to feel like I was no more than a stop along the way for her.

Do I, Landon Gibson, Amateur Relationship Participant, even know what the hell I'm talking about?

I grab my phone as it goes to voicemail. I call Hardin right back and he answers on the first ring.

"Hey," I say, looking at Tessa as she pulls the blanket up to her neck like it's protecting her from something.

"I'm about to book my flight. It's next month," he says, loud enough for Tessa to hear. And with every word from Hardin's mouth, she visibly shudders.

She stands up and walks to her room without a word.

I whisper so she doesn't hear me: "I don't know if it's a good—"

"Why?" he interrupts. "What's going on, where's Tess?"

"She just went into her room after shaking like someone was screaming at her the moment she overheard your voice." It's harsh to say it like that, I know, but it's honest.

Hardin makes a noise that pains me. "If she would just speak to me . . . I fucking hate this shit."

I sigh. I know he hates it. So does she. So do I. But he did this to himself, to her, and it's not fair of me to push her toward him if she doesn't want to go.

"Try to give her the phone," he demands.

"You know I can't do that."

"*Fuck*, man."

I can picture him running his fingers through his hair.

He hangs up the phone, and I don't call him back.

I wait a few minutes and knock on Tessa's door. She opens almost immediately and I take a step back into the hallway. I glance at the tabby cat picture and wonder again how I managed to never pay attention to these weird little pictures before.

"You okay?" I ask my friend.

She looks down at her feet, then back up at me. "Yeah."

"You're a terrible liar," I say.

She steps back into her room and leaves the door open, gesturing for me to come inside. She sits on the edge of her bed and I look around her room. It's spotless as usual, and she's done a little more decorating since I've last been in it. Her TV is no longer on the dresser; in its place are stacks of books, organized by author's last name. Three worn copies of *Pride and Prejudice* catch my eye.

Tessa lies back on her bed and stares up at the ceiling. "I really am okay with him coming to visit. He's your family and I won't keep you from seeing him."

"You're my family, too," I remind her. I sit on the opposite edge of her bed, near the blue upholstered headboard. The color matches her curtains and I can't see a single dust bunny in her windowsill.

"I'm just waiting and waiting, and I don't know how to stop . . ." Her voice is flat, detached.

"Waiting for what?"

"For him to stop being able to hurt me. Even hearing his voice . . ."

I pause to let her catch her breath, then say, "It will take a while, I assume."

I wish I hated him, too, so I could tell her how terrible he is for her, that she's better off without him, but I can't. I can't and won't pretend that they both aren't better when they're together.

"Can I ask you something?" Tessa's voice is soft.

"Of course." I prop my feet up on her bed and hope she doesn't notice how dirty my socks are on her white comforter.

"How did you get over Dakota? It makes me feel like shit that you were feeling this way and I barely comforted you. I was so consumed by my own problems that I never thought about you feeling the way I feel now. I'm sorry I'm such a shitty friend."

I laugh softly. "You aren't a shitty friend. My situation was a lot different than yours."

"That's so Landon to say that. I knew you would tell me I'm not a shitty friend," She smiles and I can't remember the last time I saw her do this. "But really, how did you get over her? Does it still eat at you when you see her?"

That's a good question. How did I get over her?

I don't even know how to answer that question. I don't want to admit it, but I don't think I ever felt as low as Tessa does now. It hurt when Dakota broke up with me, especially the *way* she did it, but I didn't drown in my own misery. I held my head up and tried to stay as supportive of her as I could and kept going on with my life.

"It was so different for me. Dakota and I had barely seen each other in the last two years, so I wasn't always around her the way you were with Hardin. We never lived together, and I think I was used to feeling alone anyway."

Tessa rolls over and rests her chin on her elbow. "You felt alone when you were dating?"

I nod. "She lived across the country, remember?"

Tessa nods. "Yes, but you still shouldn't have felt alone."

I don't know what to say. I did feel alone, even when Dakota and I talked every day. I don't know what that says about me, or our relationship.

"Do you feel alone now?" Tessa asks, her gray eyes focused on me.

"Yeah," I answer honestly.

She rolls back over and looks up at the ceiling again. "Me, too."

# chapter

## Nineteen

MY CLASSES FELT SO LONG TODAY. Well, they've felt like that all week. I couldn't focus after everything that went down with Dakota. And then with Hardin calling to tell me that he's coming just next weekend . . .

Next weekend . . .

That doesn't give me much time to get Tessa used to the idea of him being here, in her space.

When he called back that night, I didn't answer. It was the first time Tessa and I had really connected in a while and we were too busy wallowing in our aloneness. It was sad, but *nice*, too, to be there with her.

And miracle of miracles, instead of calling back several times in a row, Hardin actually left me a voicemail. Fairly amazing, really. But thinking back on it, I remembered that he claimed he had to come because he has an appointment in the city that he "can't miss."

He *has* to be applying for jobs here—why else would he have an "unmovable" appointment here in New York? It has to be for a job . . .

Or he's tired of being away from Tessa. He can't stay away from her long; he must need his fix.

When I reach my building, a loud delivery truck is idling

in the middle of the street. The deli below gets deliveries at all times of the night. Voices and the heavy sound of doors closing, opening, closing again drove me nuts at first because I was so used to the stillness and silence of the suburbs in Washington State, in the Scott "castle" on top of the hill. I still remember how big that house looked to me as we pulled up in my mom's station wagon. We had chosen the cheap way to travel, driving cross-country, despite Ken's many attempts to buy us airline tickets and have our stuff shipped. Looking back, I think my mom had too much pride to let him believe she was around for anything other than her love for him.

I remember the first time I heard her laugh in front of him. It was a new laugh—the kind that changed her face and her voice. The corners of her eyes drew up, and the joy that emerged from her throat seemed to come from deep inside her and filled the room with light and fresh air. I felt like she was a different, happier version of the mom I knew and loved.

Of course, when I talk to her now, she always mentions something about me that's worrying her. Case in point: my sleeping habits since I moved to the city. She keeps asking when I'm going to find a doctor to look into it, but I'm not ready to do most of the practical parts of living in a new city. Seeing a doctor and getting a new driver's license are things that can wait. Besides, I don't want to drive in this city, and as far as I'm concerned, the real problem I have right now is those 3 a.m. garbage trucks.

So instead of a doctor's visit, I got my white noise machine. It helped me tremendously. Tessa likes the noise, but she said she grew up next to a railroad track and missed the sound of the trains during the night. Lately, we both seem to be reaching for anything that reminds us of home. My sense in New York is that your home is truly your castle, or if not a castle, at least the cubbyhole in the city you can control. Apparently, for both Tessa and me, controlling the sounds we hear helps us feel in control in general, just in different ways.

Inside, the hallways of my building are empty and silent.

When I step off the elevator and into the hallway on my floor, it smells like sugar and spice. Nora must be here, and she and Tessa must be making a sweet, floury mess in the kitchen.

Music is playing; the crooning voice of an edgy girl taking a stand for disregarded youth who are the New Americana fills the apartment when I open the door. I kick off my shoes and leave them by the door. When I walk into the kitchen, I put the gallon of milk I bought while I was out on the counter near Tessa, but it's Nora who thanks me first.

"It's nothing," I tell her, pulling my jacket off of my shoulders and down my arms.

I really need to do something for Ellen for her birthday. She looked even less excited today when I asked her about her big day this week.

"I was walking right by the store when Tessa texted me," I add.

Still, Nora smiles at me.

God, she's even more beautiful than I remember, and it's only been a week since I've seen her.

Nora grabs the milk and walks over to the fridge. "You missed the most epic baking fail. Tessa added whipped cream instead of whipping cream to the scone recipe."

"We said that was going to be a secret," Tessa grumbles play-fully. She looks at me. "The dough fell flat."

"Yeah. After the scones burned," Nora says over her shoulder.

I think I like how comfortable she seems to be feeling here. I like that she walks with ease through the kitchen, her back straight and her full mouth partly smiling, relaxed. She opens the fridge and places the milk inside. I look away when she bends over to grab a pitcher full of cold water from the bottom shelf. I try not to let my mind linger on the tightness of her white pants. They aren't quite sweats, but they aren't really yoga pants either. I don't care what they are: her ass looks incredible with the fabric stretched over it, accentuating the melon shape.

She's wearing a long-sleeved baseball-style shirt, the arms of which are a different color from the body, and her deep-blue sleeves are pushed up to her elbows. Her thick, dark hair is pulled up into a high ponytail and her socks have little cartoon bacon and eggs printed on them. The skin of her stomach is showing, but I refuse to look, knowing I won't be able to stop.

Nora walks over to the oven and pulls out a tray of biscuits, or maybe they're scones? Probably scones. I typically don't care for them; Grind sells only incredibly healthy scones that taste like olive-oil-covered grains baked into wheatgrass bread. Not for me.

My mom's professional-level skills as a baker ruined me for anybody else's cookies or cakes. Our house was always full of sweets, which is probably why I was a pudgy kid. I have to work a little harder than normal people to be able to eat the things I like without putting on weight. It took me a while to realize that, but I'm glad I did. I remember how it felt when the ass-holes at my high school stopped having a reason to make fun of my weight—not that they didn't find another reason to treat me like shit—but I felt lighter, mentally and physically, and I started gaining a confidence I'd never felt before.

Tessa and Nora have been in the kitchen every day this week, but I've been hiding in my room, trying to get my school assignments done and just plain crashing after work. Even in my dreams I hear the displeased customers' voices as they stare at the menu board on the wall.

"Um, do you have, like, Frappuccinos here? Like Starbucks?"

"Why don't you have cashew milk?"

"What's the difference between a cappuccino and a latte?"

I only worked three hours tonight, but this week has exhausted me. As tired as I am, though, I don't think I want to hide in my room tonight. I want to talk to Tessa, and even to Nora. I hate the way my chest tightens when she looks at me, the way her eyes always catch mine. I'm making a choice to be social tonight. It's nice for me to engage with people, even if it's just the two of them.

Nora takes the scones off of the hot pan and places them on a cooling rack. They smell like blueberries. I sit down at the small three-person table and watch Nora move around the room. She picks up a plastic bag full of yellow goo and twists the end, creating a puffy triangle of creamy icing. She places a small metal tip on the pointy end and squeezes the icing on top of each scone.

Nora says something about how icing makes scones taste better, but I'm too busy trying to make sure my eyes don't linger on her ass for a beat too long to really pay attention.

I'm also suddenly struck with the question of whether I should stay out here with them or not. I don't want to be in the way.

"How was work?" Tessa asks.

She dips her finger into a bowl of thick batter, speckled with blue chunks. Blueberries, maybe? Her mouth opens and she pops her finger into her mouth.

I look over at Nora, who's pushing up her sleeves again. Which leads me to notice the material at the bottom of the shirt. It looks like it's been cut with scissors to reveal the bottom four inches of her abdomen.

I usually wouldn't mind this. Not one bit. I can't imagine that anyone would, unless they, too, were tortured by the temptation that is Nora while also knowing that nothing could come of it.

Her skin is a few shades darker than mine and I can't tell her ethnicity by simply looking at her. I do know, though, that she's a mix of something beautiful and unique. I'm not sure what it is specifically, but the almond shape of her eyes is striking, and so are her dark brows and the thick lashes that shade her high cheekbones. That shirt she's wearing looks perfect on her, just like every trendy outfit I've seen her in. Her hips are full, and the way her white cotton pants cling to her ass is hard to look away from.

Did I already say that?

I allow myself a few seconds to look at her, really look at her. It won't hurt just to stare for a second or two . . . right?

She's so oblivious to my gaze, to my longing to run my fingers along the bare skin of her back. My thoughts take me there, to a world where Nora is lying next to me, my fingers moving their way across her tanned skin. I would love to see her fresh out of a shower. Her hair would be wet, wavy at the ends, and her skin would be dewy, her dark lashes even blacker against her skin when she blinks—

"That bad, huh?" Nora asks.

I shake my head. I was so lost in my own thoughts that I didn't respond to Tessa's question about my workday. I tell her it was the same as usual, crowded and fast-paced. The first few weeks of college are a busy time for coffee shops, even across the bridge in Brooklyn.

I don't bore them with the details of the nozzle on the sink breaking off, spraying water all over Aiden. I can't say I didn't laugh when he wasn't looking—he was so pissed that his hair got messed up. It was all the funnier because it had been his idea to toy with the nozzle in the first place, claiming that he knew how to fix the leak.

Draco . . . foiled again.

Tessa tells me that she picked up extra shifts for the next two weekends, and I know that by mentioning her work schedule she's also really itching to know when Hardin is coming so she can keep her distance. I should tell her that he's coming next weekend, and I intend to, but I'm going to wait until Nora leaves so Tessa can have some time alone to get used to the idea and figure out how to prepare herself.

I've watched the light in Tessa drain away with each day she's in the city, alone, all the while that she's hearing about how Hardin is thriving under the influence of his new group of friends and the advice of his therapist. I truly think he's getting better and that this time away is necessary for him, even if he loathes it.

If the two of them don't end up married with a bunch of stubborn, shaggy-haired children, I will lose all my faith in love.

I hate the word *therapist*. It adds such a stigma to someone who spends their life attempting to heal others.

Somehow it's been deemed inappropriate to talk about your therapist at the water coolers at your day job, yet spreading gossip about your co-workers' lives is completely acceptable. Sometimes the world's priorities are really messed up.

"Have you heard from your mom?" Tessa asks me.

Nora moves comfortably around the kitchen again. She washes the cooling racks and wets a sponge to wipe the countertops clean while I explain to Tessa that my little sister is using my mom's belly for soccer training. "She swears that little Abby will be first pick in the MLS superdraft," I tell them.

My mom says her body aches and aches at night, making room for the baby growing inside. She isn't complaining, though—she's awed and fascinated by the changes her body is undergoing at her age and she's eternally grateful to have had a healthy, uneventful pregnancy.

"You lost me at MLD super-something," Nora chirps, her lips quirking up to one side in amusement.

Slight amusement. Her eyes always seem to have a touch of boredom, like her life prior to the current moment was much more exciting in some important way.

"I was talking about soccer. You don't watch any sports?" I ask. I know Tessa doesn't.

Nora shakes her head. "Nope. I'd rather cut my own eyes out and eat them with ketchup."

I laugh at her very detailed and fairly morbid reply.

"Well, then." I reach for a scone that she already covered in icing and she stops my hand just before I grab it.

"You have to let the icing cool," she explains, her hand still on mine.

"Just like three minutes," Tessa adds.

Nora's hand is so warm.

Why isn't she letting go?

And why don't I want her to?

I was supposed to be forgetting about any sort of attraction I have to her. I was supposed to get used to my spot in the friend zone. It seems pointless to keep asking myself these stupid questions about why I feel this or feel that, but I'm trying to feel slightly more in control of myself, and asking questions seems like a way to do that.

I need to constantly remind myself to stay in the friend zone. It's hard to do this when she's sitting here, looking at me like this, touching me like this, wearing that.

I glance down at our hands, hers darker than mine, and when my eyes catch hers, she seems to remember that she shouldn't be holding my hand like this; friends don't hold hands.

Tessa's phone rings and Nora jumps. Her cheeks flare, and I want to reach for her again, but I can't.

"It's my boss. I'm going to take this," Tessa says.

She pauses for a moment and glances at both of us, silently asking if we're okay to be left alone alone.

Nora gives her a small smile, her eyes saying what her mouth—and mine—can't.

With every step that Tessa takes down the hall, the air in the kitchen grows thicker. Nora keeps herself occupied by pulling a pan from the counter and tossing it into the sink. She turns on the water, grabs the bottle of dishwashing liquid, and gets to scrubbing. I don't know if I should just stand here awkwardly while she washes the pan, or if I should just go in my room and spend the night alone, again.

I pull out my phone and scroll through the last few text messages I received. I have a text from Posey, a meme about baristas. A quiet laugh rocks through me and Nora's shoulders tilt toward me.

She seems to stop herself before she completely turns around. She grabs the bottle of soap and squeezes again. Little angry bubbles float around her and I notice that she's still scrubbing the same pan.

I take a silent step toward her and look into the sink. The pan is clean, no cake residue left, its surface all shiny despite a thick and completely unnecessary coat of bubbly soap. Her hands work at the already-clean pan and I take another step closer to her. My foot catches one of the legs of the wooden kitchen chairs and she jumps at the noise.

"So, how have you been? Anything new?" I ask, like I've never spoken to her before and like I didn't just trip over a chair.

Nora's shoulders lift with a deep breath and she shakes her head, her dark ponytail waving back and forth with her movements.

"Not really" is all she says, and her hands go back to scrubbing the pan. Finally, she rinses it and lays it to dry on the wire rack next to the sink.

*Where is Tessa?* I wish she would come back and break the awkwardness in this kitchen.

"How's work going? Do you still like it there?" I just can't shut the hell up.

Nora shrugs again and I think I hear her say, "It's okay."

"Are you mad at me or something?" my mouth says for me.

*Mad at me?* Am I five, asking Carter if he's mad that my mom accidentally ran over his toy in the driveway?

Before I can stumble further and make things even more awkward between the two of us, Nora turns around to face me. The curve of her throat seems to be pulsing, her chest rising and falling in a slow throb. My own chest is on fire, a hollow feeling that doesn't belong here, not because of someone who's practically a stranger.

"Mad at you? For what?" There's sincerity in her eyes when she speaks to me; her lips are pouty and she's waiting for an answer that's somehow harder for me to give than it should be.

I rub my hand over the back of my neck, thinking, thinking, thinking, always thinking.

"Everything? The Dakota thing, the kiss, the—"

When Nora opens her mouth to speak, I stop midsentence to let her. She leans her elbow against the counter and her eyes focus on me. She's staring hard, and in this moment I wish I knew her well enough to know what she's thinking, how she's feeling. I can't read her, no matter how badly I want to.

I'm usually good at figuring out people and their behaviors. I can usually tell when someone is feeling something, even when they're trying their best to hide it. The quick movement of their eyes to the opposite side of the room or the subtle shift of their body weight . . . there are a million ways to read someone.

"I'm not mad at you at all. It's all been a little messy, yes," she says, and something about the way her voice catches at the end of her sentence makes me uneasy.

I have never wanted anything more than to know about the parts of herself that she keeps hidden.

Her whole being reminds me of some sort of secret, the closest thing to discovering a true-life mystery, one that's difficult to solve but that tantalizes you with the prospect of a solution.

"Landon, the reason why—"

But her voice is interrupted by the creak of sneakers on the clean tile floor.

I turn. The white sneakers touching the floor belong to a pair of tightly covered legs. The body is thin, wearing a sparkling tutu and black body suit.

Dakota's eyes scan Nora, standing only inches away from me, and she seems to morph into something bigger, something darker and stronger.

Dakota squares her shoulders and pushes out her chest, demanding attention.

"Dakota . . ." I instinctively step toward her and away from Nora.

"So this is where you went?" she says.

I'm confused for a moment before I realize that she's not talking to me. She's facing Nora now.

Nora's eyes meet mine. "No, I was just here with Tessa—"

Dakota cuts her off midsentence. "I told you to leave, not to come running to him."

And I'm so confused by what's going on. Dakota's voice is rising like an angry tide, ready to swallow my tiny Brooklyn apartment.

"I told you to stay away from him," Dakota says. "He's off-limits. We *agreed*."

Dakota's eyes are narrow slits and Nora's are wide saucers; she still seems shocked at seeing Dakota in the kitchen.

"I better go." Nora reaches for the dishcloth on the counter to dry off her hands. She does so quickly, and Dakota and I stand in silence as she leaves the kitchen without looking at either of us. The front door opens and closes in less than twenty seconds and she's gone without so much as a goodbye to Tessa.

She's so quick, and I'm so much in shock that I didn't even have a chance to follow her.

I briefly wonder if I would have, and how Dakota would react if I did.

# chapter

# *Twenty*

DAKOTA IS STANDING IN THE KITCHEN, her eyes on me and her mouth set in an angry frown. Her hair is down, wild ringlets running loose over her shoulders. She's picking at her fingernails, and I really don't like the way she's behaving, acting like we're in high school.

Scratch that, she's acting full-on elementary, and the tutu she's wearing isn't helping make her look like an adult.

"What was that all about? What's up with you?" I ask.

Well, it came out more like a demand, but I need some answers. None of this makes sense.

And of course she's immediately on the defensive, glaring at me as though I'm the one acting like a jealous child. Dakota doesn't say anything, she just stares at me, and suddenly her gaze softens. Her lips pout out and she leans casually against the kitchen counter as if nothing just happened.

I decide not to let this one go. "Why did you just chase Tessa's friend from our apartment?"

Dakota looks me over. I assume that she's using her silence to buy herself time to decide what to say.

Finally, after a few more seconds, she sighs and begins to speak.

"She's not just Tessa's friend to me, Landon. She's my roommate, and I don't want her hanging around you. She's not good for you. And I'm not going to let her attach herself to you."

She pauses a beat, then adds, "I refuse to let that happen."

I don't know what's worse: the tone of her voice or the jealousy and possessiveness that thread through her words, but my skin prickles and adrenaline builds in my chest.

"Okay, first of all, I had no idea you two were roommates—so I'm still processing that. And second, *you* don't get to decide who's good for me, Dakota," I say.

She blanches like I've smacked her across her face.

"So you actually *do* like her!" Dakota's mouth twists into a grimace as she hurls these words at me.

I'm getting angrier at her by the second and I can feel the tension between us building with every rise and fall of her chest.

"No. Well, I don't know what I feel about her, honestly." My answer sounds like I'm avoiding the truth, but I truly *don't* know.

I've always been honest with Dakota, save for those rare moments when the truth was better left unsaid.

What I do know is that Dakota doesn't get to be the one who decides who gets to "attach herself" to me.

Dakota walks across the kitchen to me, her glittery tutu swaying with every step. "Well, try to figure it out, because I don't want you to be confused about how you feel about me either." She rolls her eyes.

I recognize this tone, this guardedness.

"Cut it out. Turn it on," I tell her.

She knows exactly what I mean.

Dakota is good at turning her emotions off and completely detaching herself from any danger of pain, and throughout the years I've been good at reminding her to turn them on and lower the guard. Only when it's safe to do so, though . . . I've always wanted to keep her safe.

She sighs in defeat. "I've been thinking about you so much lately."

"What about me?" I ask her.

Dakota swallows and pulls her bottom lip between her teeth. "Just that I love you, Landon."

She says the words so casually, as if they wouldn't unwind something inside of me, a knot pulled so tight, stuck underneath my rib cage, waiting for her to untie it, to ease the pain.

I haven't heard those words from her mouth since before I moved to New York. Those three words used to be as natural-sounding to my ears as hearing my own name . . . but not anymore.

Now they cut at me, lashing at the progress I've made in recovering from the pain and the loneliness that came with her leaving me.

These three words threaten to break the already fragile fort I've been working on constructing since she decided she didn't want me.

These three words are much more significant to me than she can even fathom, and I feel like my heart is going to rip angrily from my chest at any moment.

I wasn't expecting a declaration of love. I was prepared for her to throw angry words at me, not this.

I don't know which would have hurt worse, to be honest.

"I do, Landon." Dakota's voice cuts through my silence, and I close my eyes. "I've loved you ever since I can remember, and I'm sorry that I keep causing trouble in your life. I hurt you, I know I did, and I'm so sorry—"

Her voice breaks at the end and her eyes gloss with tears. She's standing closer now, close enough for me to hear her breathing. "I was selfish, I still am, and as fucked up as it is, I can't bear to see you with anyone else. I'm not ready to share you. I remember the first time I saw you . . ."

I open my eyes and try to catch my breath.

I should stop her from digging up old memories, but I can't bring myself to do it. I want to hear her say them.

I *need* to hear them.

"You were riding your bike up and down the street. I could see you from the window in my room. Carter had just gotten home from some camping trip, and one of the parents called my dad with some rumor, something about Carter trying to kiss another boy."

My heart sinks as her words gnaw at me. She never talks about Carter, not in this much detail, not anymore.

"My dad came barreling down the hallway, belt in hand." She shudders at the memory.

I do, too.

"Everything was so loud. I remember thinking the house was going to fall down if he didn't stop."

Dakota is staring past me. She's no longer in New York, she's back in Saginaw. And I'm there with her.

"You were riding your bike in the street and your mom was out there with you, taking pictures . . . or videos maybe, and when Carter started to scream with every lash of that leather belt, I watched you and your mom. She fell somehow, like she tripped over her own feet or something, and you ran over to her like you were the parent and she was the child. I remember wishing I could be strong, like you, and help Carter. But I knew I couldn't."

Her lip begins to quiver and my chest is aching, pain shooting through me like a burning star.

"You know how it was. How bad it was when I tried to help."

I did know. I witnessed her father's abuse of Carter a few times. My mom called the cops twice before we learned that the system was flawed, so very flawed, and much more complicated than two kids could imagine.

My feet shuffle and bring me closer to Dakota without my mind's permission. She holds up a small hand and I stop in my tracks.

"Just listen, don't try to fix anything," she urges.

I do everything I can to abide by her wishes. I stare at the green numbers on the stove and tuck my hands behind my back. It's almost nine, the day having flown by without me.

I continue to focus on the numbers as she goes on.

"I remember the first time you talked to me, the first time you told me you loved me. Do you remember the first time you told me you loved me?"

I do remember . . . how could I possibly forgot that day?

Dakota had run away; Carter told me she had been missing for hours. Her dad, drunk and seemingly unfazed that his fifteen-year-old daughter was nowhere to be found, sat in his stained recliner, a cold beer can sweating in his hand. His stomach had grown fuller—all the liquor and beer had to go somewhere. His face hadn't been shaved in weeks, the hair on his chin was unruly, growing thick and rough in patches on his face.

I couldn't get a response from him, I couldn't even get him to glance away from the damn television screen. I remember he was watching *CSI*, and the small living room was full of smoke and cluttered with junk. Empty beer cans covered the table and unread magazines were piled on the floor.

"Where is she?" I asked him for the fifth time.

My voice was so loud that I was scared he was going to react and hit me like he did his son.

He didn't, though; he just sat there lazily staring at the screen, and I gave up quickly, knowing he was too intoxicated to do anything useful.

He moved and I jumped back a little, my fear soothed when he reached for his pack of Basic cigarettes. When he grabbed the ashtray, cigarette butts and ashes fell onto the brown carpet. He didn't seem to notice, just the way he didn't seem to notice me standing there, asking where his only daughter was.

I got on my bike and rode around the neighborhood, stopping everyone who passed. I began to panic after Buddy, one of the drunks who lived by the woods, said he saw her run into the woods. We called the rows of trees and trash the Patch, and it was full of people whose lives were empty. Drugs and liquor was all they had and they littered the woods with it.

The Patch wasn't safe, and she wasn't safe in it.

I dropped my bike at the edge of the spruce trees and ran into the darkness like my life depended on it. In a way, it did.

I ignored the drunken voices and the ache of my muscles as I ran toward the center. The Patch wasn't very big. You could run from one side to the other in about five minutes. I found her near the middle, alone, unharmed, her back against a tree.

When I found her, my lungs burned and I could barely breathe, but she was safe, and that's all that mattered. She was sitting cross-legged on the ground of the woods, dirt and sticks and leaves surrounding her, and at the sight of her, I had never been more relieved in my life.

She looked up at me and saw me standing in front of her, my hands on my knees, trying to catch my breath.

"Landon?" She sounded confused. "What are you doing here?"

"Trying to find you! Why are you out here? You know what this place is like!" I was shouting, which spurred her to look around, her dark eyes taking in the surroundings.

A blanket hung on broken branches, ripped and dirty, being used as a makeshift tent. Beer bottles lay scattered on the ground; it had recently rained, and the rain hadn't dried in some places, leaving wet trash and mud puddles all around us.

I stood up straight and reached out my hand to her. "You shouldn't ever, ever come out here again. It's not safe."

She seemed like she was in a trance when she ignored my hand and spoke.

"I could kill him. You know? I would get away with it, I think."

My heart sank with my body and I leaned against the tree and wrapped my fingers through hers.

"I've been watching a lot of crime shows, and with the way he drinks and the trouble he causes . . . I could get away with it. I could take whatever money the house is worth and get out of this shitty town. Me, you, Carter. We can go, Landon. We can."

Her voice was full of a painful urgency and it killed me to realize she was borderline-serious about this plan.

"No one would miss him . . ."

A small part of me wished I could go along with it, to ease her pain, even for a few moments, but I knew if I did, reality would sink in for both of us sooner or later anyway, and life would be harder than it already was.

I decided to distract her instead of outright telling her that of course she couldn't *murder* somebody. But she did need to get away from here, even if only by distraction.

"Where would we go?" I asked, knowing how much she loved to daydream.

"We could go to New York City. I could dance there and you could teach. We would be far away from here, but still have the snow."

Throughout our adolescence, each time I asked Dakota this question, she always had a different answer. Sometimes she would even suggest that we leave the country. Of all the cities in the world, Paris was her favorite; she had fantasies of dancing at the famous opera house there. But living in Saginaw was reality and anywhere else just a silly dream.

"We could live in a high-rise above the city even. Anywhere but here, Landon, anywhere but here." Her voice was distant, as if she was already living in a place far, far away.

When I looked over at her, her eyes were closed. She had a streak of dirt on her cheek and her knee was scuffed up. *She must have fallen,* I thought to myself.

"I would go anywhere with you. You know that, don't you?" I asked her.

She opened her eyes and the corner of her lips turned into a smile. "Anywhere?" she asked.

"Everywhere," I promised.

"I love you," she claimed.

"I've always loved you," I confessed.

Her hand squeezed mine and she leaned her head on my shoulder and we sat there until the sun came up, bringing silence to her haunted house.

And now, here, in the kitchen of my Brooklyn apartment, remembering our dreams and the roots of our love, Dakota says with a low voice, "You said you've always loved me."

"I have," is all I can say back.

Because it's the truth.

# Twenty-one

THE LAST THIRTY MINUTES have been confusing, to say the least. I don't know how to stop this spiraling into her, or even if I should try. Dakota's words mean so much to me . . . and yet there's a hint of something missing, some small part of me that isn't totally connecting to them. I'm a bit on guard, and I don't know if I should be so quick to jump when she says jump.

The spiral has much too much pull on me, and it overcomes that little niggling voice telling me that something's missing.

I don't want this moment to end.

I don't want her to go.

I want her to stay and make up for the times when she left me, to make me feel normal again. It's easier to focus on other people and make everyone around me happy than it is to come to terms with the fact that maybe I'm a little lonelier than I care to admit. It's so easy to fall back into this routine with her. I used to think that I was made to protect her, that every atom of my body was created solely for her purpose. I was happiest when I had her, when I had someone who made me feel important, needed, necessary.

Dakota came here, to my apartment—she ran *to* me. But, I wonder, does this mean that she's done running *from* me? Her body is so close now, so close that I could reach a hand out to her and pull her into my arms if I wanted to . . . and I do want to.

I just need her touch. I need to know if that familiar tingle will spread through my body in the wake of her fingertips. I need to see if she can fill the empty parts of me that she left like holes in my body.

I take another step and wrap my arm around her small frame. She leans into me without missing a beat and my lips move with caution to find hers.

Her mouth is so soft; her lips are clouds that I want to be lost in, high above the world of common sense and far away from our shared pain. I want to float in this space where it's she and I, and me and her. No breakups, no tragedy, no shitty parents or exams or long hours of work.

The moment my lips graze hers, Dakota's breath hitches and relief floods through me. My mouth is timid, careful not to rush into this. My tongue glides over hers and she's melting into me, as she always used to do.

I bring my other hand to the small of her back and pull her closer. The material of her tutu rustles against my sweats, and she uses both hands to push the sparkling fabric down to the floor, then presses her body against mine. Her body is firmer than I remember; the hard work she's put in is paying off, and I love the way she feels now, solid and mine. She's actually mine, maybe not forever, but for right now.

Dakota's mouth is slightly slack, as if she's forgotten how to kiss me. I rub her back as she tries to remember my mouth. My thumbs trace tiny circles on the small of her back and she sighs a breath between my lips. Her kiss is slow and her mouth tastes like tears and I don't know if they are mine or hers.

She sniffles and I pull away.

"What's wrong?" I ask her. My throat is full of molasses and my words are slow, stuck in my throat. "Are you okay?"

She nods and I look down at her face, taking her in. Her

brown eyes are shining with tears and her lips are wet, pouty, and turned down into a frown.

"What is it?"

"I'm fine . . ." She wipes at her eyes. "It's not that I'm sad, I'm just overwhelmed. I've missed you." She sniffles again and a single tear escapes and runs down her cheek. I tap at it with my thumb and she breathes heavily into my hand as it cups her cheek. "Will you give me time to figure my shit out? Please, Landon, I know I don't deserve another chance, but I will never, ever hurt you again. I'm sorry."

I pull her in to me, relief and anxiety flooding through me as I hug her to my body. I have been waiting for months to hear these words, even if she's giving me half a yes. Even if she needs time to figure it out, I never expected an apology or anything close to a declaration of love. Maybe that's why they sound so foreign? I've wished to hear these exact words for so long that I feel like I actually willed this to happen. Will this be a blessing or a curse? Or both?

I can't stop my mind from whirling.

I push my own thoughts aside and comfort her.

"Shh," I whisper, and rest my chin on top of her head.

A few seconds pass and she pulls away slightly to look up at me.

"I don't deserve you," she says softly. Her eyes don't meet mine as she continues: "But I've never wanted you more."

Her head is heavy on my chest as she cries. Her hands are fists, full of my T-shirt. A faint ringing sounds through the apartment and Dakota quickly reacts, snapping her head up from my chest.

Talk about bad timing.

"I'm so sorry, it's my agent," she says, rushing to the living room. "Well, not agent yet, but he might be."

*Agent?*

Since when does she have an agent? Or want one? What the heck does an agent do for a ballet student? I know she's been auditioning for small roles in commercials for the time being, but maybe she's decided to pursue acting?

From the living room, her loud voice breaks my thoughts. "I have to go!"

Then Dakota's head pops into the doorway of the kitchen. "I'm so sorry, but this is huge!" Her tears are gone, her frown replaced by a bright smile.

Perhaps my face is registering the utter confusion I'm feeling, because she walks into the kitchen, saying, "I'll come back tomorrow, okay?"

She leans onto the tips of her toes and kisses me softly on the cheek.

Her hand squeezes mine and she looks like a new person. She's happy, she's light. I've missed this version of her and I can't decide if I should be disappointed that she's leaving in the middle of . . . *whatever* the hell we were doing, or excited for whatever opportunity is coming her way.

I choose to be happy for her and not question her motives.

"I have to work tomorrow, but I'll be here Friday, all night after classes," I tell her.

Dakota beams. "I'll come Friday!" Then she adds, "And maybe I can stay over?"

She looks at me shyly, like she's never stayed with me before. She bites her lips and I can't stop my mind from recalling the last time she was in my bed. Well, not the last time, because she was drunk and I didn't touch her, but the time before that.

She was beautiful, her bare skin was shimmering under the dim light in my room at Ken's. She had woken me up in the middle of the night with her mouth around my cock. Her mouth was so warm, so wet, and I was so hard, embarrassing myself by finishing after only a few slow drags of her lips across me.

"Landon?" Dakota knocks me back into reality.

"Yes, of course." I feel the blood rushing to my cock.

Hormones are tricky and embarrassing things.

"Of course I want you to stay."

"Good. See you Friday," she says while quickly kissing my lips. She squeezes my hand and rushes out the door.

Sleep doesn't come easy. My mind is stuck on my past.

As I lie here, staring at my ceiling fan, I'm sixteen, writing notes to Dakota in class and hoping I don't get caught. She's giggling at the words I've written down, sexual innuendos that I knew would make her smile. Our teacher was so oblivious most days that we would pass notes back and forth the entire period and never get caught. On this particular day, much to our misfortune, he noticed. He caught me red-handed and forced me to read the message in front of the entire class.

My cheeks burned as I spoke, something along the lines of her tasting like chocolate-covered strawberries and that I couldn't wait to devour her.

Oh, man, I was lame as hell.

The class snickered, but Dakota sat with her back straight, smiling at me. She looked at me like she wasn't a lick embarrassed, like she couldn't wait to jump my bones.

I honestly thought that she was only trying to make me feel less mortified, to show solidarity against a teacher that would make me reveal such a thing to everyone.

But when we were walking home, she did, in fact, push me into a corner of her backyard and jump my bones.

It's hard to believe we were only teens when we were together. We went through so much, so many firsts, good and bad. We were good together and we still can be. Memory after memory floods through my dark bedroom and my bed has never felt so empty.

Friday can't come soon enough.

Friday is here, faster than I expected.

Yesterday, after classes, I worked at Grind until closing. Posey and Aiden were both there, but Aiden was surprisingly quiet. Uncharacteristically so. He seemed to be concentrated on something somewhere else, or maybe he got a therapist who told him that being an obnoxious douche was at the core of his problems.

Whatever the reason, I was glad for it.

Dakota texted me twice yesterday, and once this morning, just to tell me that she can't wait to see me. Her sudden return to affection is still slightly confusing, but with each bit of attention she feeds me, my loneliness fades.

It's such an instinctual thing, needing companionship. I never thought of myself as a person who needed someone else to make himself feel complete, and sometimes I question why humans are made this way.

Why is it that since the beginning of our history, we crave company, and we strive to find love? The goal of life, whether you're religious or not, is to find companionship in friends and in lovers.

Humans are needy creatures, and it turns out I'm very, very human.

# chapter

## Twenty-two

IT'S SEVEN NOW, and since I haven't heard back from Dakota after this afternoon, I text her that I can't wait to see her.

She texts back a contented-looking smiley face. I don't know how to read emoji, so I decide it's a happy smiley, not a bored one.

I hope she's not standing me up.

I really, really hope she's not standing me up.

I sort of hate that she's unpredictable now. A really big piece of me misses when I was a part of her life. I was her best friend and her lover. She shared her thoughts with me, her hopes, and even her dreams. We dreamed together, we laughed together—I knew every thought she had, every tear she shed.

Now I'm an outsider, waiting for her to decide to call me. I miss the days when it wasn't even a question if I was worth her time.

Why am I getting so down? I need to perk up and stop thinking of the worst when it comes to her. I'm sure she's just busy and she will call or text when she can.

If she was going to flat-out cancel on me, she would tell me.

I think?

Lying on my bed, staring at the hockey game on my television, I watch a big guy in a teal jersey get slammed against the glass. The San Jose Sharks. I recognize the jerseys of both the

Sharks and their opponent. I don't really care for either team, but I'm bored out of my mind and I don't know what to do besides stare at my phone and wait for Dakota to call.

"Landon . . ." A soft voice is accompanied by a softer knock on my bedroom door.

It's Tessa, not Dakota, and I'm trying not to be disappointed. I almost tell her to come in, but I need to get out of my bed. I can't just lie here and wait for Dakota. I can at least go to the living room.

Yes, I know it's still pathetic, but sitting on the couch is a little less pathetic than lying in my bed, right?

I stand up and walk to the door. When I open it, Tessa is standing in the doorway wearing her work uniform. The lime-green tie makes her eyes look even lighter and her blond hair is in a long braid resting on her shoulder.

"Hey," she says.

"Hey." I run my hand over the stubble on my jaw and step in front of her to go toward the living room.

Tessa sits down on the opposite end of the couch and I rest my feet on the coffee table.

"What's up? Are you okay?" I ask her.

"Yeah . . ." She pauses. "I think so. Do you remember that guy named Robert? The one who I met when we went to the lake with your mom and Ken?"

I try to remember the details from that trip. The red panties floating in the hot tub, Tessa and Hardin barely speaking to each other, the brunette in the black dress, playing I Spy with Hardin and Tessa on the way down.

I don't remember a guy named Robert, except maybe . . . the waiter?

Oh, shit, I do remember him. He drove Hardin half-mad.

"Yeah, the waiter?" I confirm.

"Yes, the waiter. So, guess who works with me, starting today?"

I raise a brow. "No way. Here in Brooklyn?"

What a freaking coincidence.

*"Yes way,"* she half jokes, but I can see she's not really finding it funny. "He came in and I was so surprised to see him here, all the way across the country. He's starting his training as I finish mine. It's so weird, right?"

It's definitely weird. "A little, yeah."

"It's like the universe is giving me some sort of a test or something." Her voice is heavy with exhaustion. "Do you think it's okay for me to be friends with him? I'm not even close to being ready to date anyone." She looks around the room. "But I could use more friends. That's okay, right?"

"What? More friends than just me? How could you!" I tease.

Tessa kicks out at me and I grab hold of her pink-socked foot, tickling the sole. She screams and lunges at me, but she's easy to stop.

I hold my arms up and wrap them around her, preventing her from whatever revenge she was planning to exact. She screams and her laughter rings through the apartment.

God, I have missed her laughter so much.

"Nice try," I say, laughing, tickling her sides.

She shrieks again, thrashing around like a fish on a line.

"Landon!" Tessa shouts dramatically, trying to get free from my grip.

This must be what it's like to have a sister. I can't wait for little Abby to come into the world. I better stay in shape so I can keep up with her. Sometimes I worry that the gap in our ages will be too big, that she won't want to be close to me.

Tessa is still kicking and I've loosened my hold on her. She's red-faced and her hair is messy. Her green tie is thrown over her shoulder and I can't help but burst into laughter. She sticks her tongue out at me. Hearing something, I look toward the hallway.

Dakota is standing in the doorway staring, stone-faced, at Tessa and me on the couch.

"Hey." I smile at her, relieved that she didn't stand me up.

"Hi."

"Hey, Dakota." Tessa waves with one hand while trying to fix her braid with the other.

I stand up from the couch and walk toward Dakota. She's wearing a white T-shirt, hung off one shoulder and barely covering her pink sports bra underneath. Her pants are workout capris, the tight black material clinging to her skin.

"I'm going back to work. If you guys need anything while I'm out, text me," Tessa says. She grabs her purse from the table and tucks her keys into her apron.

We never finished our conversation about Robert, but I don't think she feels comfortable enough around Dakota to talk about it. Still, it's so strange that he's here, living in Brooklyn. If this were a comic book, I would swear he was a creepy stalker, or some kind of spy.

A spy would be more interesting, for sure.

"Will do," I say just as she walks through the door.

Turning to look at Dakota, I notice that she hasn't moved from the spot she was standing in when she came in.

"You look beautiful," I tell her.

She fights a smile.

"So beautiful . . ." I go over and kiss her on her cheek. "How was your day?"

She relaxes and I can't tell if she's in a bad mood or if she's nervous to be alone with me after all this time.

"It was good. I had another audition, that's why I'm late. I came as soon as I could. Although it seems you were fine waiting, though," she says with a hint of sarcasm.

"Yeah, I was talking to Tessa. She's having a hard time lately." I shrug my shoulders and reach for her hand.

When she lets me take it, I lead her to the couch.

"Still? Is it Hardin still?" she asks.

"Yeah, it's always Hardin." I half smile, trying not to think too much about his visit next weekend and the fact that I'm a chickenshit and still haven't told Tessa. She knows he's coming, just not how soon.

I'm going to try to keep the new-old waiter thing under wraps for now.

Even though it's a coincidence, Hardin will make way more of it.

"Well, she seemed fine to me," Dakota says, looking around the living room.

"Is something wrong?" I ask her. "You seem mad or something. How was your audition?"

She shakes her head and I reach for her feet and place them on my lap. I pull off her sneakers and start rubbing her arches. Dakota's eyes close and she leans her head against the back of the couch.

"It was okay. I don't think I'm going to get it. The line for open auditions was still out the door when I left. I was the third—they probably already forgot about me."

I hate when she thinks so low of herself. Doesn't she know how talented she is? How unforgettable she is?

"I doubt that. There's no way anyone could forget about you."

"You're biased." She gives me a little smile and I return the gesture with a huge grin.

"Hardly," I scoff. "Have you *seen* yourself?"

She rolls her eyes and winces when my fingers press gently at her toes. I pull off her socks and they stick to her toes.

"Is that blood?" I ask her, slowly peeling off the black cotton.

"Probably," she says like it's no big deal.

Like it's a paper cut that she barely noticed.

Sure enough, it's blood. Her toes are crusted with it . . . I've seen what ballet shoes do to her feet even before she was dancing full-time. They were bad then. But this is worse than I've ever seen.

"Jesus, Dakota." I peel off the other sock.

"It's fine. I got new slippers and they just aren't broken in yet."

She tries to move away, but I put my hand on her leg to stop her. "Stay here."

I lift her feet off of my lap and get up from the couch.

"I'm getting a washcloth," I tell her.

She looks like she wants to say something, but doesn't.

I grab a clean washcloth from the bathroom cabinet and run it under warm water. I check the cabinet for aspirin and shake the bottle. Empty, of course. I can't imagine Tessa leaving an empty bottle of anything around, so the blame is mine for this.

I glance in the mirror while the washcloth soaks with water, and try to tame my hair. The top is getting long, too long. And the back needs trimming; it's starting to curl up on my neck, and unless I want to look like Frodo, I need a haircut soon.

I shut off the water and ring the excess out of the washcloth. It's a little too hot, but it will cool down by the time I get back into the living room. Grabbing a dry towel, I walk back to Dakota.

But when I find her, she's fast asleep on the couch. Her mouth is slightly open and her eyes are tightly closed. She must really be exhausted.

I sit back down, careful not to wake her, and, as gently as I can, dab the cloth on the damaged skin of her feet. She doesn't stir, just lies silently sleeping as I clean her cuts and wipe away the dried blood.

She's working herself too hard. From the bloody feet to the pure exhaustion she's wearing on her face right now. I want to spend time with her, but I want her to rest, so gathering up the bloodstained washcloth and the towel, I grab the blanket from the chair and cover her sleeping body with it.

What can I do to occupy myself while she sleeps?

Tessa is at work, Posey is at work . . . and thus ends my long list of pals.

# chapter

## Twenty-three

*I*N THE END, ASPIRIN AND GATORADE were the friends I decided to call upon, which meant a trip to the deli.

Ellen is working, and since her birthday is tomorrow, I killed some time seeing what she was up to (nothing much) and asking what she thought her parents might get her (again, nothing much).

Which sounds terrible. So I try to ferret out what she likes so maybe I can get her something fun.

On the way back, I gave my mom a call and talked to her and Ken for a few minutes.

When I get back in the apartment, I hang up and hear noise from the living room and figure Dakota's woken back up. Going in, seeing her there looking at me with a sort of confused where-the-heck-have-you-been look, I set my cell phone down on the table as slowly as I can.

I do it somewhat comically, but I feel like I'm trapped in an interrogation room or something. Only in this room there're Cheez-Its and bottles of Gatorade. So, maybe not so much like an interrogation room.

Though . . . Dakota would make a sexy-ass cop. I can imagine her body dressed in a tight uniform, just for me to peel off. The look on her face right now, though, says that if she were a cop, she would arrest me. And not in a sexy, playful, handcuff-me-to-the-bed-and-tease-me way.

"It was my mom and Ken on the phone. They had an appointment today for little Abby," I say with a somewhat fake smile.

Not fake in that I'm *not* happy about the baby's progress, or that Ken is still head over heels for my mom, but fake because I suddenly get paranoid that Dakota overheard me talking to my mom about Nora right at the end of the conversation.

But Nora is my friend, if barely. Still, Dakota hearing her name as I said it to my mom would only further fuel the fire of jealousy she's creating over her roommate. The match in her hand is burning pretty bright now and I want her to understand that there's nothing to be worried about. Nora wouldn't give me a chance even if I pursued it. It would be messy because of her friendship with Tessa, and I barely know her anyway—so why is this a thing?

Dakota gets up and stretches out her back. "So, how is she?" she asks. "Abby. How is she doing in there?"

I let out a little tension-breath I didn't realize I was holding and step into the kitchen with my haul. Dakota follows me in, wrapping her arms around my neck and leaning her head on my shoulder. Her hair smells like coconut and her curls are soft against my cheek.

"She's good. They sounded a little worried for a second, but I think I'm just overthinking things."

Dakota's breath is warm against my skin. "*Overthinking? You?* You don't say!" She chuckles and her laugh is beautiful, like she is.

I reach my hand up and gently squeeze her arm.

"I'm glad she's doing okay. It's still kind of weird to think of your mom being pregnant, at her age." Seemingly aware of how her words sound, she quickly recovers, adding, "Not in a bad way. She's the best mom I've ever seen, and both you and Abby are so lucky to have her, at any age. I don't know Ken very well yet, but from what you tell me, he's going to be a great dad."

"He will be," I say, and kiss her arm as I put the snacks away in the cabinets.

"Let's just hope Abby is more like you and less like Hardin." She laughs again and little needles prick my skin.

I don't like the way she said that. Not one bit.

"What's that supposed to mean?" I lift her arms from mine and turn around to face her.

Dakota's face gives away her surprise at my reaction.

Am I overreacting?

I don't think that I am.

"I was just joking, Landon. I didn't mean anything by it. You two are so different, that's all."

"Everyone is different, Dakota. It's not your place to judge him. Or anyone."

She sighs and sits down at the kitchen table.

"I know. I wasn't trying to judge him. I'm the last person who can judge anyone." She looks down at her hands. "It was a shitty joke that I won't make again. I know he means a lot to you."

My shoulders relax, and I start wondering why I got so irritated so quickly. It's like it came out of nowhere, although I do get tired of people piling on my stepbrother.

Dakota seems remorseful . . . and Hardin really *is* a tough pill to swallow. I can't really blame her for her opinion of him. She only knew him as the guy who smashed a cabinetful of dishes my dead grandma gave my mom. And as the guy who refused to call her by her actual name.

Hardin does this thing where he pretends that he doesn't know any female names except Tessa's. So Dakota became "Delilah" every time he addressed her. I don't know why he does it, and sometimes I actually wonder if, in fact, he really hasn't forgotten every woman's name except Tessa's.

Weirder things have happened between those two.

But I would rather not spend the entire night at odds with Dakota over one remark.

"Okay. Let's just talk about something else. Something lighter," I suggest.

Since she's already apologized and seems like she genuinely didn't mean anything by her comment, I want to move on. I want to talk to her. I want to hear about her days and her nights.

I want to lie next to her in bed and reminisce about our wild teenage years when we had movie marathons on school nights and held pizza-roll-eating contests on my futon. My mom never questioned why I blew through bag after bag of pepperoni pizza rolls. She had reason to wonder what was going on when I started asking for the combination varieties, because she knew I hated them. But she never once asked me why Dakota ate so much every time she came over. I think she knew that since a couple of forty-ounce beers cost just as much as a bag of pizza rolls, the chances were slim that Dakota's freezer would have any food in it, much less name-brand pizza rolls.

"Thank you." Dakota looks down and I smile at her and move closer.

"Come on, you." I dip down and lift her body into my arms and she shrieks.

She's light, even lighter than I remember, but it sure feels good to hold her in my arms.

The twenty-two steps to the couch isn't long enough to make up for the last few months, but I drop her onto the cushions. She lands with a soft thud and her body bounces up a few inches and she shrieks again.

I step back and she's on her feet in no time, running after me with a huge grin. She's giggling, face red and hair wild.

When she lunges at me, I jump out of the way. I slide on the thick rug that I was supposed to tape down the second day I moved in and jump onto the chair, missing her fingertips by mere inches. Something creaks beneath me.

I really hope I don't break this damn chair.

I leap off of it and slide across the floor with the help of my socks. I lose my balance, and as my leg muscles strain, unsuccessfully, to right myself, I realize that my pants are so freaking tight that my legs are bending in a painful, unnatural way. Sitting on the floor, I pull one leg in and twist my body and Dakota rushes over to me. Her face is worried when she puts one hand on my shoulders and tucks the other one under my chin, forcing me to look up at her.

I can't stop laughing and my stomach hurts from it, but my leg doesn't.

Dakota's panic turns to amusement and her laughter is my favorite song.

I grab her shoulders and pull her down into my lap. Her hands wrap around my neck and she pulls me closer to kiss her.

Her mouth is softer than my touch, and not for the first time, I'm a fool for her as I trace her tongue with mine.

# chapter

## Twenty-four

DAKOTA'S HANDS SLIDE FROM MY NECK to my arms and she rubs them. Up and down she rubs, staying a few moments extra on my biceps.

I can't pretend that I'm not proud of my body. Especially after years of hating it. It makes me feel strong and sexy for the first time in my life, and I'm on cloud nine with her hands all over me.

"I've missed you so much." Dakota's words are something between a cry and a moan, and they speak to me, to the man I am now, not just the boy I was when I met her.

"I've missed you more," I promise her.

Dakota's brown eyes are nearly closed, so heavily lidded that I can barely make out their color. Except I already know the color; I memorized her eyes long ago. I've memorized every single inch of her from the birthmark on her left foot to the shade of her eyes. They're a soft brown with a flake of honey in the right one. She used to tell the kids at school that the light mark on her face was a scar from some fight she was in at her old school, but it wasn't true. She always told stories that made her sound as intimidating as possible, since she was nothing of the sort at home.

"I need you, Landon." Dakota's voice is a desperate whisper as she kisses me.

Her hands are on my back now, pulling my shirt up. Her

mouth traces the nape of my neck and her small hands work to take my shirt off. The floor is cold, but she's so damn hot and I feel nervous and excited and my mind is racing.

"Help me," Dakota says, still tugging at my fabric. "I can't take it off like this," she says, and licks at my neck.

I move quickly, hating that I have to pull away from her but beyond ready to take off all of my clothes—and hers.

I tug at the fabric and toss the WCU T-shirt across the room . . . only it catches on the lamp and stays there, making the light slightly red.

I'm so damn awkward that I can't even throw a T-shirt in a sexy way? Really?

I'm hoping she noticed that I wore red, her favorite color on me, and sweats, just like she always loved. I used to find it weird that she liked my lounging-about clothing so much, but given how I feel about her sports bra and yoga pants, I get it.

"Come here," Dakota says, her voice like candy. Sweet and addicting.

I move back to her and wonder if we should go into my room. Is it weird to be sitting on the living room floor and taking off my clothes?

Dakota answers that question for me. She pulls her shirt over her head and somehow manages to bring her sports bra with it. Between her exposed breasts, her wet lips, and the way she's looking at me, I may just embarrass myself before we even begin.

I know that look. The one where her eyes are hooded and her mouth is slack. I've seen that look so many times, and here it is again.

She's desire wrapped in sugar and I need to taste her.

I move to her, taking one soft breast in my hand and the other into my mouth. Her nipples are hard pebbles under my tongue, and hell, I've missed her body.

She's moaning now and I'm growing harder by the second.

I've missed her, I've needed her. Dakota is moaning as she pushes her body into me, rising to her knees so I have better access to her. My hand moves from her breast down her stomach, and my fingers find her pussy, soaked and throbbing. I use my index finger to draw small circles over her wetness.

I know how crazy that drives her.

Dakota's body has always been so responsive to my touch. She's usually dripping for me, so this comes as no surprise. What does kind of amaze me is that I'm thinking clearly while touching her. With my mouth sucking at her nipples and my finger drawing small circles over her swollen clit, I'm aware of every single thing. I'm aware of her hair pulled over her shoulder, her hand tugging at my hair as she gasps, "More, please, more."

I'm not used to being so present when I'm touching her. I was always so lost in the sensation that I could barely form a thought.

I use the tip of my tongue to trace the outline of her taut nipples and Dakota yanks her body away from me.

I pull back, worried that I did something wrong.

She lies back a little and tugs at her tight pants, yanking them down her legs, letting me know that everything's more than fine. When I look down at her exposed body, she's not wearing panties.

Jesus freaking Christ, she's not wearing panties and she's literally glistening. She's so wet that she's probably going to leave a puddle on my floor, and I caused that.

Knowing that feels pretty damn good.

"Make love to me, Landon."

It's not a request, I know this. I know her.

She lies on her back and I suddenly remember when she said our sex life was "boring" and my cheeks flush in embarrassment.

*Boring, huh?*

Dakota is completely naked and my door is locked, and she's

waiting for me to climb on top of her and probably expects we'll have normal, "boring" sex like we had in the past.

Only to me, it wasn't even close to boring.

Still, I'm going to show her that I'm not boring at all. I have a few tricks up my sleeve.

I've watched enough porn that I'm practically an expert.

Though if Dakota knew I watched porn, she would probably be pissed. She broke up with me once when she found a *Playboy* magazine under my mattress. Man, these teenage boys nowadays don't know how easy they have it, having porn on their phones and not even needing to worry about their mom finding it when she cleans their room.

Okay, I'm getting distracted.

Back to being all adventurous and sexy and stuff.

"Stay still," I tell her, and she looks up at me.

She nods, but she looks confused as I take my sweats and boxers off. I don't try to throw them. I just lay them next to us and act as if I'm continuing on in my plan.

Except I don't have one.

I want to blow her mind.

I want her to remember me and never forget me and want me and need me all in one second of my touch.

It's a lot to pull off, but I'm going to amaze—

"Are you okay?" she asks, impatience clear in her tone.

I nod and crawl to her, naked and hard and nervous. My hands touch her thighs and she quivers as I slowly trace the tips of my fingertips over her soft skin. Goose bumps rise on her brown skin and she's so beautiful, it's like she's the sun burning through me.

I gently touch both of her knees and spread her thighs. She moves like she's going to sit up, but I push my hand out, willing her to stop.

"Let me try something."

I move back and lower my mouth to her body. Her skin tastes like salt and I'm so hard that it hurts.

I kiss her skin, from her navel to her perky breasts and back down again. She trembles beneath me, her breath so heavy that it makes me shake with desire. I need to be patient, to show her that I can please her, not be "boring" . . .

My mouth travels lower and I forge a trail of gentle kisses down her body. To her hipbones and down between her thighs. She gasps as the tip of my tongue meets her clit. My cock is throbbing and my palms are probably sweating.

Am I any good at this?

I struggle to push all doubts from my mind and flatten my tongue over her. She moans my name when I lap around, licking at her wetness and sucking her swollen bud between my lips. Her fingers claw at my shoulders and she says my name again and again. I must be doing something right. Her legs tighten and I move my tongue faster, then slower, savoring her sweetness with my mouth.

When her legs tighten around my neck, I bring one hand up to her breasts and move the other down between her legs. Slowly, I tease her entrance with my finger, and she groans, compliant and needy, and I feel like a damn king.

"I can't wait anymore." She pulls at my hair, then my shoulders, and I take one more lick and raise my body to cover hers.

"Please," she begs, and I line the tip of my cock between her thighs and she's panting and I can't wait to be inside of her. I try to kiss her but she moves her head, pushing her neck to my mouth.

I suck on her skin, just enough to make her crazy, but not enough to leave a mark.

I grab myself and push at her entrance while I grab her ass . . . but nothing happens.

I reach back between my own legs and grip my cock in my hand and shrink back.

*Shrink* is the right word . . . *Why am I not hard?*

Is this some sick joke the universe is playing on me?

I move my hand up and back down again, taking another look at Dakota's sexy body. The way her curly hair is a wild frame around the work of art that is her beautiful face, her full lips. I take in the way her breasts rest on her chest, small nipples still hard.

What the hell is wrong with me? She's so sexy, so ready, and I'm soft?

I keep touching myself, praying that I can get hard. This has never happened to me before.

Why, oh why, is this happening now?

"What's wrong?" Dakota asks, catching on to my unease.

I shake my head and curse at my traitorous body. "Nothing, I'm just . . . I'm having difficulties."

I hate to admit it and the embarrassment I feel right now is like nothing I've ever felt before, but I'm not really in a position to lie. This problem is literally impossible to hide.

Yep, I've never been this embarrassed. Not even when my mom caught us having sex in my room when she was supposed to be at work all day. Not even when Josh Slackey pulled my pants down in front of the entire fifth-grade class.

Not even when I fell in the shower while masturbating and Nora ran in to help me.

And that last one was definitely up there on the embarrassment level.

"Difficulties?" Dakota questions.

She lifts herself up and I want to crawl into a hole. A dark, dark hole where no one can find me.

"Um, yeah" is all I can think to say.

"You can't get hard?" she guesses, and I really, really want to disappear.

I lift my hands up and stay on my knees.

"I was, just a moment ago. I don't know why—"

Dakota raises her hand into the air. "I don't get it. How can you not?"

Her eyes move to my cock, soft and hanging, and I feel about two inches tall.

"I'm sorry. I don't know what the hell is wrong with me." I move my hand quickly and run it through my hair, some part of me hoping she'll follow its arc and stop looking down *there*. "Maybe we can try something else?"

Dakota nods. But she doesn't look anything like she did a few moments ago. Her eyes no longer look like a wild animal ready to devour me. She looks confused and embarrassed, and I hope she doesn't think this has anything to do with her or how she looks.

She's so beautiful, so sexy, and any man would be stupid not to think so. I don't know what the hell is wrong with me right now, but I do know it's not her fault.

"No . . . let's try *this*," she says, and shifts, then lowers her body so her mouth is level with my cock.

She takes me in her mouth and I try to focus only on its warmth, the way her tongue feels tracing the head of my cock. The way I *want* this, really, really want this.

Still, nothing happens.

She stops after a few seconds and pulls back. Her face is stone as she looks at me, then away quickly.

"I'm so sorry," I explain. "I don't know what the hell is wrong with me, but this is in no way your fault or anything to do with how I feel about you."

Dakota looks away, and I can feel her shutting down inside.

"I can . . ." I don't know how to word what I'm trying to say. "I can finish you, you know, with my mouth?" I offer.

She whips her head around, and the look she shoots me is one with a sharp end. She's clearly not into that idea at all.

"I really am sorry," I say again.

"Just stop talking. Please." She stands up and gathers her clothing.

I know better than to follow her when she walks down the hallway and into the bathroom.

When the door slams, I think I can feel it reverberate through me, but I stay put.

I feel like an asshole and I am at a huge loss about how to fix this. I have no clue how to handle something like this, and I know Dakota enough to know that when she's shut down, she's shut down. That's it. I've embarrassed her and I didn't mean to. I would never, ever mean to.

I grab my pants from the floor and pull them on.

I can't believe after all this time thinking and fantasizing about her, I couldn't even get hard when it came time.

I look down at my uncooperative dick. "Way to go."

I try to think . . . *Think, Landon!*

I glare at the cats in hats on the wall lining the hallway, hoping they can help. The odd pictures offer no advice. Go figure.

I stand outside the bathroom door and try to think of something to say, some way to apologize that will make her understand how sorry I am for making her feel like she isn't enough for me.

She's more than enough, she's everything I've ever wanted.

She's the only person I've ever been with.

She was my first love, my only love.

"Dakota." I use my knuckles to tap on the door.

She's silent. Seconds later, she turns the sink on and I wait.

Time seems to move incredibly slow when you've made a fool of yourself and someone else all in one quick motion. I knock again and she doesn't answer. The water is still running and it's been at least three minutes. I knock again.

She doesn't answer.

"Dakota, are you okay?" I say against the bathroom door.

The running water is the only noise I hear when I press my ear to the door.

Is she okay? Why is the water still running?

On instinct, I turn the knob and open the door.

"I'm sorry . . ." I begin again, but when I look around the small bathroom, it's empty.

The window is open.

The curtains are blowing in the wind.

And I curse at my building for having a fire escape.

# Twenty-five

*I*T'S BEEN LESS THAN TEN MINUTES since Dakota left my house and I'm more and more ashamed by the minute. I hate that this happened to me, to her.

I can't imagine how my inadequacy made her feel.

Well, I can *sort of* imagine, given that she climbed down my fire escape and obviously preferred just getting the heck away from me. I wish she would have talked to me, even *yelled* at me, instead of sneaking out my bathroom window. I feel like shit about it.

I imagine that she may feel even worse.

Her words ring through my ears:

*"I don't get it. How can you not?"*

*"I don't get it. How can you not?"*

I felt so much worse in that moment and now those words won't stop looping through my mind.

*I*
　　*don't*
　　　　*get*
　　　　　　*it.*
　　　　　　　　　*How*
　　　　　　　*can*
　　　　　　*you*
　　　　　*not?*
　　*???*

I sit on the couch and bury my face in my hands. Dakota is probably not going to want to talk to me for a while, maybe never again. The thought of that makes my head spin. I can't imagine her being completely out of my life. The notion is so strange. Too strange. I've known her half of my life, and even when we broke up, I still knew she was out there, not hating me. Her having bad feelings toward me for the rest of our lives just wouldn't be right. It would be like messing with the universe.

A knock on my door pulls me from my thoughts and I jump up.

It *must* be Dakota—back to hear my apology . . . or possibly even offer her own?

As I rush to the door, another knock sounds and I yank it open.

Only it's not Dakota. It's Nora, with some groceries.

"Can you grab something, please?" she asks, struggling with the bags, and I grab as many as I can, careful not to accidentally make her drop them as I help.

When I glance inside them, there's lots of green stuff. I can't tell what any of it is, except that it's green and looks kind of fluffy. The heaviest of the three bags makes a clinking sound when I put it on the counter, and when I peek inside, I find three bottles of wine.

"Sorry," she says as she puts the other bag on the kitchen counter. "I was either going to lose an arm or the wine. And after today, I'd rather lose an arm."

She begins to pull stuff out like she lives here and I watch her silently navigate my kitchen and place her food inside my fridge. She pulls out the bottles of wine, one by one, and puts them in the freezer.

I thought that, unlike liquor, wine froze, but I don't want to ask her and look like an idiot.

"Are you waiting for Tessa or something?" I ask, unsure how to start a conversation with her, or if I should.

Things feel distant between us since Dakota yelled at her for being around me.

Nora nods. "Yep. She's having a rough night, too, a twenty-top just walked in and they put them in her section even though she's still new." She rolls her eyes. "I got bitched out for bitching out the hostess."

"Seems fair?" I shrug, smiling so she knows I'm joking.

She smiles. "Touché."

I watch as she opens a drawer and pulls out the cutting board. She doesn't do anything with it, she just leaves it sitting next to the microwave while she empties the last bag.

I lean awkwardly against the counter and think of an exit plan before I become a burden.

"Oh my God," Nora says, touching her forehead with the tips of her fingers. "I'm sorry. Are you busy or having company? I just barged in here and started unloading groceries and didn't think to ask if I'm in the way."

She's not in the way, now.

I'm so, so, so glad she didn't come ten minutes earlier.

"No, not at all. I'm just going to study and go to bed. You'll have the kitchen to yourself," I tell her.

She blows a loose strand of dark hair out of her face and it falls right back down in front of her eyes. She's still wearing her work uniform. The same one Tessa wears: black pants, white button-up shirt, and that bright green tie.

Nora's shirt is tighter than Tessa's, or so it seems.

"Thank you. I just really needed to not go home to my apartment tonight. I had such a shitty shift, and frankly, I can't handle any of those bitches right now," she huffs.

Her eyes meet mine and she covers her mouth. "No offense."

"None taken," I tell her, meaning it.

I don't ever want to be in the middle of Dakota and Nora's friendship, or lack of friendship, or roommateship, or whatever. I would rather be in Madam Undersecretary Professor Umbridge's office staring at cat pictures while she tortures me.

Both Dakota and Nora are raging fires, and I'd rather not become a pile of ash by being too close to their flames.

"I'm going to make some food if you want to eat? I just grabbed a bunch of stuff and I'm going to see what I can whip up," Nora offers.

This is the most we've spoken in a while and I'm sort of glad she's speaking to me again. I figured we would both avoid each other and make things awkward, but this is a much better alternative.

"I'm not really hungry," I say, even though I am. "I just ate," I lie.

I'm pretty sure Nora got stuff to make her and Tessa dinner, not Tessa's dorky roommate, and I don't want to lurk around longer than I'm wanted. Nothing is worse than the feeling of questioning whether you're wanted or not. It's even worse than knowing you aren't, because at least then you know for sure. There's no desperate hope lingering that maybe your company is wanted.

"Okay. I'm going to leave the extras out for Tessa if you change your mind," Nora says, her eyes on my chest. I should have put a shirt on because now all I can think about is the first time she touched me.

And the second.

And when she kissed me.

And the way her lips tasted like candy and I wanted more.

I need to think about something else. Anything else.

Cakes. Big fluffy cakes with piles of purple ice cream and intricate little flowers.

*Not* the icing that was smeared on her shirt. Cakes and cooking and nonsexy things, like her cooking.

I do enjoy Nora's food. She's a hell of a cook.

Thinking about her cooking reminds me of cakes, which reminds me of Ellen's birthday tomorrow. I still have no idea what to get her. I was going to ask Dakota for help, but that's obviously not in the cards now.

"Are you good at getting people gifts?" I blurt out.

Nora turns to me, her brows furrowed, and she cocks her head. "Huh?"

I cringe at my own awkwardness. "Like for birthdays and stuff."

"Sort of. I mean, I haven't bought anyone a gift in a while, but I can try to help. Who's it for? Dakota? Maybe you can get her something dance-related, or a new yoga mat or something."

I didn't even know Dakota was into yoga. It's a strange thought that Nora knows things about her that I don't.

"It's not for Dakota. It's for this girl I know."

Yikes, that sounded weird. Maybe I should explain it's for this seventeen-year-old girl, so not really someone . . . no, wait, that sounds worse. And would it be even worse still if I now backtracked and explained that it was for a neighbor, like I was expecting Nora to care, like I was somehow hitting on Nora or something?

Ugh, I don't understand these things.

"Okay?" Nora looks puzzled, but doesn't comment on my obvious discomfort. "What types of things does she like?"

Nora continues to put the food away and I wonder if I should be helping her. I honestly have no idea where this stuff goes or how she's going to make a meal out of a can of almonds and a bag of brussels sprouts.

I have haunting memories of being made to eat brussels sprouts as a kid.

I wonder if Nora makes them taste better, somehow.

"I'm not sure. I know she studies a lot and she doesn't like flowers."

"Smart girl. I hate flowers, too. At first, they're so beautiful, but soon enough you're forced to watch them wither and waste away and you just end up having to throw them out, and they're messy. A complete waste of time. Like relationships."

Her voice is so flat that I can't tell if she's joking or not.

I try to defend love, even though I'm clearly not in a place to do so. "Not all relationships are like that."

Nora pulls the plastic bag off of some broccoli and I watch her eyes look everywhere except at me.

"So how long have you known her? What else do you know about her?"

"Nothing really." I shrug my shoulders.

Nora takes the bunch of broccoli over to the sink and turns on the water.

"Nothing else?" she questions. "Then why are you getting her a gift? Are you close friends?"

I get the feeling she's trying not to be too nosy, but I'm bringing all this up quite awkwardly. And since she's given me an entrée to explain, I say, "She works downstairs at the corner store. I wouldn't say we're friends really, but her birthday is tomorrow and I don't think anyone even cares."

Nora turns around from her spot at the sink, the broccoli in her hands dripping water on my floor, and says, "Wait. What?"

I shrug, uncertain of what her tone means. "Yeah. It's terrible. She's turning eighteen and all she does is work down there. And study. She's always studying."

Nora holds up her hand, wet broccoli and all. "You're doing

something for the girl downstairs? The one that always wears the headbands?"

I nod. Her eyes find mine and rest there. She tucks her bottom lip between her teeth and I have to look away from her stare. Her thick eyebrows are bunched together again and her cheeks are glowing. She's wearing more makeup than she usually does, but it looks nice.

She reminds me of the women in those videos Tessa always watches on YouTube. She always says she's going to try to recreate the way they put on makeup, but when all is said and done, the products usually end up in the trash and her eyes are puffy from tears, not covered in color.

"You're something else, Landon Gibson," Nora says, and my cheeks flush.

I turn a little, pretending that I'm thirsty, and open the fridge to grab a Gatorade.

I don't say anything else. I don't know what to say and I know that if I stand here any longer I'm going to make a fool of myself somehow. I've already done that enough for one day and I don't want to scare Nora away from the apartment. Tessa needs as many friends around her as possible, and Nora seems to be a good one.

"I'm going to finish my paper."

*The one that's already completed.*

"If you need anything, I'll be in my room," I tell her, shoving my hands into the pockets of my sweats.

Nora nods and turns back to the sink to rewash her broccoli.

When I get to my room, I close the door and lean my back against it.

The wood is cold against my bare skin and I'm exhausted. Today freaking *sucked*, and I'm so glad it's over.

I don't bother opening a textbook to even pretend like I'm

studying. I don't even bother turning on my light. I just lie down on my bed and close my eyes. I move around for a while, willing sleep to come to me, but my mind is still reeling from Dakota.

And now from Nora. She's in my kitchen, and I have to keep my distance from her, even though I'm not sure that I want to.

# chapter

## Twenty-six

**A**FTER A FEW MINUTES OF SILENCE, music begins to play from the kitchen.

I know the song. I sit up, not ready to get out of bed, but impressed that Nora knows Kevin Garrett, too. This is one of my favorites.

Ironically, the lyrics speak to me more now than ever before. I hear the humming of Nora's voice in my kitchen and imagine her moving her body to the slow beat, singing the words, gliding effortlessly around my kitchen.

I lie back on the bed again, this time with my back against the metal headboard. This bed took hours to put together yet still creaks when I move. The day I got it, Tessa and I spent the entire afternoon at IKEA—and it was absolute hell. The store was crowded and way too big. As we tried to follow the map, Tessa kept going on about a red ladle in some book she was reading about a murderous stalker guy who, for some weird reason, she was in love with. She literally told me that Beck (the main woman, aka his prey) "doesn't deserve him." I rolled my eyes and told her she needs to get out more, but when I googled the book, a lot of people seemed to have the same reaction. It's fascinating the way a narrator can have you questioning what you think you know about the world.

No matter how great the book was, or how many red ladles

IKEA sells because of it, I would be perfectly fine if I never have to go there again. They have these small pencils so you can write the numbers down of the items you want, and after walking through the entire showroom, we wanted everything. So when we got home we had a million items that were hell to carry upstairs and even worse to put together. To top it off, we were missing a bundle of screws and I waited on hold with customer service for forty minutes before I hung up and decided to just go to the hardware store down the street. And all that was *after* having to hire and haggle with a guy with a van to take us to the store and haul our stuff back. All that created another place to avoid: Craigslist's odd-jobs listings.

Nora's hum-singing grows louder and I grab my laptop from the desk and switch the light on. I need to keep myself occupied and distracted. I really shouldn't go out there.

But I'm beginning to feel all rebellious because the more I focus on why I shouldn't go back into the kitchen, the more I want to. Being friends with Nora is fine and dandy. It's not like Dakota's going to burst back in here now.

We can be friendly when Tessa is around, but there's something about Nora that screams danger, and I'm already in a mess as it is. I know we would never date, or anything close to it, but if she kissed me again, or if I keep thinking about her kissing me, things will get awkward for Tessa . . .

Ugh. It's not even easy inside my own *home*.

I press the power button on my laptop and try to remember my password. I keep having to change it because I can't remember it, and the more times I change it, the more difficult Apple makes me make it. For example, the first password was LANDON123 and the last one I can remember was LaNdON123123!@#. I thought I saved it in my phone somewhere, but I don't remember that either.

Finally, after four tries, I get in. My research paper for U.S.

History 201 is still on the screen, even though I finished it. I have three windows open, my iTunes, my paper, and Yelp. Since I moved to Brooklyn, I use Yelp nearly every day . . . except when I did zero research on the bar Nora was taking me to, I suddenly realize. That's weird; I normally check everything out first. It feels so long ago now, even though it hasn't been long at all.

It's hard to believe that Dakota left less than an hour ago. I feel like it's been hours, days even. I'm going to wait until tomorrow to call her. I know that when she needs space, I should give it to her.

The next song starts in the kitchen, and it's Kevin Garrett again. He's singing about being pushed away and feeling alone, and I've loved him since I heard his cover of "Skinny Love," but I've never related as much to him as I do now. Come to think of it, nearly every song on his EP describes what I'm going through right now with Dakota.

Nora's voice is louder now as she sings along. Could it really be such a bad thing for me to go out there and just make casual conversation?

It's not like we've got something going on, and I'm still . . . whatever this is with Dakota, so it's not like she's going to kiss me or anything. Without thinking, I raise my fingers to my lips and I shove my laptop away.

I'm a grown man, I can surely handle being friends with someone I'm attracted to. It happens all the time in movies.

Except they usually end up together in the end . . .

I really should stop comparing movies to reality and porn to actual real-life sex. Movies and porn are so far-fetched compared to life—especially to my life. This is the second time I've thought about porn today. I swear I'm not as obsessed with it as it seems. I've actually watched less of it than most guys my age, I'm sure.

I really need to stop rambling inside my head and go out there and socialize.

I should put a shirt on first, right?

Definitely.

I open my closet and grab the first sweatshirt I see. It's blue and green and the logo for the Seahawks is in a big circle on the chest. The Seahawks remind me of when Hardin and I went to a game last year and he nearly got into a fight over some guy being a jerk to me. I don't usually condone violence, but that guy was a douche.

Now that I'm dressed, I go into the kitchen, and Nora's still singing when I enter. Her back is to me and she's standing over the stove, turning one of the burner knobs. She's taken off her long-sleeved work shirt and is now wearing a black tank top. The straps of her white bra are visible and I can see that she has a tattoo on the top of her back, just above her bra line. A dandelion, with half of the seeds detached and scattered across her back, as if someone had made a wish and blown on it. I guess I'm not surprised that she has a tattoo; her body seems to be made for it somehow.

I lean against the doorway and watch her, waiting for her to notice me. She grabs a bottle of olive oil and pours some into the sauté pan on the burner. Her hips move slowly and her voice is softer now, like both cooking and singing this song are second nature.

I watch as she takes the chopped broccoli and slides it into the sizzling pan. She turns the heat down when it sizzles a little too much and grabs a spatula from the utensil holder on the counter and stirs.

I feel creepy, like the guy in Tessa's book, as I watch her. She hasn't even caught on that I'm here watching her. Is she completely lost in her own thoughts? Or does she just zone out when she's cooking? These are simple things I will never know about this mystery woman.

The song changes again and now it's The Weeknd. I don't

know if I can stand here and watch her dance to him . . . his songs are already sexual enough . . . her hips are so curvy and her pants are so tight.

I should take my ass back to my room and go to bed.

Yet thirty seconds later, I'm still watching. Nora stirs the broccoli, pouring some sort of sauce on it, and then turns around, spotting me.

She doesn't act surprised or embarrassed at all when she sees me lingering in the doorway. Her lips turn up into a smile and she waves the spatula for me to come closer. The oven beeps and she sings her way to it. I don't say anything, I just walk over and sit down at the kitchen table. The kitchen is small; the table is in the corner, but still only a few feet away from the stove and fridge.

Nora grabs a sunflower-printed potholder from the counter and opens the oven. She pulls out a cake and sets it on the empty side of the stove top. She's definitely good at multitasking. I can barely bake a store-bought cake mix and breathe at the same time, let alone make a cake from scratch and cook something on the stove simultaneously.

"Tessa just texted me. The twenty-top just got their food. She's going to be a while," Nora tells me.

I glance at her and nod, trying desperately to ignore the way her breasts threaten to spill out of her tank top.

Would it be rude to ask her to put her other shirt back on?

Yes, I'm positive that it would be. And it would reveal that I've been watching a little closer than I'd like to let on.

"That sucks." I stop staring at her boobs. "How's she liking it there? She tells me that she likes it, but you know she would never complain."

I keep the conversation neutral. Unrelated to any part of her body. No matter how sexy those parts may be.

Nora grabs a fork and sticks it into one of the corners of the cake. She tosses it into the sink and turns to me. "She says she likes it. And now that that Mr. Blond Doctor Guy Robert is there, I'm sure she'll like it even more."

I glance at her, then at the wall, then back at her. "Hmm." I don't know what to say.

I don't know how much Nora knows about Tessa and Hardin's breakup, and I don't want to overshare. It's not my place.

"He's cute. Tessa says you met him before, too. He's cute, right?"

Is he attractive? I don't even remember what he looks like.

"Oh, come on. Please don't tell me you're one of those guys who's too insecure about his own masculinity to say another man is attractive." Nora rolls her eyes.

I laugh. "No, no, I'm not. I just don't remember what he looks like."

She smiles. "Good. I didn't peg you as the type. He's hot, though, take my word for it."

He wasn't that hot. All I remember is blond hair. I'm sure he's not that hot. Maybe it's that he's in medical school that makes him more attractive to women? I don't know.

"Sure." I shrug my shoulders.

Nora lifts the pan and dishes the steaming broccoli onto a plate.

"Look, I know Hardin is your brother and all," she begins. "And I also know that Tessa is still madly in love with him, but I don't think her being out in the dating world is such a bad thing. She isn't ready now, but as her friend, and completely biased and loyal to her, I want her to be happy."

I didn't expect the conversation to go this way.

"I've tried to fix a guy before and . . ." She doesn't finish her sentence. Her voice catches like she caught herself saying something she shouldn't.

"You're entitled to your completely biased opinion." I smile at her to ease the discomfort of whatever it is going on in her mind. "Even if it's wrong."

She laughs at this and walks over to sit next to me at the table. "What's he like, this Hardin guy?"

"You've met him, haven't you?" I have to think back to a few months ago. Yeah, he met her once or twice, maybe. To my knowledge they never spoke directly, but they definitely crossed paths. I think I remember him calling her the wrong name.

"Yes. I've met him, but what's he really like? Is this one of those situations where she's better off without him, and as her friend, I should give her a push in the right direction, or do they actually have a shot at getting their shit together and *being* together?"

Nora speaks quickly, like this is important to her. Like Tessa's well-being is important to her. I like that.

"It's complicated." I pick at the chipped paint on the table. IKEA fails, once again.

"But as her best friend and his stepbrother, I try to stay as neutral as possible. I care about them both, and if I ever thought it was a waste of either of their time, I would tell them. But I honestly don't. I truly believe they'll be fine. Somehow. And if they're not . . . well, my whole family is screwed because we all love both of them."

Nora stares at me, seeming to examine every inch of my face. "Do you always say exactly what you feel?"

Her question surprises me, and she lifts both of her elbows onto the table and rests her chin in her hands.

I shrug. "I try to."

*Except that it's not like I'm going to say I can't stop thinking about how beautiful you are.*

"But sometimes, less is more."

"I thought that rule only applied to plastic surgery and douche capes," Nora challenges.

"What the heck is a douche cape?" I must know the answer to this.

Nora grins, obviously happy to lay on me her knowledge of whatever a douche cape is.

"You know those shirts that men wear that are covered in rhinestones and big crosses? The ones that are always too tight and the men wearing them are always too greasy and look like they just shot up steroids in the bathroom?"

I don't even try to stop my laughter.

She tilts her head and lifts up her hand. Her index finger touches the tip of my nose and she giggles. What an odd but adorable gesture.

"You know exactly what I'm talking about."

And I do. Thank God I've never worn one, but half of the guys at my high school did. Her description is spot on, and thinking about it again makes me laugh even harder.

"I do," I admit.

She smiles again, and when she closes her mouth, her lips look like a heart, full and plump, and pink.

"Do you want to help me decorate the cake? After what you said, I made one for your friend downstairs. Everyone should have a cake on their birthday," Nora says, kindness dripping from her words like honey.

I love that she would make a cake for Ellen, even though she spent her entire day at work baking and having a shitty day.

"That's so amazing of you!" I say with a smile. Then add, "When's your birthday?" I don't know why I just asked that.

"Next week, actually. But if we are going to be friends, you have to promise me something." Her voice is lower now, serious even.

"Okay?"

"You won't ever, ever do anything for me for my birthday."

What a weird promise to make.

"Um, okay?"

She shifts in the chair and stands up. "I mean it. No cards, no cakes, no flowers. Deal?"

Her eyes are dark and her lips are pulled tight.

"Deal."

And with that, she nods, letting me know she's happy with my agreement. Instantly the tension that had filled the room dissipates.

I don't know why she's requesting this, or if she's joking or not, but I don't know her well enough to pry. If the day comes when we're close enough for her to tell me, I'll gladly listen, but I get the feeling that there are very few people that know anything about this woman.

"So, what color do you think we should go with?" Nora goes to the farthest cabinet lining the wall.

I've never even opened that cabinet before; maybe that's why I didn't know it was full of food.

Nora pulls out a bag of powdered sugar and a little box with a rainbow on it. Food coloring maybe? My thoughts are confirmed when she opens the box and pulls out four little bottles with white caps. Red, yellow, green, and blue.

"Can you grab a stick of butter and the milk from the fridge?" she asks.

Her hands tear at the bag of powdered sugar and she opens the drawer in front of her. She pulls out measuring cups and I find it funny that I live here and didn't even know half of this stuff was in here.

"Yes, ma'am," I tell her, and she turns around, her lips forming a devilish smile . . . and I'm too innocent for her to be looking at me like this.

# chapter

## Twenty-seven

**T**URNS OUT I'M AN AWFUL BAKER. Awful as in I can't even decorate a plain sheet cake without making a mess.

"Just one or two drops this time," Nora reminds me, as if I didn't learn my lesson thirty seconds ago when she shrieked and shouted at me for dumping half the bottle of food coloring into the first bowl of icing.

How was I supposed to know that this little bottle held enough power to turn Ellen's mouth red for a week?

"We need more sugar," Nora says, and I grab the bag from the counter next to me.

The powdered sugar moves to one side and I realize that she cut the end open. I try to grab it before it spills out, and fail. The sugar dumps out of one end and onto the counter and the floor. A cloud of white dust puffs up in my face and Nora waves her hand around as the sugar cloud covers her.

"Oh my God!" she shrieks, humor evident in her voice.

I sit the plastic bag on the counter and look at the mess I made. As if it's mocking me, the bag falls to the floor and the last bit of sugar puffs out. My sweatshirt is so covered in white that the seahawk printed on the front is barely visible. When Nora smiles, her eyes crinkle at the corners and I sort of like it.

"Sorry! I didn't know it was open." I wipe my hand across the counter, and while I like the way the soft sugar feels against my skin, I should never, ever, try to bake anything again. Noted.

Nora's black tank top is covered in blotches of powdered sugar. Along with her arms, her hands, her cheeks, and her dark hair.

"It's okay." Her smile is contagious and I'm not even embarrassed at the mess I made. It feels weird that she's not mad about it, and I don't know why. She's just smiling, looking from the mess to me, and shaking her head with her lips pressed into a smile.

Nora moves the mixing bowl out of the way and grabs a roll of paper towels. She turns the water on in the sink and uses her hands to push as much powder into the basin as possible.

"During my first semester at culinary school, I forgot to put the guard on a forty-quart mixer. A ten-pound bag of confectioners' sugar went everywhere. Needless to say, I had to stay an extra three hours to clean and redo my assignment, and my teacher was such a prick he wouldn't let anyone help me." Her hands are moving quickly to clean the mess I made and I should probably be helping her.

"Did you pass the class? I mean, after you redid the entire thing?" I ask her.

"Nope. Like I said, my instructor was a real prick."

I look at her and she lifts her sugary hand to scratch her face. She wipes at her cheek, smearing white on her tanned skin.

I grab a paper towel and start to help her. "That's why I want to be a teacher."

She tosses the empty sugar bag into the trash. "To be a prick?"

I laugh and shake my head. "No. To be the opposite. I had this teacher in tenth grade, Mr. Haponek, who went above and beyond his job. He was everything a teacher was supposed to be, but the older I got, the less my teachers cared about their jobs, and when I looked around my school, I saw so many kids who needed that one good teacher. It makes a difference, you know?"

"What was your high school like?" Nora asks.

*Terrible.*

*A shithole.*

"It was okay," I say.

I don't think she wants to hear about my actual experience.

I don't think I'd want to tell her.

It's kind of like when people ask "How are you?" and really only want you to say "fine." Any further explanation makes them uncomfortable.

"I didn't get to go to a real high school. I went to a small private school near Seattle. It was awful," Nora says, surprising me with another small glimpse into who she is.

"My school was awful, too," I admit.

Nora regards me with a skeptical look. "I bet you were one of the popular kids. You played sports, didn't you?"

I nearly laugh at the idea of me being a popular kid.

*A jock? Me? Not even close.*

"Not quite." My cheeks get red. I can feel it. "I wasn't anything, really. I wasn't cool enough to be popular, but I wasn't smart enough to be considered a nerd. I was just in that middle ground where no one gave a shit about me. I was chubby then, so I got teased when the popular kids got bored with their usual prey. But honestly, I didn't realize how bad my high school was until I moved to Washington halfway through my senior year. My experience in Washington was so different."

Nora walks over to the utility closet and grabs the broom and dustpan. She starts to sweep the floor and I prepare to fill the silence with more ramblings about my high school days as I wet a paper towel and clean the rest of the counter.

"Nothing is worse than a bunch of assholes who peak in high school," she observes.

I bark out a little laugh. "That's one of the truest things I've ever heard."

"I guess I wasn't missing much," Nora says, her eyes distant. She has that expression on her face again, the one that looks like she's grown bored.

"Did you always want to be a pastry chef?" I ask. The sugar is close to being cleaned up now, but I don't want the conversation to end. I almost wish there was another bag of something for me to *accidentally* dump on the floor.

I've never heard Nora talk this much before, aside from her and Tessa gushing over the two boys kissing on that demon-hunting show Tessa's obsessed with. Usually, I'm never a part of their conversations, I'm in my room studying or at work when she's here, and now that we are alone and she's being uncharacteristically chatty, I want to gather in as many words as she's willing to say.

She moves the broom across the tile floor and looks over at me. "Thanks for remembering not to call me a baker. And no, I actually wanted to be a surgeon. Like my dad and his dad and his dad."

*A surgeon?* That's the last thing I expected her to say.

"Really?"

"Don't be so surprised. I'm actually very intelligent." She cocks her head to the side and I decide that I really like her playful attitude. It's different from Dakota's, not as harsh or as hard.

*Dakota.*

I haven't thought about her once in the last thirty minutes, and her name sounds foreign inside my head.

Does that make me a bad guy? Naked with her one minute, not thinking about her the next.

Is she sitting at home, waiting for me to call her?

. . . Somehow, I doubt that.

"I'm not doubting that." I raise a sugary hand to her. "I just thought you would say something more . . . art-related."

Nora regards me with a thoughtful look on her face. "Hmm, why is that?"

She rests the broom against the counter and leans closer to me to turn on the faucet. Her arm brushes against the fabric of my sweatshirt and I move out of her way.

"I don't know. I just picture you being some sort of artist." I run my hand over my hair and little bits of sugar fall onto the floor. "I don't really know what I'm talking about."

"You should have taken that off before I swept." Nora's fingers wrap around a string from my sweatshirt and I look down, watching her hand.

"Probably," I say, and she takes a step closer.

I hold my breath.

Her eyes catch mine and she sucks in a quiet breath between her teeth. "Sometimes it feels like you know me more than you should," she whispers—and I can't move.

I can't breathe, or move, or even speak when she's this close. Even with sugar covering her, she's so painfully stunning that I can barely look at her.

"Maybe I do," I tell her, somehow feeling the same.

Truthfully, I barely know anything about her, but maybe it isn't about knowing the factual things. Maybe it doesn't matter if I know her mom's name, or her favorite color. Maybe it doesn't take years to know people like we assume; maybe the important things are much, much simpler. Maybe it matters more that we see deeper, that we know what kind of friend they are, or that they bake cakes for people they don't know without being asked.

"You shouldn't," she says, still staring up at me.

Without thinking, I take a step closer to her and she closes her eyes.

"Maybe I should."

I don't know who I am in this moment. I don't feel nervous about being so close to such a beautiful woman. I don't feel like I'm not good enough to be touching her face.

I barely have any thoughts running through my mind.

I like the silence inside my head that she seems to bring.

"We can't," she says, in a voice that's barely audible.

Her eyes are still shut and my hand is on her cheek without me even knowing that I put it there. My thumb traces the outline of her pouty mouth, and I can feel the quickening of her pulse where my palm rests on her neck.

"Maybe we can," I whisper.

In this moment, all I know in the world is that her hands are gripping the fabric of my sweatshirt, and despite the doubt in her words, she's pulling me closer.

"You don't know how bad I am for you." The words rush out of her mouth and her eyes peer open just a fraction . . . and my heart swells.

There's pain there, a deep pain shredded through the dark green and the flakes of brown. Her pain is visible to me for the first time, and I can feel the weight of it in her hooded gaze. Something shifts and locks into place inside of me and I don't have the words to explain it. I want to heal her. I want her to know that everything will be okay.

I want her to know that pain is only permanent if we allow it to be.

I don't know the origin of hers, but I'm certain that I would do anything to take it away from her. My shoulders can bear the weight of her pain. They are strong, built for supporting, and I need to her know that.

I feel fiercely protective of her now, as if she's been mine to guard for my entire existence.

"You don't know what you're getting into," Nora warns, and I quiet her with my thumb against her lips. She parts them under my touch and exhales a quiet sigh.

"I don't care," I say, and mean it.

Her eyes close again and she pulls me closer, closer, until our bodies are pressed together, molded like they're supposed to be, like they were made to be.

I lean down and lick my lips and she whimpers as if she's been waiting an eternity for my lips to find hers, and it does feel that way. I feel a powerful sense of relief, like I've found a part of me that I didn't know was missing.

I rest my hand on her cheek and there's barely an inch between our mouths. She's breathing so softly, as if I'm the fragile one, and she's being careful not to break me.

Her lips taste like sugar and she's my favorite dessert.

I'm gentle with her, gently pressing my lips against the corners of her mouth, and she makes a noise in the back of her throat that makes my head swim. I feel dizzy when her mouth opens and her tongue gently meets mine.

It's the best kind of disoriented and I never want to think straight again. The hand of mine that's not on her cheek moves to her back and I press her soft body against mine until there's not a single inch between us.

Through her soft lips, she whispers my name, and I've never felt this type of rush before. She pulls away for a moment and I feel lost, like I'm swimming out in the middle of nowhere, and when her mouth finds mine again, she's found *me* and anchored me to her.

A vibration buzzes against the counter and the music I had forgotten was even playing fades out.

It's like I've lost the last few minutes of my life, but I never, ever want them back. I want to stay here, lost with her.

But reality has other plans and Nora pulls away, taking the silence in my mind with her.

She grabs her phone from the counter and looks at it quickly as she swipes her finger across the green circle. I lean against the counter to steady myself and she apologizes and steps into the hallway.

A few seconds of silence pass and I can hear her talking but I can't make out any of the words. Her voice gets louder and I force myself not to move closer to eavesdrop on her conversation.

"I have to go," she says when she comes back into the room. "But I'll be back in the morning to help you decorate the cake. I'll wrap it up so it won't get stale."

She moves across my kitchen and I notice the change in her demeanor. Her shoulders are slouched, and every time I try to catch her eyes, she avoids mine.

A thrumming rises in my chest.

"Is everything okay? Is there anything I can do to help?" I ask. I decide in this moment that there are only a few things in this world that I wouldn't do for her.

I know I'm insane and that I barely know her. I'm aware that it's hard to protect someone that won't allow you to. I'm also aware that I have a messy on-and-off relationship with someone else, but there's nothing I can do to go back now. I can't make the last few minutes disappear—and even if I could, I never would.

"Everything is fine. I just have to go back to Lookout, my boss needs me," she says with a weak smile I can see right through.

I stand in silence as she layers Saran Wrap around the cake pan and grabs her shirt from the back of the chair. She tucks her tie into the back pocket of her black pants and walks to the entry of the kitchen.

Her eyes still won't meet mine and it makes my stomach hurt. "Don't worry about those dishes, I'll get them in the morning."

I nod, not knowing what else to say. The bliss from our kiss is evaporating faster than I can blink, and the endless questions I have for her are filling my head.

"I'm sorry," she says, and I truly feel like she means it. At least there's that.

She disappears through the doorway and I stand still for a few minutes, recollecting every moment we just shared. From the sweet taste of her sugary kiss to the desperation in her fingers as she clutched the fabric of my sweatshirt.

The apartment is so silent, unlike my mind, and I turn on the faucet and open the door to the dishwasher. I toss out the un-eaten broccoli and put the olive oil back into the cabinet. By the time Tessa gets home, I'm still sitting in the kitchen, at the table. The dishes are clean and put away, and there's no trace of pow-dered sugar anywhere to be found.

She unties her apron and lays it on the back of the chair. "Hey, what are you doing up?"

I look at the time on the stove. It's nearly one in the morning. "I don't know," I lie.

She's having a hard enough time lately, I don't want to bur-den her with my problems, especially when I don't even under-stand them.

Tessa looks at me and I can see the speculation in her eyes. She glances around the room and spots the cake on the counter.

"Where's Nora?" she asks.

My throat is dry as I explain. "She came by for a little bit, then she got called back to work."

"Back to work? By who? I just left there and Robert and I were the last people there."

I should be surprised by this, but I'm not.

I wave an unconcerned hand. "I must have heard her wrong. How was work?"

I change the subject, and Tessa lets me.

# chapter

# Twenty-eight

THE MORNING CAME faster than I expected.

When I wake up, I lie in bed for a while, just staring at my ceiling fan. I wonder who lived here before me, and why they decided to paint the fan mismatching colors. Every blade is a different color. Blue, then green, then purple, then yellow, and lastly, red. I wonder if it was a child's room. If not, the inhabitants must have had quite the quirky side.

I don't know what time it is when I finally push myself to get out of bed. All I know is that I'm exhausted, like I've been through a war in the night. When I grab my phone to check the time, it's dead. I plug it into the charger and make my way to the living room.

The living room is dark and the television is on. Tessa's sleeping on the couch and an episode of *Cupcake Wars* is playing on the screen, the volume low. I grab the remote from where it lies on her stomach and turn off the TV. She's still wearing her work uniform. She must have been drained by the time she got home. I could tell by the way her eyes were closing while she ate the plate of food she brought from work last night. We sat at the table for less than thirty minutes and she gave me a play-by-play of her night.

A group of professors from NYU came in, twenty minutes before closing, and sat in her section. It had to have bothered her a little, even though she didn't say, that they were from NYU, since the university hasn't accepted her yet. I'm sure they will, just not for this semester. She doesn't want Ken to use his position at WCU to try to help her, but I believe he's going to if they don't take her for the winter semester. It would be pretty cool to have her on campus with me, even though we have different majors. During our sophomore year, a few of our classes will overlap since I'm going for early childhood education and she's going for English.

I walk into the kitchen to check the time. It's only eight. It's sort of weird that the stove is our only clock in the entire apartment. We rely on our phones to tell us the time; I wonder how the clock business is handling that.

It would be so strange to live in a time when you have to walk into a building or the town square to check the clock. And what if it was wrong—you wouldn't even know. If Hardin lived back then, I could see him having the wrong time on all his clocks just to mess with people.

I really need to tell Tessa that Hardin's coming next weekend. I'll tell her when she wakes up.

I will.

Really this time.

The kitchen is quiet; only the soft buzzing from the fridge is audible. The undecorated cake is still sitting on the counter, covered in Saran Wrap.

I wonder if Nora's going to come back, or if whatever took her away last night will keep her today.

I look in the fridge for something to eat before I start getting ready for work.

*Fuck!*

Work.

I was supposed to be there at six today to cover Posey's shift.

I rush to my room to grab my phone to call my boss. My foot catches on something hard and I stumble over it, and try to balance on one foot. Of course that doesn't work, and my toes smash into the leg of my desk.

*Dammit*, it hurts.

I grab my foot and finally reach my phone. Of course it's still dead.

*Double dammit.*

I'll have to use Tessa's phone to call work.

I toss my phone at the bed and bounce on one foot out to the living room, my toe still throbbing. When I reach Tessa's sleeping body on the couch, I scan her and the furniture. Her cell has to be around here somewhere.

Why didn't I listen to my mom about getting a landline?

*You never know what could happen, Landon.*

*The cell service could stop working.*

*You may lose that cell phone and have to use the landline to call and find it.*

*The aliens could invade Brooklyn and steal all technology to further their plan of taking over Earth for their evil doings.*

Okay, so I made the last one up when I teased her about her concern.

However, this is one of the many times in my life when I've come to realize that my mother usually knows what the heck she's talking about. Most twenty-year-olds would never admit it, but I'm smart enough to know that I'm lucky to have a parent like her.

I spot Tessa's phone wedged between the back of the couch and her hip. I slowly reach for it and hold my breath, trying not to wake her. Just as my fingertips reach the phone and I grab hold of it, Tessa's body jerks and her eyes dart open.

I pull back and give her time to understand that it's only me, and she's asleep on the couch in her own living room.

"Are you okay?" Tessa groans. Her voice sounds like she's still asleep.

"Yeah, sorry. My phone is dead and I'm late for work."

She nods and reaches her phone out to me.

I take it and go to dial the number, but I'm asked for the passcode.

Tessa starts naming numbers and I type them in quickly.

"Zero, two, zero, one," she says, and closes her eyes. She rolls on her side and lifts her knees up toward her chest.

"Thanks."

I grab the blanket from the back of the couch and drape it over her. She thanks me with a smile and I unlock her phone. Her phone feels weird in my hand; it's so small compared to mine.

She teases me for the size of mine, calling it an iPad, and I tease her for always breaking or losing hers. I bring up the one she dropped in the toilet, the one that "went missing" in an Uber, the one that she threw at a spider on the rooftop of our building. The only one left, the one I don't mention, was her first phone.

That's the one whose screen she busted purposely and stomped it under her feet at least twenty times. I came home from work to find her smashing it. She swore she was never going to use an iPhone again, and I had my suspicions that it had nothing to do with the technology. Rather it's the same reason she only drinks cold coffee now. The same reason she can barely listen to her favorite band anymore.

She quickly gave up on her promise after using another phone for a week. She lost all of her music, all of the information she had saved. All of her auto-login websites, her saved credit cards. She cursed Apple all the way to the store, saying that they are taking over the world, and it pissed her off that they have such good products because they leave consumers no other choice but to use them. Quite the paradox.

She also mentioned more than a few times that they should make more affordable products. I agreed.

When I get to the call screen, I realize I don't know the number to Grind by heart. I usually rely on the number already in my phone. I can barely remember the days before smartphones took over the world. I did have an old Nokia when I was twelve that my mom made me bring with me everywhere I went, just in case something happened. I used to kill the battery playing Snake all day.

Man, I feel old.

What the heck would we do without technology? I'm ashamed of my reliance on it, but at the same time I cringe at the thought of having to find a phone book and search for the number to my work.

Man, we humans are spoiled.

Scratch that, we Americans are spoiled. There are many, many places in the world where people have never even seen an iPhone, and here I am pondering my existence without Apple products.

I have it pretty damn easy.

I google the number for Grind, and when I call the line goes straight to busy.

What the hell?

I don't even have Posey's number. Again, technology as hindrance.

I used to have all my friends' phone numbers memorized. It helped that I only had two friends, and they lived in the same house, but still.

"I'm just going to hurry and get dressed and run there," I explain in a rush.

I set Tessa's phone on the coffee table and walk to my room.

My toes still hurt.

If I leave now, I can get there in less than fifteen minutes. I could be halfway there already if I'd just gotten dressed instead of trying to call them. I glance at the phone on my bed. I also could have used my phone by now if I'd left it on the charger.

You win some, you lose some.

I rush around my room and throw on dark jeans and a plain gray T-shirt. I hurry to the bathroom and brush my teeth. I take a piss and wash my hands. Without even looking in the mirror, I shut the light off and go back into the living room. The feeling is coming back to my toes, and I'm glad, since I'll have to practically run there. I'm sure I look like complete hell, but once I get to work, I'll run my fingers through my hair, or something.

My shoes . . . where are my shoes? I scan my floor and look inside my closet.

Living room. They must be by the door.

*Where they belong.* I hear Tessa's voice in my head and laugh to myself.

I'm at the door, pushing my feet into my sneakers, in less than five minutes since I tried to call Grind. I grab my keys and yank the door open to find someone standing in front of me.

Nora.

With a trash bag in one arm and a box at her feet.

Her eyes widen when she sees me and I look down at the box. There's a book, a picture frame, and some random stuff that's unidentifiable and buried.

"Hi." Nora's lips shape the word and she stares at me with what looks like hesitation.

"Hi," I respond, trying to piece together what she's doing here.

With her stuff.

"Are you okay?" I ask her, and she nods.

Suddenly her eyes well up with tears and I watch her clench her free hand into a tight fist. She takes a deep breath, and just like that, she straightens her back and holds her tears at bay.

"Can I come in?" Her voice is low, defeated, but she's putting on a good front.

I bend down, grab the box, and hold it in one arm. I reach out my hand for her to give me the trash bag and she does.

Her eyes are hard. She's a fighter. I can see it in her eyes.

Her bag is heavy and I set it down on the living room floor next to my grandma's table. I lay the box down and wave for Nora to come inside. She steps in slowly and Tessa sits up on the couch.

I look at her phone on the table.

Shit.

I look at Nora apologetically. "I have to go to work. I'm *really* late."

She nods and smiles at me, but it's the smallest smile I've ever seen.

The self-promises I made to protect her last night surge back up in my chest. I never want her to look this way, to feel this way.

Tessa stands up and assesses the situation. I can't stay around for the explanation, even though it's going to drive me crazy to not know what's going on.

What happened?

Why is Nora here with her belongings?

Was it something with Dakota?

My stomach twists at the possibility.

When I leave, will she tell Tessa that we kissed, again?

I wish I could stay, but I can't. Too many people are counting on me, and I've already messed up big-time this morning.

I rush down the hallway and take the stairs. I don't have time to wait for the world's smallest elevator to get to my floor.

# chapter

# *Twenty-nine*

WHEN I PUSH THROUGH THE DOORS at Grind, the place is packed.
Oh no.

A long line is snaked around the shop, from the pastry display case to the pickup area. Women and men dressed in casual business clothing are scattered around the room, chattering and sipping on caffeine. As I scan the line, I notice a few irritated faces toward the back. I immediately walk through the crowd and go behind the counter. I don't even bother to grab an apron. Aiden is taking orders, his fingers quickly navigating the familiar register and his usually pale face bright red. His neck, too. Sweat has soaked through the back of his shirt.

*Well, shit.* He's not going to be very happy with me.

As I step up behind him, he hands a black-haired woman in a red pantsuit her change. For her part, the woman is clearly irritated, her hands moving around angrily in the space between them, trying to communicate her frustration, I guess.

"Hey, I'm here. Sorry, man. My phone died and my alarm—"

"Save it." Aiden glares at me. "Just help me get this line down," he says quietly.

I wish I could call on Hermione to turn him into a ferret.

Still, I nod, sort of understanding his frustration. This line is no joke and sometimes people are just crappy.

Draco—I mean, Aiden—shouts an order at me. "Macchiato. Extra foam!"

I grab a small cup and get to work. As I steam the milk, I look back at Aiden. He's filthy: black coffee grounds stain the front of his shirt, and he has a wet spot on his chest. It would be much more amusing if it wasn't my fault. If I'd arrived on time, we still would have been busy and overwhelmed, but it would have been much easier to handle with two people.

As I pour the frothed milk over the dark espresso, Aiden gives me another order. We continue like this until the line shrinks down to three people. Aiden is calmer now, back to smiling and being friendly with customers. This is good news for me.

It's helping keep my mind off of Nora showing up at my apartment, and the fact that I'm an idiot for not bringing my phone to text Tessa to make sure everything's all right. I could have found power for it somewhere.

Every table is still full and there are at least twenty people standing up, coffee in hand. I notice that they're all wearing lanyards and assume that it's the usual electronics conference that happens every couple months nearby. It's a much bigger crowd than we usually get at one time, but it's good for business. That's another cool thing about New York City; there's always something going on.

I start to refill the canisters of beans and wipe down the grinders while Aiden tackles the condiment station, refilling the creamers and restocking the seven different types of sugar we offer. Before I moved to the city, I'd never seen a lump of sugar pressed into the shape of a cube, like on Bugs Bunny. I honestly thought that was just cartoon shorthand.

Back in Saginaw, every once in a while, I would hear a customer ordering a nonfat something or other, but that was about as complicated as it got in small-town Michigan. Dakota and I would sit in the local coffeehouse for hours. We would switch tables when we got tired of the view. We'd get a sugar high and walk home, holding hands and dreaming under the stars.

My mind moves down that familiar memory lane and I remember when Dakota and I got into a fight in Starbucks. I remember that her hair smelled like coconut and her new lip gloss was sticky. I chased her down the street and she sprinted, reminding me that she could run faster than anyone I knew. The track coach at our high school knew it, too—not that Dakota was interested in sports. She would humor me and watch the meets with me and ask a million questions every time a whistle blew.

She wanted to dance. She always knew it. I envied her that certainty. Dakota ran and ran farther away from the Starbucks, and I chased her, as I always did.

She turned a corner down an alleyway, and I lost her. I felt like I couldn't breathe until I found her. It was too dark for her to be running through that part of town. I found her a few minutes later, right outside the Patch. She was sitting on the ground next to a half-torn-down fence, the black of the woods behind her.

The chain-link fence had huge holes in it and it was dark outside, and after a minute I could finally breathe again. Dakota was picking at the gray rocks and tossing them into a pothole in the street. I remember how relieved I felt when I saw her. She was wearing a yellow shirt with a smiley face on it and glittery sandals. She was mad at me because I thought it was a bad idea to try to track down her mom.

Yolanda Hunter had been gone for too many years. I felt that if she wanted to be found, she wouldn't be hiding.

Dakota was angry, telling me that I didn't understand what it was like to have no parents. Her mom ran away, leaving her children with a drunk father who liked to smack his son around.

When I caught up to Dakota, she was crying, and it took her a few seconds to look at me. It's so strange the way my mind remembers the exact details of that night. I had started to get worried about her. Sometimes, I would think she was going to disappear, like her mom.

*"There's no proof that she wouldn't let me live with her,"* she told me that night.

*"And there's no proof that she would. I just want you to consider how you'll feel if she doesn't say what you want her to, or if she doesn't say anything at all,"* I said to her as I sat down next to her on the crunchy gravel.

*"I'll be fine. It couldn't possibly be worse than not knowing,"* she said.

I remember grabbing her hand and that she laid her head on my shoulder. We sat in silence, both of our heads tilted up toward the sky. The stars were so bright that night.

Sometimes, like that night, we wondered why the stars even bothered to shine over our town.

*"I think it's to torture us. To mock those of us who are stuck in bad places and living crappy lives,"* Dakota would say.

I'd say something like *"No, I think they're here to give us hope. Hope that there's more out there. Stars aren't evil like humans."*

She would look at me and squeeze my hand, and I would promise her that someday, somehow, we would get the hell out of Saginaw.

She seemed to trust me.

"Sorry it took so long!" I recognize Posey's voice through the cloud of memories in my head. She's talking to Aiden. A woman in a black dress holds up a sign and tells everyone it's time to go. As the crowd spills out of the shop, I listen to the exchange between Posey and Aiden.

He lifts his shirt up to wipe his sweaty face as she talks to him. "It's all right. Landon finally showed up."

Posey's head turns and she finds me, wiping a rag across the metal counter.

Not eavesdropping at all.

"I'm so sorry!" Posey says, walking toward me. Her hands are behind her back and she's tying her apron. Her red hair is up today, pulled back into a bun.

"I could have sworn we switched shifts today, I must have forgotten to ask you," she explains.

I shake the rag over the trash can before soaking it in the soap bucket. "No. We did switch. I was just out of it last night and let my phone die. Sorry you had to come all the way down here."

She looks toward Aiden and I follow her eyes. He's not looking at either of us; he's talking to a customer about decaf coffee being despicable and pointless.

"It's like alcohol-free beer. Waste of time," the middle-aged man Aiden's talking to says in a raspy voice. He looks like he's had a few beers today himself.

"I kind of need the hours, anyway," Posey whispers to me, and nods toward the table against the back wall, closest to the short hall that leads to the restroom. Her little sister, Lila, is sitting there patiently, with her chin on the table. "I brought backup."

She reaches into her pocket and pulls out three little cars. Hot Wheels, maybe?

"She likes her cars." I smile at the little girl, but she doesn't notice.

Posey nods. "Oh yes she does."

"You're sure you want to stay? I can. I don't have anything to do," I offer.

The terribly selfish part of me wants her to stay so I can go see how Nora's doing, but I would never admit this out loud.

"Nope. I'm good, honestly. I only needed the two hours this morning for my grandma's doctor appointment. She's not doing very well." Posey looks to her sister and I can spot a hint of fear.

As a college student working at a coffee shop, it would be nearly impossible for Posey to raise her little sister on her wages alone. I don't know too many of the details of her family life, but I assume that her parents aren't going to magically return.

"I can take Lila with me for a few hours. I'm just going back to my apartment. She can come there, or we can go to the park across the street."

I wouldn't mind watching her for a little while so Posey can work the last two hours of her shift.

And this means that I can go back to my apartment.

I'm a terrible person.

Posey's eyes return to her sister every few seconds. She looks after her so well, even when she's working behind the counter. The little girl is still sitting with her chin resting adorably on the table.

"Are you sure? You don't have to."

"I know," I respond. "But I'd like to help."

Man, I'm going to hell for pushing this.

Posey looks at her sister again and seems to consider the little girl's boredom. "Okay. But take her to your apartment. It's hot today and we were already out all morning." She laughs. "It's too early for her to be worn out."

"Got it. I'll clean up these tables before I go."

"Thanks, Landon." Posey smiles at me. Her freckles are extra noticeable today. It's cute.

"No prob, Bob."

I grab the dish bucket and she lifts the divider in the cash wrap and waves me by.

The tables are dirtier than I've ever seen them. I have to change towels three times to wipe up the spills and rings of coffee.

At least the crowd is gone. Only one customer is left, a young hipster typing away on his little gold MacBook. He seems content.

When I'm ready to go, Lila is still in the same seat. Her chin is no longer resting on the table. Instead, she's zooming a little purple car along its surface, making sound effects and all.

"Hey, Lila. Remember me?" I ask her.

Her little round face looks up at me and she nods.

"Cool. Do you want to hang out with me while your sister works? We can go to my house for a little bit? I have a friend who would love to meet you." I bend down to her level and she looks back at her car.

"Yes." Her voice is soft but clear.

Posey says my name and I tell Lila that I'll be right back to get her.

When I stand in front of Posey, she has a serious expression on her face.

"You know how to be around kids, right? She's so young and I trust you, otherwise there's no way I would ever leave her alone with you, but do you know how to handle kids? What to do if she's hungry? Or if she falls and scrapes her knee?" Posey's voice is low and she sounds like a mom. "You have to hold her hand when you walk outside. At all times. And she only eats fries and peanut butter crackers."

I nod. "Fries and peanut-butter crackers at all times. Hold hand. Don't let her fall down. She's too young to write my essays for me. Got it." I grin at her and she sighs, smiling at me.

"You're sure?" she asks again.

"Positive."

"Call me if you need anything," she says.

I nod and promise her over and over that everything will be fine. I don't tell her that my phone is at my apartment, but I'm going straight there, and telling her that I won't be reachable until I'm home will only make her more panicky, if that's possible.

Posey explains to Lila that she's going to work for a little bit, then come to my house and pick her up. Lila doesn't seem to mind one bit.

When I say goodbye to Aiden, I notice a deep purple mark on the side of his neck, just above the collar of his shirt. My stomach turns a little, and I try not to picture the type of women he brings home.

During the walk to my apartment, Lila holds my hand and points to and names every bus, van, and ambulance as they pass. Any car with lights on it qualifies as an ambulance in her book.

The walk is quick and she's chatty, though it's hard to make out some of her words. As I look around, it seems like there are a ton of women out and about today. Either that, or women really do pay more attention to men with kids. I've gotten more smiles and more hi's in the last twenty minutes than I have since I moved here. Weird. It's like in that movie with the dog, where Owen Wilson's friend uses his puppy to get attention from women.

Probably best I don't compare kids to puppies, though.

When we reach my building, I let Lila press the button on the elevator and I count the seconds as it climbs to my floor. I really hope Nora is still here.

The TV is on when we walk through the door. Tessa is still on the couch, her hair pulled on top of her head. She still looks tired when sits up to greet our guest. She's sitting alone, I notice immediately.

"Well, hi," she says with a smile for Lila.

Lila waves and pulls her blue car from the pocket of her tiny jeans.

"This is Posey's little sister. I'm keeping an eye on her for the next hour and a half or so."

This seems to wake her up a little. She beams and waves at Lila. "What's your name?"

Lila doesn't answer. She just sits down on the floor and starts rolling her car around our printed rug, making little noises as she drives the car along the lines.

"She's adorable," Tessa observes.

I nod in agreement. "I'm going to put my phone on the charger and run to the bathroom. Can you watch her for a minute?"

I try not to make it obvious when I scan the room for Nora for the second time.

"Of course," Tessa says, and I go into my room and plug in my phone.

My bed isn't made and my laptop is open on the floor next to it. Good thing I didn't step on it when I was rushing around this morning. I wait a minute or two for my phone to turn on so I can text Posey and tell her that we made it just fine. No falls. No problems whatsoever.

But when my phone turns on, I see I have a text from Nora:

**Please don't tell Tessa anything. She doesn't need the drama right now :/**

I reply, asking her where she went.

A few seconds pass and I don't get a response, so I text Posey and leave my phone to charge for a little bit. I glance out into the living room and then go into the bathroom and close the door behind me. While I'm washing my hands, the door opens and Nora appears in the mirror.

# chapter

## Thirty

*I* STARE INTO THE MIRROR for a few seconds, and Nora stares back at me.

She doesn't move closer. She just stands in the doorway with her eyes on mine. Without looking away from her, I turn off the water and grab a towel to dry my hands. She must have been in Tessa's room when I arrived.

"Hi," Nora's reflection says.

"Hi," I repeat.

We seem to be saying this a lot today.

"What happened?" I ask. I had planned on waiting for her to volunteer the information, but I couldn't stop myself from blurting out the question.

She takes a deep breath and I watch her chest rise and fall. I turn around and she takes a few steps into the bathroom and closes the door behind her.

When she approaches me, she seems subdued, not the same woman who was in my kitchen last night. Her hands are held in front of her, not clenching my sweatshirt. Her lips are pursed, not kissing me.

Nora's hair is tied into a braid and resting over one shoulder. She's not wearing any makeup and I notice a few freckles on her cheeks. Her eyes look tired, giving away that she hasn't slept much. She's wearing a white T-shirt, another one that hangs off of one shoulder, and black leggings. Her feet are covered in pizza-print socks. This is the second time I've seen her wear odd socks. I like them.

"I'm okay," Nora says, and licks her lips.

I reach for her hand and pull her closer to me. She hesitates for a moment, then steps to me.

*The trash bag full of clothes says otherwise, Nora.*

"You don't seem okay." I raise my free hand and touch the end of her braid. Her eyelids fall closed.

"You can talk to me. You know that, don't you?" I take my hand from her hair and lift up her chin, just slightly, so I can get a good look at her.

Tired-looking blue circles line the bottom of her almond-shaped eyes. They are puffy and my stomach aches at the thought that she's been crying. I run the pad of my thumb over one of her closed eyes and her lips part.

Her eyelashes are so long that they remind me of the feathers on a bird.

A very, very pretty bird.

Oh, my mind is in a weird place.

She nods and I move my thumb back under her chin. Her eyes open, just enough for me to see that she's hiding something.

Her voice is soft and she moves her face away from my touch when she says plainly, "I'm taking care of it."

I take a step back, wanting to give her space, and she surprises me by grabbing my shirt and pulling me closer. She wraps her arms around my back and buries her head in my chest. She doesn't cry; she just stands there, taking shallow breaths and not speaking.

I rub one hand up and down her back, letting her have the silence she seems to be wanting.

After a few more seconds, she raises her head and stares up at me.

*I want to take care of you,* my heart says. Then my mouth says the same.

She takes in my words, her eyes pouring into mine. "I don't want to be taken care of."

Her honesty stings, but I have to remember that she's a few years older than me and has been doing this life thing by herself for a while.

"I don't want my parents' help. I don't want your help. I don't want anyone's help. I just want to figure my shit out and cause the least amount of problems possible along the way. I will only bring you trouble . . . it's what I do. It's who I am. I'm not saying this to be dramatic—I'm serious, Landon."

She looks at me, her eyes begging me to listen. To really listen. "I carry too much baggage, and I'm not looking for a knight in shining armor to rescue me."

I don't know what to say. I don't know how to fix this, or if she even needs to be fixed.

I'm not used to not being needed. I've always been the fixer. Who I am without that role?

I don't know.

"I know, princess," I say, trying to add a little humor, break some of this tension I don't know what to do with.

"Eew." She makes a face of pure disgust. "I'm no princess."

"What are you, then?" I ask her, genuinely wondering how she views herself.

"A human."

There's more to her words than sarcasm.

"I'm no damsel in distress, no princess. I'm a woman who is human in every sense of the word."

My eyes meet hers and she hugs me again.

"Can we just stand like this for a few seconds? Can you just hold me for a few seconds so I can memorize how it feels?"

I hate that her words sound so ominous, like she's saying more than goodbye.

I don't respond. I just hold her in my arms until she lets go a few seconds later.

"I wish you would tell me what's going on," I finally say when she pulls away.

Her eyes don't meet mine when she says, "So do I."

Nora stands up straight and opens her eyes wide. "Okay. Let's decorate this cake and give Ellen the best birthday of her life."

The change in her demeanor is immediate and total. It worries me how quickly she can shut down and change the subject.

I want more from Nora. I want answers. I want to know the magnitude of her problems so I can offer a solution. I want to hold her in my arms until she believes that I'll be here for her. I want to kiss her pain away and make her laugh until she forgets why she keeps herself hidden from me. I want her to know that I see her, even though she doesn't want me to.

I want so many things, but I can't want them alone . . . she has to want them, too. But I give her the response she seems to need right now and plaster a fake smile on my face.

"Let's." I raise my hand to high-five her and she cracks a smile.

She lifts her hand to mine and smacks it. "You're the corniest person I know," she says, opening the bathroom door.

I follow behind her. "I'm fine with that."

And just like that, we're "friends" again.

Tessa and Lila are still in the living room when we walk down the hallway together. Lila is still entranced by her car and Tessa is sitting cross-legged on the couch, watching the little girl with a big smile on her face.

Tessa looks at me, then at Nora, then back to me. Her face

doesn't hide her curiosity or her suspicion, but she doesn't say a word.

"Lila." I bend down to talk to the little girl. "We're going to decorate a cake. Do you want to come into the kitchen with us?"

Lila looks up at me and grabs her car. "Car," she chirps, holding the shiny Hot Wheel up to show me.

"Yep. You can take your car with you." I reach for her hand and she takes mine.

"I'm going to close my eyes for a few more minutes and rest," Tessa says, lying back down.

I tell her to go back to sleep and I walk Lila into the kitchen. Nora follows.

"Well, hi, beautiful. What's your name?" Nora asks.

Lila doesn't look at her, but she says her name and sits down at the table.

"What a beautiful name. Do you like cake?" Nora asks her.

Lila doesn't answer.

I touch Nora's arm to get her attention. She turns to me and I hold my hand up to block my mouth from Lila as I speak.

"She's autistic," I explain.

Realization dawns on Nora's face and she nods and sits down next to Lila at the table.

"Cool car," she says to her.

Lila smiles and rolls the car over Nora's hand, saying "zoom, zoom." I take it as her stamp of approval.

"Do you remember how to make the icing?" Nora asks from her seat at the table.

I nod. "Powdered sugar, butter, vanilla, and something else . . ."

I can't recall the last ingredient even though we had to make the stuff just last night.

"Milk."

I nod. "Right. Milk. And seventeen drops of food coloring."

She glares at me. "One or two drops."

"Okay, so ten drops. I get it."

She laughs, rolling her eyes. I watch as a sparkle of life comes back to them. *"Two* drops."

I walk over to the cabinet and grab the box of food coloring. "Well, if I'm supposed to get this right, I may need supervision. Do you know any bakers?"

*Take that,* pastry chef.

She shakes her head. "Nope. Sure don't, sorry." A playful smile lights up her face.

I sigh dramatically and grab a new bag of powdered sugar from the cabinet.

"That's too bad. I can't promise I won't mess this up."

Nora watches me with amusement in her eyes. "He's an awful baker," she loudly whispers to Lila.

Lila looks at her and smiles.

I wave a big spoon at the two of them. "Hey, don't go ganging up on me."

Nora laughs.

I make my way to the fridge and grab the milk and a stick of butter, then I get the mixing bowl out of the dishwasher. I actually do remember how to make the icing.

I think . . .

Nora stays quiet as I start. After the sugar and butter are blended, I add the vanilla and milk. I carefully add two drops of green food coloring and Nora claps her hands as I mix it in the silver bowl.

After a minute or two of quiet, Nora stands up and walks over to me. She unwraps the cake and throws the Saran Wrap into the trash. I dip the spoon into the icing and spread it across the vanilla cake.

"Aw. Look at you. Decorating the cake all by yourself. You've come a long way, young grasshopper."

I laugh at Nora's banter and she nudges me with her shoulder.

She looks at Lila. "Who does she belong to? I didn't think to ask."

"She's my friend Posey's sister. Posey had to work this morning, so I offered to watch her. She'll be here in an hour or so to get her."

Nora looks at me in that way that she does and I feel like she's reading every thought of mine. My pulse quickens.

"You're something else, Landon Gibson," she tells me for the second time in two days.

I flush under her compliment and I don't even care if she notices.

"You're good with her." I point the green-icing-covered spoon toward Lila.

"Me? Good with kids?" she says with genuine surprise.

"Yes," I tell her, and press the tip of my index finger into her nose the way she pressed mine yesterday.

"Hey, you stole that from me!" She turns her shoulders so she's facing me, only inches away from my face.

I rub the spoon over the top of the cake, making sure to get the corners. "I have no idea what you're talking about."

I look up at the ceiling, then back at the cake.

Nora nudges me again. "Liar."

"I'm a liar and you keep secrets. We're the same—"

The words are out before I can stop them, and I hate the way her face immediately changes from carefree to guarded.

"That's not the same. Secrets and lies aren't the same," Nora defends herself.

I turn to her and drop the spoon onto the edge of the pan. "I didn't mean it like that. I'm sorry."

Nora doesn't look at me, but I can see her guard lowering with each breath. Finally, she speaks. "Promise me something?"

"Anything."

"You won't try to fix me."

"I . . ." I hesitate.

"Promise me." She holds her ground. "Promise me that and I'll promise not to tell lies."

I look at her. "But you'll keep secrets?" I ask her, already knowing the answer.

"No *lies*."

I sigh in defeat. I don't want her to keep secrets.

"Is this my only option?" I ask. Again, already knowing the answer.

She nods.

I contemplate her offer for a few seconds. If this is the only way she'll let me get closer, it's all I've got.

I don't know if I'll be able to keep that promise, but this is my only chance.

With a deep breath, I nod slowly. "I promise not to try to fix you."

She exhales and I suddenly realize that she'd been holding her breath.

"Your turn."

She's hesitating this time. "I promise not to tell lies."

She holds out her pinkie and I loop mine through it.

"It's a pact now. Don't break it," she warns.

I glance at Lila sitting at the table, content with her car.

"And what happens if I do?" I ask her.

"I disappear . . ."

Nora's words cut at me and I'm terrified by them because I know—I know without a doubt—that she means them.

# acknowledgments

*I* PLANNED TO WRITE THIS BOOK a while ago, back when I hadn't even spoken with a publisher about the After series. I was writing on Wattpad, trying to figure out what to do with my life. I was so excited to write it, and I couldn't wait to get inside of Landon's head.

Then, when I finally sat down to write it, I was surprised when I wasn't having very much fun. I loved the story, but it felt off, like something was missing and I didn't know what. I typed and typed, sitting in hotel lobbies and crowded coffee shops, but when I read the words back, they felt only half-there, as if I was reading someone else writing my story. (Think fanfiction, but less awesome.)

So with my deadline approaching I knew the story was okay, but I wasn't having as much fun as I did when writing my first series. I went through phases of "OMG, am I even a writer?" and "What if After was the only story in me?"

But then I began to send pieces of it to a small group of my friends who started as readers back when I first began writing but had become some of my best friends. The moments they would read the parts and text me their responses, something clicked. It was so exciting having their reactions and opinions, though most of the texts were: OMFGGG. (Thanks Bri, Trev, Lauren, and Chels. I love love love you guys.)

I soon began reworking the story and basically wiping out the whole first draft, but I still had a little problem. I wanted to write the chapters, mostly live, on Wattpad before sending them to my editor. The concept of this is soooo not common and honestly a little scary for publishers. I understand why, but I really felt like writing on Wattpad was the key. I love the socialized writing, the comments, the adrenaline of posting a new chapter.

The idea of a writer is someone who writes in solitude and quiet, and would never dream of letting thousands of people read their work before an editor does. I panicked for a minute and crossed my fingers that my publisher would understand and consider my idea.

I held my breath and explained my situation to my editor, Adam Wilson, and the first thing he said was "That makes so much sense"—and I could have screamed, I was so happy. He got it, he gets it, he's always understood that not all writers are the same. From the moment I met him, I knew that he got me. (I have used this word about ten times now, LOL.)

Adam is always so open and curious about the new and unique ways of writing. He knows that writers from the inter-webs are different, and he has never made me feel like I have to conform to the idea of a traditional writer. He has always encouraged my quirks and praised my ability to do things my way. The publishing industry is lucky to have someone like him.

So Adam, I need to acknowledge you x39394. Thank you for your patience and for always having my back. I can't imagine writing a book without you.

Ashleigh Gardner: Thanks for always having my back and being a major force in the modernization of traditional publishing.

Ursula Uriarte: Thank you for being my brain, and my best friend. And for sending me Malec gifs when I'm stressed. I would forget everything without you.

Aron Levitz: Thanks for making me fancy. Now, put this book down and take a DAMN VACATION. *bunny emoji*

Wattpad: Thanks for being my home base.

Jen Bergstrom: Thank you for being so willing to let me try new things. It means a lot to me and makes me really happy. I love everyone at Gallery so so much.

Thank you to the copyeditor and production staff—you guys rock at moving fast.

A huge, huge, massively massive thank-you to my foreign publishers for always working so hard for me. I've had such an incredible time meeting so many of you, and I appreciate your hard work on my behalf.

# Connect with
# Anna Todd on Wattpad

The author of this book, Anna Todd,
started her career as a reader, just like
you. She joined Wattpad to read stories
like this one and to connect with the
people who wrote them.

**Download Wattpad today to
connect with Anna:**

 **imaginator1D**

# LOOK FOR

## Once Upon Now

A collection of
modern tales with a
fantastical twist!

by the  authors